Walt Disney's STORY LAND

55 FAVORITE STORIES

adapted from Walt Disney films

Illustrated by the Walt Disney Studio

Stories selected by Frances Saldinger

A GOLDEN BOOK • NEW YORK
Western Publishing Company, Inc., Racine, Wisconsin 53404

TABLE OF CONTENTS

BAMBI

Based on the original story by Felix Salten

Bambi came into the world in the middle of a forest thicket. The little, hidden thicket was scarcely big enough for the new baby and his mother.

But the magpie soon spied him there.

"What a beautiful baby!" she cried. And away she flew to spread the news to all the other animals of the forest.

Her chattering soon brought dozens of birds and animals to the thicket. The rabbits came hurrying; the squirrels came a-scurrying. The robins and bluebirds fluttered and flew.

At last even the old owl woke up from his long day's sleep.

"Who, who?" the owl said sleepily, hearing all the commotion.

"Wake up, Friend Owl!" a rabbit called. "It's happened! The young Prince is born!"

"Everyone's going to see him," said the squirrels. "You come, too."

With a sigh the owl spread his wings and flew off toward the thicket. There he found squirrels and rabbits and birds peering through the bushes at a doe and a little spotted fawn.

The fawn was Bambi, the new Prince of the Forest.

"Congratulations," said the owl, speaking for all the animals. "This is quite an occasion. It isn't often that a Prince is born in the forest."

The doe looked up. "Thank you," she said quietly. Then with her nose she gently nudged her sleeping baby until he lifted his head and looked around.

She nudged him again, and licked him reassuringly. At last he pushed up on his thin legs, trying to stand.

"Look! He's trying to stand up already!" shouted one of the little rabbits, Thumper by name. "He's awfully wobbly, though, isn't he?"

"Thumper!" the mother rabbit exclaimed, "that's not a pleasant thing to say!"

"Bambi, a Life in the Woods," translated by Whittaker Chambers, copyright 1928 by Simon and Schuster, Inc.

The new fawn's legs were not very steady, it was true, but at last he stood beside his mother. Now all the animals could see the fine white spots on his red-brown coat, and the sleepy expression on his soft baby face.

The forest around him echoed with countless small voices. A soft breeze rustled the leaves about the thicket. And the watching animals whispered among themselves. But the little fawn did not listen to any of them. He only knew that his mother's tongue was licking him softly, washing and warming him. He nestled closer to her, and closed his eyes.

Quietly the animals and birds slipped away through the forest.

Thumper the rabbit was the last to go.

"What are you going to name the young Prince?" he asked.

"I'll call him Bambi," the mother answered.

"Bambi," Thumper repeated. "Bambi. That's a good name. Good-by, Bambi." And he hopped away after his sisters.

Bambi was not a sleepy baby for long. Soon he was following his mother down the narrow forest paths. Bright flowers winked from beneath the leaves.

Squirrels and chipmunks looked up and called, "Good morning, young Prince."

Opossums, hanging by their long tails from a tree branch, said "Hello, Prince Bambi."

The fawn looked at them all with wondering eyes. But he did not say a word.

Finally, as Bambi and his mother reached a little clearing in the forest, they met Thumper and his family.

"Hi, Bambi," said Thumper. "Let's play."

"Yes, let's play," Thumper's sister cried. And away they hopped, over branches and hillocks and tufts of grass.

Bambi soon understood the game, and he began to jump and run on his stiff, spindly legs.

Thumper jumped over a log and his sisters followed.

"Come on, Bambi," Thumper called. "Hop over the log."

Bambi jumped, but not far enough. He fell with a plop on top of the log.

"Too bad," said Thumper. "You'll do better next time."

Bambi untangled his legs and stood up again. But still he did not speak. He pranced along behind Thumper, and soon he saw a family of birds sitting on a branch.

Bambi looked at them.

"Those are birds, Bambi," Thumper told him. "Birds."

"Bir-d," Bambi said slowly. The young Prince had spoken his first word!

Thumper and his sisters were all excited, and Bambi himself was pleased. He repeated the word over and over to himself. Then he saw a butterfly cross the path. "Bird, bird!" he cried again.

"No, Bambi," said Thumper. "That's not a bird. That's a butterfly."

The butterfly disappeared into a clump of yellow flowers. Bambi bounded toward them happily.

"Butterfly!" he cried.

"No, Bambi," said Thumper. "Not butterfly. *Flower*."

He pushed his nose into the flowers and sniffed. Bambi did the same, but suddenly he drew back. His nose had touched something warm and furry.

Out from the bed of flowers came a small black head with two shining eyes.

"Flower!" said Bambi.

The black eyes twinkled. As the little ani-

mal stepped out, the white stripe down his black furry back glistened in the sun.

Thumper the rabbit was laughing so hard that he could scarcely speak.

"That's not a flower," said Thumper. "That's a skunk."

"Flower," repeated Bambi.

"I don't care," said the skunk. "The young Prince can call me Flower if he wants to. I don't mind."

"Flower," Bambi repeated.

So Flower, the skunk, got his name.

One morning Bambi and his mother walked down a new path. It grew lighter and lighter as they walked along. Soon the trail ended in a tangle of bushes and vines, and Bambi could see a great, bright, open space spread out before them.

Bambi wanted to bound out there to play in the sunshine, but his mother stopped him. "Wait," she said. "You must never run out on the meadow without making sure it is safe."

She took a few slow, careful steps forward. She listened and sniffed in all directions. Then she called, "Come."

Bambi bounded out. He felt so good and so happy that he leaped into the air again and again. For the meadow was the most beautiful place he had ever seen.

His mother dashed forward and showed him how to race and play in the tall grass. Bambi ran after her. He felt as if he were flying. Round and round they raced in great circles. At last his mother stopped and stood still, catching her breath.

Then Bambi set out by himself to explore the meadow. Soon he spied his little friend the skunk, sitting in the shade of some blossoms.

"Good morning, Flower," said Bambi.

And he found Thumper and his sisters nibbling sweet clover.

"Try some, Bambi," said Thumper.

So Bambi did.

Suddenly a big green frog popped out of the clover patch and hopped over to a meadow pond. Bambi had not seen the pond before, so he hurried over for a closer look.

As the fawn came near, the frog hopped into the water.

Where could he have gone? Bambi wondered. So he bent down to look into the pond. As the ripples cleared, Bambi jumped back. For he saw a fawn down there in the water, looking out at him!

"Don't be frightened, Bambi," his mother told him. "You are just seeing yourself in the water."

So Bambi looked once more. This time he

saw *two* fawns looking back at him! He
jumped back again, and as he lifted his head
he saw that it was true—there was another
little fawn standing beside him!

"Hello," she said.

Bambi backed away and ran to his mother,
where she was quietly eating grass beside another doe. Bambi leaned against her and
peered out at the other little fawn, who had
followed him.

"Don't be afraid, Bambi," his mother said.
"This is little Faline, and this is your Aunt
Ena. Can't you say hello to them?"

"Hello, Bambi," said the two deer. But
Bambi did not say a word.

"You have been wanting to meet other deer,"
his mother reminded him. "Well, Aunt Ena
and Faline are deer like us. Now can't you
speak to them?"

"Hello," whispered Bambi in a small, small
voice.

"Come and play, Bambi," said Faline. She
leaned forward and licked his face.

Bambi dashed away as fast as he could run,
and Faline raced after him. They almost flew
over that meadow.

Up and down they chased each other. Over
the little hillocks they raced.

When they stopped, all topsy-turvy and
breathless, they were good friends.

Then they walked side by side on the bright meadow, visiting quietly together.

One morning, Bambi woke up shivering with cold. Even before he opened his eyes, his nose told him there was something new and strange in the world. Then he looked out of the thicket. Everything was covered with white.

"It is snow, Bambi," his mother said. "Go ahead and walk out. It is all right."

Bambi stepped out onto the snow very cautiously. His feet sank deep into the soft blanket. He had to lift them up high as he walked along. Now and then, with a soft plop, a tiny snowy heap would tumble from a leaf overhead onto his nose or back.

Bambi was delighted. The sun glittered so brightly on the whiteness. The air was so mild and clear. And all around him white snow stars came whirling down.

From the crest of a little hill he saw Thumper. Thumper was sitting on the top of the pond!

"Come on, Bambi!" Thumper shouted. "Look! The water's stiff!" He thumped with one foot against the solid ice. "You can even slide on it. Watch and I'll show you how!"

Thumper took a run and slid swiftly across the pond. Bambi tried it, too, but his legs shot out from under him and down he crashed on the hard ice. That was not so much fun.

"Let's play something else," Bambi suggested, when he had carefully pulled himself to his feet again. "Where's Flower?"

"I think I know," said Thumper.

He led Bambi to the doorway of a deep burrow. They peered down into it. There, peacefully sleeping on a bed of withered flowers, lay the little skunk.

"Wake up, Flower!" Bambi called.

"Is it spring yet?" Flower asked sleepily, half opening his eyes.

"No, winter's just beginning," Bambi said. "What are you doing?"

"Hibernating," the little skunk replied. "Flowers always sleep in the winter, you know."

Thumper yawned. "I guess I'll take a nap, too," he said. "Good-by, Bambi. I'll see you later."

So Bambi wandered back to the thicket.

"Don't fret, Bambi," his mother said. "Winter will soon be over, and spring will come again."

So Bambi went to sleep beside his mother in the snug, warm thicket, and dreamed of the jolly games that he and his friends would play in the wonderful spring to come.

HIAWATHA

Based on the Walt Disney motion picture "Hiawatha"

IN THE far-off Indian country lived a boy called Hiawatha. More than anything else, Hiawatha wanted to learn to become a great hunter.

One day Hiawatha paddled his canoe across a shining lake until he came to a green island.

Many little animals were scampering around the island, so Hiawatha landed his canoe and waded ashore.

Eagerly Hiawatha looked at the animals around him. Here were squirrels, birds, beavers, rabbits, and even a fawn to stalk!

Hiawatha aimed his arrow at a little rabbit. But before he could shoot, the laughing animals had scampered away and were safe in their holes.

Hiawatha was turning to go when he saw strange tracks on the ground. Quickly he bent down to study them. He was sure he had never seen them before, and his heart beat high.

"Perhaps I have found a new kind of animal," he thought.

Suddenly a shrill whirring startled him. Before him, rubbing its wings together, stood a giant cricket. This was the new kind of animal Hiawatha had found!

Speechless, Hiawatha stared at the cricket.

Then, with a yelp, Hiawatha fled.

Of course, many little eyes watched Hiawatha's flight! Squealing and chirping with laughter, the forest animals popped out of their holes.

"Hiawatha is afraid of a cricket!" they cried. Shamefaced, Hiawatha stopped running.

But the little animals could not stop laughing. "Afraid of a cricket!" a little rabbit choked, drumming his paw on the ground. "Oh my, afraid of a cricket!"

Hiawatha's face turned redder. No impudent little rabbit was going to make fun of him!

Grabbing his bow and arrow, Hiawatha chased the rabbit. The rabbit ran and dodged among the great tree trunks, but at last Hiawatha cornered him. He aimed his arrow.

Trembling, the rabbit sat up and begged for mercy. In spite of himself, Hiawatha was touched.

"All right," he said crossly. "Shoo! Scat! You won't get off so easily again!"

The rabbit ran off, and immediately Hiawatha was surrounded by joyful, grateful animals.

Seeing how friendly they were, Hiawatha made a resolution. He swore never to hunt them again.

He took his bow and arrow and smashed them across his knee.

Since he no longer wanted to be a hunter,

Hiawatha decided to become an explorer. He started off to explore the island, and soon found great paw marks on the ground.

Creeping forward quietly, Hiawatha followed the mysterious paw marks.

Suddenly, there he was, face to face with a bear cub hidden behind a rock!

The cub squealed with fear and dashed off as fast as his shaggy little legs could carry him.

Hiawatha ran after him. He did not understand why the cub should be frightened. "Stay and play with me! he shouted. "Stay and play with me!"

But the cub would not listen to Hiawatha. He headed for his cave, with Hiawatha close behind.

Suddenly Hiawatha made a pounce. He felt something shaggy. "Got you!" he laughed, and wrapped his arms tightly around the squirming cub.

But then a terrible roar shook the forest.

This was no cub! This was the mother bear he had caught!

Again the chase started!

Hiawatha fled, panic-stricken, from the roaring mother bear.

Fortunately Hiawatha's new forest friends saw his danger. The beavers pounded out an SOS.

The first to answer were the weasels. "Quick, this way!" they urged Hiawatha.

He fled past them, and behind him they spread out a trap of vines for the furious mother bear.

Then the friendly beavers took over.

At a riverbank, Hiawatha dashed out on a tree trunk. The beavers ferried him across.

The mother bear hesitated a moment at the cold water. But then she, too, plunged in and crossed over.

When he had crossed the river, Hiawatha climbed a tree. Unfortunately, the mother bear climbed up the tree right after Hiawatha.

Hiawatha would have been caught, had not the squirrels helped him down. Quickly they set him in a harness hitched to the fawn and pressed the reins into his hand.

"Giddyap!" they shouted, and Hiawatha was off.

By fawn express, Hiawatha was carried swiftly through the forest. Soon the growls of the bear faded out behind him, and he knew he was safe.

When they came to the lake, Hiawatha climbed into his canoe. "Good-by," he called to all his new forest friends. "I'll be back soon!"

A happy Hiawatha turned the bow of his canoe homeward. He had not learned to become a great hunter, but he knew that he had made many new friends.

Donald Duck
PRIVATE EYE

HELP!" cried Minnie Mouse. "Mickey, my jewel box is missing. I can't find it anywhere. Someone must have stolen it."

"Now, now," said Mickey, "keep calm, Minnie. I will help you find it."

Together they searched Minnie's house . . . upstairs, downstairs . . . and even in the garden. There was no sign of the jewel box.

"Oh, dear, oh, dear," sobbed Minnie, "what shall I do?"

"There is only one person who can help us," answered Mickey, "and that person is Donald Duck, the great Private Eye. I will go to him at once."

Donald was in his office, and as usual, he was very busy.

"Donald! Donald! Wake up!" said Mickey. "Minnie's jewel box is missing. We need you to help us find it."

Donald opened a sleepy eye.

"I'll take the case, Mickey," he said. "I'll search the underworld tonight, and find the jewel box in no time."

It was midnight when Donald entered the underworld. His coat collar was pulled high and his cap was pulled low to hide his face, and he carried all his detective tools.

It was dark and spooky, and glittering eyes watched him from under lowered curtains. Donald was so busy searching for clues that he didn't notice a huge figure hiding in the deep shadows.

As Donald moved further into the darkness, a huge shadow tiptoed silently after him.

"I'll find Minnie's jewel box," Donald said aloud, "or my name isn't . . ."

"Donald Duck, the great Private Eye," a great voice boomed out.

Donald leaped into the air, dropping his tools. The voice went on:

"That's not a very good disguise you have there, Donald."

And, as the moon came out from behind a cloud, Donald saw that the voice belonged to Black Pete.

"Everybody can recognize you in that outfit," added Black Pete kindly. "Better try another disguise."

"I will," said Donald, "and nobody will ever see through it."

The next morning, Donald looked through all his books about disguises, but he didn't find any that he liked. Then he happened to look in a mirror.

"Say," he chuckled, "I've found the answer."

"First," he said, "I'll fluff up my feathers and add a hair ribbon. Then I'll put on a blouse and skirt and . . . OUCH! . . . a pair of tight high-heeled shoes! Now nobody will know me from *Daisy Duck.*"

He smiled proudly as he walked out the front door of his house.

His three little nephews were playing marbles on the sidewalk.

"Hello, Unca Donald," they all shouted.

Donald stopped short. He was very surprised that his nephews recognized him.

"I guess my disguise isn't quite perfect," he thought. "I'll have to try a different one."

Back he went to his disguise closet. He took off the hair ribbon, and he pulled an old-fashioned blouse over his sailor shirt. Next, he added a pair of steel-rimmed eyeglasses.

"There," he said, as he put on a white wig, "nobody will know me from *Grandma Duck.* Now to search the underworld for Minnie's jewel box."

Just as Donald was coming out of his front door, Goofy walked by.

"Hello, Donald," said Goofy gaily. "Are you going to a fancy dress party?"

Poor Donald!

"How did Goofy see through my disguise?"

he asked himself. "If he recognized me, everybody else will, too!"

"This makes me angry," grumbled Donald, as he peeled off the blouse. "But I'll fool everyone yet. I'll leave on the glasses. Then I'll slip on this old smoking jacket and, with a few odds and ends of whiskers, nobody will know me from my own rich uncle, *Scrooge McDuck!*"

Just then, Mickey and Minnie Mouse came running down the street, at the head of a happy parade.

"Oh Donald," they called, "we won't need your help after all. We've found Minnie's missing jewel box."

Minnie's nephew, Morty, had borrowed it to keep his fishing worms in.

"I'm glad you found the jewel box," sighed Donald. "But how did you all see through my disguises? I thought they were perfect."

"This Uncle Scrooge disguise was almost perfect," laughed Mickey and Minnie. "But you forgot one thing. Uncle Scrooge would never be without his spats."

"That goes for your Daisy Duck disguise, too," chimed in Huey, Dewey and Louie.

"We thought you were Daisy Duck until we noticed that her long black eyelashes were missing."

"You almost had me fooled," chuckled Goofy. "Then I saw something, you weren't wearing — Grandma Duck's high-buttoned shoes."

Toy Sailboat

From the Motion Picture "Chips Ahoy"

THERE!" said Donald Duck. "At last it's done!"

He stood back to look at his toy sailboat. Making it had been a big job. It had taken him all summer long. But now the boat was finished. And it was a beautiful boat.

The mantel was just the place for it, too.

The whole room looked better with the sailboat up there.

"Building sailboats is very hungry work," Donald said to himself. So he fixed himself a fine big lunch.

"Now to try out the boat in the lake," he thought. But his hard work had made him sleepy, too. So Donald settled down for a nap. After that he would try out the boat.

Now outside Donald's cottage in the old elm tree, lived two little chipmunks, Chip and Dale. And they had had no lunch at all.

"I'm hungry," said Chip, as he rubbed his empty middle.

"Me too," said little Dale. But suddenly he brightened. "Look!" he said.

Chip looked and looked. At last he spied it—one lone acorn still clinging to the bough of an oak down beside the lake.

Down the elm tree they raced, across to the oak, and up its rough-barked trunk.

"Mine!" cried Chip, reaching for the nut.

"I saw it first!" Dale cried.

So they pushed and they tugged and they tussled, until the acorn slipped through their fingers and fell *kerplunk* into the lake.

The two little chipmunks looked mighty sad as they watched the acorn float away. But Dale soon brightened. "Look!" he cried.

Chip looked. On a little island out in the middle of the lake stood a great big oak tree weighted down with acorns on every side.

Down to the shore the chipmunks ran. But br-r-r! It was too cold to swim.

"How can we get to them?" wondered Chip.

"I don't know," said Dale. But he soon had an idea. "Look in there!" he said.

On the mantel in Donald Duck's cottage they could see the toy sailboat.

"Come on," said Dale. So away they raced, straight in the cottage door.

They had the sailboat down and almost out the door when Donald stirred in his sleep.

"Nice day for a sail," he said dreamily, as the boat slipped smoothly past his eyes.

Soon after, Donald woke up completely.

"Now to try out my boat!" he cried.

Suddenly something outside the window caught Donald's eye. It was his sailboat, out on the middle of the lake!

"I'll fix those chipmunks!" Donald said.

He pulled out his fishing rod and reel and chose a painted fly. It looked just like a nut.

"This will do," Donald grinned.

From the pier he cast—as far as he could fling that little fishing fly. With a *plop* it landed beside the toy boat.

"Look! Look at this!" cried Dale. He leaned way over the edge of the boat to pull in the floating fly.

"Good! A nut!" said Chip. "We'll toss it in the hold and have it for supper tonight."

As soon as it was fast in the hold, Donald pulled in the line. He pulled that little boat right in shore. The chipmunks never suspected a thing. They did not even notice Donald pouring water into the cabin of the boat.

Chip discovered that when he went into the cabin. "Man the pumps!" he cried.

Those two chipmunks worked with might and main while Donald watched and laughed.

22

"Ha ha!" At Donald's chuckle, the chipmunks looked up.

"So that's the trouble!" Dale cried.

He pulled out the fishing fly from the hold and flung it at Donald so that he was soon tangled up in fishing line.

Chip and Dale set sail once more.

Before Donald could launch his swift canoe, they had touched at the island's shore.

As Donald was paddling briskly along, he heard a brisk *rat-a-tat-tat!*

The oak tree on the island seemed to shiver and shake as its store of acorns rained down.

The busy little chipmunks finished dancing on the branches. Then they hauled their harvest on board the sailboat.

"Oh, well," said Donald, watching from his canoe. "At least I know the sailboat will sail."

And can you guess what the chipmunks did? They stored their nuts in a hollow tree. And they took Donald's toy sailboat right back, and put it where it belonged!

BONGO

Based on an adaptation of the original story "Bongo"
by Sinclair Lewis

Bongo was a circus bear, a smart and lively circus bear. He was the smartest little bear any circus ever had. Yes, Bongo was the star of the show!

When the drums went tr-r-rum, and the bugles shouted, that was the signal for Bongo's act. Then the spotlights all pointed their long fingers of light down at an opening in the tent, and in rode Bongo!

In rode Bongo on his shiny unicycle, all aglitter under the glare of the lights. And his act began.

He juggled and danced on the highest trapeze. He walked a tightrope with the greatest of ease. Then up, up, up to the top of the tent went Bongo. And when he'd gone so high that he couldn't go higher, he rode his unicycle on the high tight wire!

"Hurray for Bongo!" he heard voices call below.

"You know, he's the star who makes the show!"

Bongo was king of the circus while his act was on!

But when it was over, and Bongo the star rode out of the ring to the roar of applause, then clang went an iron collar around his neck. Rattle went a long chain as Bongo was led away to his boxcar. Slam went the barred door as it locked behind him. There sat Bongo, the star of the circus, just a bear in a gilded cage.

Poor Bongo! Oh, he was well enough treated. He was fed only the finest selected bear food, from his own tin dishes. He always had fresh water to drink. He was washed and combed and curried and clipped, and kept in the finest condition.

But after all was said and done, "I'm still just a slave," thought Bongo sadly.

He was lonely, too. And from somewhere deep in his past, the voice of the wild called to him.

"Bongo, Bongo, yoo-hoo, Bongo!" it sang.

He heard it in the scream of the train whistle, as the circus moved from town to town. He heard it in the clatter of the speeding wheels.

Each time the circus stopped in a new town Bongo went through his act as though he were in a dream. And when he was put back into his cage he lived in that dream—a dream of the wide-open spaces.

In the dream the voice of the wild kept calling, "Bongo, Bongo, BONGO!"

One day that call got into his blood so that he could not sit still. He paced around his cage as it jolted with the motion of the train. He shook the bars. He hammered at the door. And the boxcar door swung open! Bongo was face to face with the great out-of-doors.

The train was moving slowly around a curve. Quickly Bongo swung out on his little cycle, dropped to the roadbed, and zipped away down a long hillside.

Behind him in the distance the train whistle faded, the hurrying cars disappeared from sight. And Bongo at last was free!

On down the hillside he sped, and into the woods he had dreamed of for so long. Bongo was wide-eyed at the wonder of this new world. For the trees towered taller than cir-

cus tent poles. The flowers were brighter than colored balloons. The crisp air smelled better than popcorn and fresh-roasted peanuts. It was wonderful!

"Yes, sir, this is the life for me!" said Bongo.

He felt so good that he just had to run and jump and sniff and snort. He even tried to climb a tree, but, plunk! down he came, flat on his back.

Poor Bongo—he had never even seen a tree before, except through the windows of the circus train.

"Well," said Bongo, "I guess that takes a little practice!"

So he backed away again, and took another little run. And plunk! Down he fell!

Now the branches above him were filled with twitterings and chatterings. The little woodland animals had all come out to meet Bongo.

"Hello," said Bongo shyly. "Let's be friends."

So they taught him which were the most fragrant flowers to sniff. They showed him how to peek at his reflection in a quiet pool.

"I've never had so much fun," Bongo told them happily. "Your forest is wonderful."

And as the sun dropped behind the trees, Bongo looked up at the velvet sky twinkling with stars, while all around him stretched the sleepy quiet of the woods.

"Yes, this is the life for me," Bongo yawned contentedly, as he curled up for a good sleep.

He dozed off, but soon he woke up with a start. The night, which had seemed so peaceful, was full of sounds. Far off somewhere a coyote howled. Just then a chilly gust of wind shivered through the forest. Bongo shivered.

"Maybe this wood is not the place for me after all," he thought lonesomely.

Then storm clouds blotted out the stars. Across the inky blackness, yellow lightning flashed, and thunder rumbled angrily. Cold, soaking rain poured down on poor Bongo.

"I wish I'd never left the circus," he thought, with a sad sigh and a shiver.

At last, though, the rain did stop. The clouds parted, and a friendly moon shone through. And Bongo slept.

He woke up next morning, stiff as a board and cranky as an old bear—and hungry! He tried picking berries, but they were not very filling. Then he tried fishing, but the fish all got away.

At last he turned from the pool with a discouraged sigh. But what was this?

Right before his very eyes Bongo saw another little bear. And the bear was smiling at him!

For a moment Bongo thought he must be dreaming. He pinched himself, but the little bear was still there. So Bongo scampered over to get acquainted.

"Hello," he said shyly. "My name is Bongo." And he tipped his little circus cap.

"My name is Lulubelle," said the other little bear. "Let's play something."

This was wonderful. For the first time in his life Bongo had a playmate! Off they went through the woods together.

Bongo was so busy thinking how happy he was that he didn't pay much attention to the crashing of underbrush and the crunching of stones as Lumpjaw, the biggest, toughest bear in the forest, came stamping out.

"H-hello," said Bongo shyly. Perhaps this was another playmate, he thought.

Lumpjaw did not bother to speak. He just swung one great paw at the little bear, and bong! Bongo crashed against a tree trunk, headfirst! As he pulled himself to his feet and shook his dizzy head, Lumpjaw lunged forward to hit him again.

But Bongo's new friend stepped between them. While Lumpjaw fumed, she stepped up to Bongo—and slapped him soundly on the cheek.

Bongo couldn't believe it. But it was true enough. So that there could be no mistake, the bear he thought his friend slapped him on the other cheek.

Bongo's heart was broken. He turned and slowly rode away. He did not dream that when he did this, it hurt the feelings of his friend. For no one had ever told him the ways of bears. How could he know that when a bear likes another bear, he says it with a slap?

Off into the woods went Bongo, heartsick. And the farther he rode, the sadder he felt.

"I should never have left the circus," said Bongo to himself. "Nobody likes me here." And he sighed.

Soon, as Bongo rode along, he heard near by the pounding rhythm of heavy feet. It sounded as though they were dancing. And he heard deep voices rumbling in what sounded like a song.

Quietly Bongo crept to the edge of an open clearing. The clearing was full of bears, a double line of them. They were shuffling about in a clumsy bear dance, and singing a tuneless bear song, and exchanging clumsy bear slaps.

"Why, they're slapping each other," Bongo whispered to himself in surprise. "And they're not cross. They like each other!"

Then the words of the song reached him—

"Every pigeon likes to coo
When he says, 'I like you,'
But a bear likes to say it with a slap."

"With a slap!" cried Bongo. "Then Lulu-belle—she likes me! We're still friends!"

So Bongo raced out into the clearing, where his playmate was dancing with Lumpjaw, and gave her a sound slap.

Bongo's friend was delighted, but not Lumpjaw. He did not want any strange bear making friends with his playmate He roared. He snorted. He fumed! He chased Bongo through the forest, tearing up trees and hurling them at the little bear as he went.

Up the mountainside raced Bongo, with Lumpjaw close behind him. Down the other side Bongo hustled, while the great rocks Lumpjaw was hurling rolled past on either side.

Lumpjaw cornered Bongo at last, on the edge of a cliff. There they teetered and tottered and struggled and fought, until Cr-r-runch! Sw-w-wish! Spl-lash!

The rock beneath them crumbled away, and they tumbled down, down, down, into a roaring river.

Now the other bears gathered on the river bank far above to watch as Lumpjaw and Bongo rode the current on a twirling, plunging log.

Closer and closer they came to the great white-foaming falls. The watching bears all held their breath! Then over the falls tumbled the great log, with Lumpjaw still clinging to it! Over the falls and down the river went the log and the bear, until at last they floated out of sight!

And Bongo? All the bears shook their heads and sighed when they thought of him.

But wait! What was this? Up the steep

river bank a wet little bear came climbing, with a dripping little circus cap still upon his head. Yes, it was Bongo, a tired Bongo, but a proud and happy little bear.

"I'm back," he told Lulubelle, and he said it with a real bear slap.

"I'm glad," said his friend, with a pat that knocked him down.

"This is the life," cried Bongo happily, as he scrambled back to his feet again. "This is more fun than the circus ever was. Yes, sir, this is the life for me!"

He felt so good that he juggled a handful of pine cones, and he did a little dance with a twisty twig for a cane.

Then his new friends showed him where to find the fattest, sweetest grubs to eat, and a honey tree running over with delicious honey. And they found him a cave that was dry and warm, and just right for him.

"This is the life," cried Bongo happily. And he threw his little old circus cap away, high up into the branches of the nearest forest tree.

"Yes, sir," said he, "I'm Bongo the woods bear now!"

Pedro

Once upon a time in a little airport near Santiago, Chile, there lived three little airplanes. There was a papa plane, a mama plane, and a baby plane.

The papa plane was a big, powerful mail plane. The mama plane was a middle-sized female plane. And the baby was a little boy plane named Pedro.

Pedro's great ambition in life was to grow up to be a big plane. Like his father, he wanted to carry the mail between Chile and Argentina. So he drank his gasoline every day like a good little plane, and went to ground school to learn the ABC's of flying.

In the little airport schoolhouse he studied reading, sky writing, and arithmetic—all in Spanish, of course, because he was a little South American plane.

He also studied history and geography. And in geography he learned the mail route between Santiago and Mendoza, over the mighty Andes, past Aconcagua, highest mountain in the western hemisphere.

This was the most fun, because Pedro could picture himself slicing through the clouds and skimming past the mountain peaks, carrying the mail over that route.

That day came sooner than he expected.

One morning the papa plane was laid up with a cold in his cylinder head, so he couldn't fly the mail. He just stayed in his hangar sneezing and wiping his windshield.

The mama plane couldn't stand the altitude because she had high oil pressure, so she couldn't fly the mail.

But everyone knows the mail must go through, and there was only Pedro to take it. The papa plane and the mama plane talked it over in low whispers, and finally they called little Pedro.

"You, my son," mumbled the papa plane, "will have to carry the mail today." And he gave him a long list of instructions.

"And," the papa plane said sternly, "whatever you do, don't go near Acon—katchoo! Acon-ca—kachoo! Aconcagua!"

"Flight Two leaving for Mendoza," chanted the signal tower.

"That's me!" grinned Pedro, and he swung into position on the runway, with his propeller whirring briskly.

"All clear, Pedro," called the papa plane from his hangar. "Let 'er go!"

Pedro waved a wing in the direction of his parents' hangar. Then, looking as stern and grown-up as he could, he took off!

Down the runway Pedro hopped.

"Give 'er the gun, boy!" he heard his father's hoarse voice call behind him.

Pedro took a deep breath and cleared a stone wall at the end of the runway—that is, he almost cleared it. A few small stones clattered to the ground as he zoomed over.

"Don't lose your flying speed!" he heard his father shout from the ground.

And up into the air flew Pedro. The radio tower ducked as he swept past; the school bell clanged as he flew right through the tower; but Pedro kept on!

He had a hard time of it, struggling for altitude, but he put everything he had into it. After all, this was his first big chance to carry the mail just as his father did.

Soon Pedro was in the mountains. Looking right and left, he kept a careful distance between himself and the mountain peaks.

But suddenly—oh-h-h-h-h-h!

Down fell Pedro, slipping between the jagged peaks at such terrific speed that his

dered in every cylinder. He stared ahead open-mouthed, then dashed behind a cloud. From this hiding-place he popped his head out for another look.

Sure enough, he was face to face with that towering monarch of the Andes, Aconcagua! And most frightening of all, the jagged crags of the mountainside seemed to form a huge, evil, forbidding stone face which glared fiercely at little Pedro through the clouds.

Taking a deep breath, Pedro shot forward, raced behind a huge cloud, and came out on the other side of the peak, safe and sound and pleased with himself. The worst was over now. Now it was clear sailing to Mendoza.

Pedro came into the Mendoza airport just as he had been taught, and soon spied the mailbag on the hangar hook. It was waiting for the mail plane, and he—Pedro!—was that mail plane. Almost bursting with pride, Pedro rolled over on his back and floated down toward the dangling sack. He hooked it neatly over one wing, and in another moment he was flying off again.

Now the mountains loomed ahead once more, but Pedro was not disturbed. He was homeward bound—and ahead of schedule!

"I'll bet my mother and dad will be proud of me," he thought.

Just for practice he did a few barrel rolls and loop-the-loops. He sailed on his back in lazy circles. He dove through clouds. He had a wonderful time. But he forgot all about being a grown-up mail plane with a job to do. He forgot all about the mountains, and his mother and father waiting beyond them.

He spied a giant condor, and chased the ugly bird all over the sky.

Before long Pedro lost track of the condor in a dense fog which shrouded the mountains. He was flying blindly through the fog, making brave little machine-gun noises to keep his spirits up.

Before him loomed Aconcagua, shrouded in low clouds. The monster-face formed by

muffler and cap were ripped loose and floated down behind him.

Pedro was caught in a dreaded down draft! He fought against the downward pull with all his strength. At last he managed to push his nose up and pull out. For the moment he was safe again!

Now, Pedro was heading into the range of snowy peaks.

He was doing all right! In fact Pedro felt on top of the world when—suddenly he shud-

its rocky, snow-filled crags frowned threateningly at poor Pedro.

The oil froze in little Pedro's cylinders; his motor knocked with fright. All the warnings he had ever heard came back to him now—the treacherous cross currents, the sudden mountain storms. Bravely he headed toward the peak.

Now the storm broke loose with a roar of fury and fastened itself upon Pedro. The lightning lashed out at him, the thunder roared its threats, rain blinded him, and the wind kept shoving and buffeting him toward the mountain.

Suddenly his windshield wipers shuddered, and he spun around in midair. The mountain's solid wall of rock loomed just ahead of him! Pedro hurled his weight to one side in a steep bank. One wing clipped a shower of rocks loose from the mountainside, and Pedro spun dizzily. Before he could right himself, the mailbag dropped from his wing!

"I really need altitude—fast!—to get out of this," Pedro thought grimly, "but I've got to deliver the mail."

So instead of climbing to safety, the brave little plane dove through the storm after the lost mailbag. Straining his eyes through the blackness, he caught sight of the mailbag, being tossed by the wind below him. Down he shot, into the heart of the storm, and grabbed the bag on a wing.

"Now I've got to climb!" he told himself, while the wind tossed and buffeted him.

Up, up into the storm Pedro climbed. Snow coated the plane, and heaped up on the mailbag. The extra weight dragged Pedro back.

"More altitude!" he thought. "I need twenty-five thousand feet!"

Pedro flashed a glance at his altimeter; it read fifteen thousand. He tilted his nose up and flew hard. The altimeter crawled up to twenty thousand.

Up and still up he fought his way, shaking off the snow as the air cleared around him. Now the altimeter hand pointed to twenty-five thousand!

"Boy, I made it!" Pedro managed a tired

grin. "Now all I have to do is level off and head for home."

But just as he got his nose pointed safely toward the home airport, Pedro started coughing and sputtering, and he couldn't stop it. Suddenly an awful thought flashed through Pedro's mind. He glanced at his fuel gauge. He was out of gas!

And, still coughing and sputtering, poor Pedro began to fall toward the mountains.

Back at the home airport, Pedro's parents searched the empty skies in vain. They saw the blackness gather over the mountain peaks, and knew that it meant a storm. The hours passed, but there was no sign of their little son, Pedro.

34

From the signal tower lights combed the sky. At last they went out, and the tower slept.

The papa and mama planes strained to see through the fog, but their eyes blinked sadly. Their brave little son was gone—another martyr to the mail service. Poor little fellow, and on his first flight, too!

Suddenly a distant whir of sound caught their ears. They looked up hopefully. The eyes of the tower opened, and searchlights flashed into the sky.

It couldn't be—but, yes it was Pedro! He hit the runway headfirst, and bounced along upside down. But he had made it!

His parents taxied out to meet him.

"Pedro! Petey, boy, are you all right?" the mama and papa planes cried.

As the searchlight beamed on him, Pedro opened his eyes, smiled wearily.

"Ahem! It may not have been exactly a three-point landing," said the proud papa plane, "but he did fulfill his mission. Pedro did the most important thing. He brought the mail through."

Pedro wiggled one wing, and his papa unhooked the mailbag and opened it.

There was one card inside.

The papa plane looked at it.

"*Está divertiendome*," it read. "Having a wonderful time."

"Hmmm," said the papa plane. "Well, it *might* have been important. And he *did* bring in the mail."

Pedro nodded his sleepy head and smiled.

And so the papa plane, the mama plane, and little Pedro flew happily ever after. And in time, Pedro became the most famous plane ever to fly the route from Santiago to Mendoza!

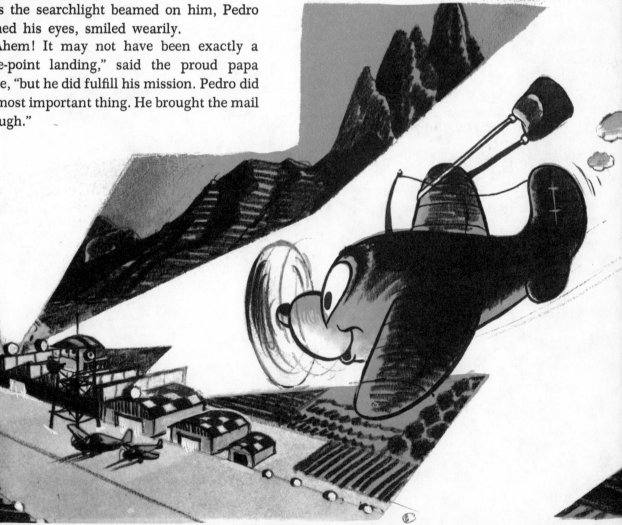

SNOW WHITE

ONCE UPON A TIME in a far-away land, a lovely Queen sat by her window sewing. As she worked, she pricked her finger with her needle. Three drops of blood fell on the snow-white linen.

"How happy I would be if I had a little girl with lips as red as blood, skin as white as snow, and hair as black as ebony!" thought the Queen as she sewed.

When spring came, her wish was granted. A little daughter was born to the Queen and King. She was all her mother had desired. But the Queen's happiness was very brief. As she held her lovely baby in her arms, the Queen whispered, "Little Snow White!" and then she died.

When the lonely King married again, his new Queen was beautiful. But, alas, she was also very heartless and cruel. She was very jealous of all the lovely ladies of the kingdom, but most jealous of all of the lovely little Princess, Snow White.

Now the Queen's most prized possession was her magic mirror. Every day she looked into it and asked:

> *"Mirror, mirror on the wall,*
> *Who is the fairest of us all?"*

If the magic mirror replied that she was the fairest in the kingdom, all was well. But if another lady was named, the Queen flew into a

dreamed—Snow White grew more beautiful day by day.

At last came the day the Queen had been dreading. She asked:

"Mirror, mirror on the wall,
who is the fairest of us all?"

and the mirror replied:

"Her lips blood red, her hair like night,
Her skin like snow, her name—
Snow White!"

The Queen's face grew pale with anger. The Queen rushed from the room and called her huntsman to her.

"Take Princess Snow White into the forest and bring me back her heart in this jeweled box," she said.

The huntsman bowed his head in grief. He had no choice but to obey the cruel Queen's commands.

Snow White had no fear of the kindly huntsman. She went happily into the forest with him. It was beautiful there among the trees, and the Princess, not knowing what was in store for her, skipped along beside the huntsman, now stopping to pick violets, now singing a happy tune.

The huntsman watched Snow White as she skipped and sang through the forest. At last the poor huntsman could bear it no longer. He fell to his knees before the Princess.

"I cannot kill you, Princess," he said, "even though it is the Queen's command. Run into the forest and hide, but you must never return to the castle."

Then away went the huntsman. On his way back to the castle, he killed a small animal and took its heart in the jeweled box to the wicked Queen.

Alone in the forest, Snow White wept with fright. Deeper and deeper into the woods she ran, half blinded by tears. It seemed to her that roots of trees reached up to trip her feet, that branches reached out to clutch at her dress as she passed.

furious rage. She would summon her huntsman and have her killed.

As the years passed, Snow White grew more and more beautiful, and her sweet nature made everyone in the kingdom love her—everyone but the Queen.

The Queen's chief fear was that Snow White might grow to be the fairest in the land. So she banished the young Princess to the servants' quarters. She made Snow White dress in rags, and forced her to slave from morning to night.

But while she worked and lived in the servants' quarters, Snow White dreamed dreams of a handsome Prince who would come some day and carry her off to his castle in the clouds. And as she dusted and scrubbed—and

At last, weak with terror, Snow White fell to the ground. As the sun began to set, she lay there, sobbing her heart out.

Ever so quietly, out from burrows and nests and hollow trees, crept the little woodland animals. Bunnies and chipmunks, raccoons and squirrels gathered around to keep watch over her.

When Snow White looked up and saw them there, she smiled through her tears. At the sight of her smile, the little animals crept closer, snuggling in her lap or nestling in her arms. The birds sang their gayest melodies to Snow White, and the little forest clearing was filled with joy.

"I feel ever so much better now," Snow White told her new friends. "But I still do need a place to sleep."

One of the birds chirped something, and the little animals nodded in agreement. Then off flew the birds, leading the way. The rabbits, chipmunks and squirrels followed after, and Snow White came along with her arm around the neck of a gentle mother deer.

At last, through a tangle of brush, Snow White saw a tiny cottage which was nestled in a clearing up ahead.

"It's just like a doll's house," and she clapped her hands in delight.

Skipping across a little bridge to the house, Snow White peeked in through one window pane. There seemed to be no one at home, but the sink was piled high with cups and saucers and plates which looked as though they had never been washed. Dirty little shirts and wrinkled little trousers hung over chairs, and everything was blanketed with dust.

"Maybe the children who live here have no mother," said Snow White, "and need someone to take care of them. Let's clean their house and surprise them."

So in she went, followed by her forest friends. Snow White found an old broom in the corner and swept the floor, while the little animals all did their best to help.

Then Snow White washed all the crumpled little clothes, and set a kettle of delicious soup to bubbling on the hearth.

"Now," she said to the animals, "let's see what is upstairs."

The woodland animals followed Snow White up the stairs. There they found seven little beds all in a row.

"Why, they have their names carved on them," said Snow White. "Doc, Happy, Sneezy, Dopey—such funny names for children! Grumpy, Bashful, Sleepy! My, I'm a little sleepy myself!"

Yawning, Snow White sank down across the little beds and fell asleep. Quietly the little animals stole away, and the birds flew out the window. All was still in the tiny little house in the forest.

"Hi ho, hi ho,
It's home from work we go—"

Seven little men came marching through the woods, singing on their way. As they came in sight of their cottage, they stopped short. Smoke was curling from the chimney, and the door was standing open!

"Look! Someone's in our house!"

"Maybe it's a ghost—er a goblin—er even a demon!"

"I knew it," said one of the little men with a grumpy look. "I've been warning you for two

hundred years something awful was about to happen!"

At last, on timid tiptoe, in they went.

"Someone's stolen our dishes," growled the grumpy one.

"No, they're hidden in the cupboard," said Happy, with a grin. "But hey! My cup's been washed! Sugar's all gone!"

At that moment a sound came from upstairs. It was Snow White yawning and turning in her sleep.

"It's up there—the goblin—er demon—er ghost!" said one of the scared little men.

Shouldering their pick axes, up the stairs they went—seven frightened little dwarfs.

The seven little men stood in a row at the foot of their beds. They all stared at the sleeping Snow White.

"Wh-what is it?" whispered one. "It's mighty purty," said another. "Why, bless my soul, I think it's a girl!" said a third. And then Snow White woke up.

"Why, you're not children," she exclaimed. "You're little men. Let me see if I can guess your names." And she did—Doc and Bashful, Happy, Sleepy, and Sneezy, and last of all Dopey and Grumpy, too.

"Supper is not quite ready," said Snow White. "You'll have just enough time to wash and change your clothes."

"Wash!" cried the little men with horror in their tones. They hadn't washed for oh, it

seemed hundreds of years. But out they marched, when Snow White insisted. And it was worth it in the end. For such a supper they had never tasted. Nor had they ever had such an evening of fun. All the forest folk gathered around the cottage windows to watch them play and dance and sing.

Back at the castle, the huntsman had presented to the wicked Queen the box which, she thought, held Snow White's heart.

"Ah ha!" she gloated. "At last!" And down the castle corridors she hurried straight to her magic mirror. Then she asked:

"Now, magic mirror on the wall,
Who is the fairest one of all?"

But the honest mirror replied:

"With the seven dwarfs will spend the night
The fairest in the land, Snow White."

Then the Queen realized that the huntsman had tricked her. She flung the jeweled box at the mirror, shattering the glass into a thousand pieces. Then, shaking with rage, the Queen hurried down to a dark cave below the palace where she worked her Black Magic.

First she disguised herself as a toothless old woman dressed in tattered rags. Then she searched her books of magic spells for a horrid spell to work on Snow White.

"What shall it be?" she muttered to herself. "The poisoned apple, the Sleeping Death? Perfect!"

In a great kettle she stirred up a poison brew. Then she dipped an apple into it—one, two, three—and the apple came out a beautiful rosy red, the most tempting apple you could hope to see.

Cackling with wicked pleasure, the Queen dropped her poisoned apple into a basket of fruit and started on her journey to the home of the seven dwarfs.

She felt certain that her plan would succeed, for the magic spell of the Sleeping Death could be broken only by Love's First Kiss. The Queen was certain no lover would find Snow White, asleep in the forest.

It was morning when the Queen reached the great forest, close to the dwarf's cottage. From her hiding place she saw Snow White saying good-by to the seven little men as they marched off to work.

"Now be careful!" they warned her. "Watch out for the Queen."

But when the poor, ragged old woman with a basket of apples appeared outside her window, Snow White never thought to be afraid. She gave the old woman a drink of water and spoke to her kindly.

"Thank you, my dear," the Queen cackled. "Now in return won't you have one of my beautiful apples?" And she held out to Snow White the poisoned fruit.

Down swooped the little birds and animals, pecking and clawing at the wicked Queen. "Stop it!" Snow White cried. "Shame on you." Then she took the poisoned apple and bit into it, and fell down lifeless on the cottage floor.

Away went the frantic birds and woodland animals into the woods to warn the seven dwarfs. Now the dwarfs had decided not to do their regular jobs that day. They were hard at work, making a gift for Snow White, to tell her of their love.

The seven little dwarfs looked up in surprise as the birds and animals crowded around them. At first they did not understand. Then they realized that Snow White must be in danger. "The Queen!" they cried, and they ran for home.

The little men were too late. They came racing into the clearing just in time to see the Queen slide away into the shadows. They chased her through the gloomy woods until she plunged into a bottomless gulf and disappeared forever. But that did not bring Snow White back to life.

When the dwarfs came home, they found Snow White lying as if asleep. They built her a bed of crystal and gold, and set it up in the forest. There they kept watch, night and day.

After a time a handsome Prince of a nearby kingdom heard travelers tell of the lovely Princess asleep in the forest, and he rode there to see her. At once he knew that he loved her truly, so he knelt beside her and kissed her lips.

At the touch of Love's First Kiss, Snow White awoke. There, bending over her, was the Prince of her dreams. Snow White knew that she loved him, too.

She said good-by to the seven dwarfs and rode off with the Prince to his Castle of Dreams Come True.

Once Upon a Wintertime

Adapted from the Walt Disney Motion Picture "Melody Time"

It was once upon a wintertime, a long time ago. Sleigh bells were tinkling and runners were twinkling over the sparkling snow.

"Let us go for a ride in the cutter. Come, Jenny," said Joe.

So he put a fur robe in the cutter, and he hitched up his spanking bays.

And Jenny put on her warm little jacket, and her mittens, each one with a flower upon it, and a scarf for her chin, and a bonnet and all—and her stout little boots.

Then away they sped, down the country roads, between towering banks of snow.

What a fine crisp, sparkling day it was! On the boughs above them the snowbirds sang.

The cutter's sleigh bells gaily rang, and the sound of them brought the bunnies to the doorway of their oak-tree home.

"What fun!" cried the bunnies. "Let us go for a sleigh ride, too."

So out they jumped, and they rode away, seated on the runners of the speeding sleigh.

44

Soon the road curved down close beside the pond, stretching smooth as glass to the woods beyond.

Joe drove up with the horses so smart and nice. And they sat and looked at the sparkling ice.

"Oh, let's skate!" said Jenny.

"Fine," said Joe.

So out they hopped, and in a trice, their skates were fastened; they were on the ice.

Joe was a star, and he loved to show Jenny the way that real skaters go, swooping and

sliding, and gracefully gliding over the ice.

On his swift twinkling skates he did fine figure eights—or nines! Or valentines!

Jenny clapped her hands at the wonderful show. But, oh woe! Down she goes!

Now Joe could not help it; he started to smile. And it grew to a chuckle after a while.

That made Jenny furious. She got to her feet, and her face was as red as a freshly scrubbed beet.

She spun on her heel, and she skated ahead so fast that she never saw a sign that said
DANGER!
Thin Ice!

Crunch! Crack! went the ice, and before Joe's eyes it broke into pieces, and Jenny's cries came back to him on the wintry air.

Joe couldn't reach Jenny, standing there, because her ice chunk was floating down, faster and faster, toward the town. And there were falls in the river ahead — steep, rocky rapids!

Joe sprang to the rescue! He raced down the bank. He tried to reach Jenny's ice cake with a plank. But that did not work.

The birds and the bunnies were all worried, too. They fluttered and chattered and wondered what to do.

The horses stood ready to help if they could. And now Joe had a plan that really was good!

He jumped to the sleigh. At his whistle, the team raced off through the snowdrifts. Behind them, Joe made a loop in his reins like a cowboy's rope at the rodeo.

He coiled the lasso; he let it fly. But just as it left his hand, oh my!

Head over heels over toes went Joe, plunkety thud in a bank of snow!

And the rope missed Jenny!

Now what to do? Joe couldn't help her. He was through, until he could dig himself out.

But the birds came swooping down through the air, and picked up the rope end lying there.

While the bunnies tied one end to Joe, who was still heels up in the bank of snow, the birds flew to Jenny on the ice. The rope dropped around her, neat and nice.

Then horses and bunnies and snowbirds all pulled Jenny back, away from the falls, up the stream and into the pond, smooth as glass, that still stretched away to the woods beyond.

Back came Jenny, and there was Joe. And they never knew how she happened to be off the ice and back under the tree.

The birds and the bunnies never told. The horses just stamped their feet with the cold, and rattled their bells and shook the sleigh, as if they were thinking, "Let's be on our way."

So in hopped Jenny, and after her Joe. He cracked his whip, and he cried, "Let's go!"

Oh, the snowbirds warbled sweetly, and the horses neighed, and the bunnies hopped aboard again, for they were not afraid.

And away they all went merrily, across the frosted snow, once upon a wintertime, long, long ago.

CHIP 'N' DALE
AT THE ZOO

Adapted from the Motion Picture "Working for Peanuts"

CHIP 'N' DALE, two little chipmunks, were having a busy day.

They were gathering nuts for their winter's food. Chip 'n' Dale had made a pile at the foot of their tree.

Now Dale tossed the nuts up one by one to Chip. And Chip swiftly stored them away.

Toss, catch, toss, catch, they had been at work all day.

Suddenly Dale seemed excited about something. "Look at this one!" he cried.

Chip took a look at the nut that sailed up. It was long and strangely shaped.

"Open it," said Dale, scrambling up the tree.

So Chip snapped the nut open. The shell of the nut was paper thin. Inside was not one nut but two!

"Let's try them," said Chip.

So they each ate one. And how good those peanuts did taste!

"Let's find some more of those," said Dale.

"Okay," said Chip. So away they went, racing from branch to branch through the trees. And their bright eyes kept searching for more peanuts on all sides.

Soon they came to a high brick wall. But they could see over the top.

Beyond was a zoo. There were lots of big animals, safe behind fences. But best of all, beyond the fences were people tossing peanuts to the animals!

"Look at that!" cried Chip.

"Let's go!" said Dale.

Where should they go first? The monkeys looked too lively, and there were so many of them they caught every peanut or pounced upon it as soon as it hit the ground.

The bears looked too brawny, and rather

fierce. Chip 'n' Dale did not want to have trouble with them.

No one threw any peanuts to the camels or lions or tigers.

"How about this?" asked Dale when they came to the seal's pool. The seals looked very friendly, sitting on their rocks. And they were clapping their flippers as if they'd just had a treat.

"I'll try it," said Chip. So he scrambled up onto the rocks beside the seals. But instead of crispy peanuts, the keeper threw him a fish!

That was enough of the seals for Chip 'n' Dale! They wandered on, feeling rather sad.

Then they came to the elephant.

The elephant stood there, big and slow, in a sea of peanuts, it seemed.

"This is for us!" said Chip to Dale. So in through the fence they climbed.

They scooped up peanuts—whole big armloads. Then ever so quietly they started for the wall leading home to their hollow tree.

They did not notice that the branch they climbed was the elephant's trunk. Dale tossed his armload into what he thought was their doorway in the hollow tree.

"Hey!" said Chip. "Where are your nuts?"

"In the tree," said Dale.

"That's the elephant's mouth!" cried Chip.

"Mouth!" cried Dale, and he ran so fast to get away from there that he bumped into Chip at his top speed—and scattered Chip's peanuts, too.

They were not ready to give up, though.

They waited in the shadows till the elephant was busy again, waiting for people to throw peanuts to him.

Then they filled their arms up high once more, and started again for the wall.

They made the top of the high brick wall with their armloads safe that time.

Then rat-a-tat-tat! They were pelted with nuts from behind. The elephant had spied

Back to work they went on their own store of nuts, Dale tossing them one by one from below, Chip catching them up above. But they were so tired now the work seemed slow.

"Let's take a little rest," said Chip.

It was while they were resting that they heard a sound like the patter of rain on leaves.

"What's that?" cried Dale. For the sun was shining.

them at the last minute and was squirting peanuts from his trunk!

Poor Chip 'n' Dale dropped their loads and ran. They hid behind boughs till all was quiet again. Then, feeling sore all over, the chipmunks crept back home.

"We can get along without peanuts, I guess," said Chip sadly.

And what do you think it was?

The elephant's trunk was pointing over the wall. And with his keeper on his head to help him aim, the elephant was squirting a year's supply of peanuts into their hollow tree!

And ever since, those chipmunks, Chip 'n' Dale, and the elephant in the zoo have been the very best of friends! Just think of that!

The Sorcerer's Apprentice

From the Motion Picture "Fantasia"

THERE WAS ONCE a great sorcerer who knew more about magic than anyone else in the whole world. He lived deep in an underground cavern, alone but for one little apprentice, who was Mickey Mouse.

There was a lot of work to be done in that underground cavern, and Mickey did it all. He did the meal cooking and the floor sweeping and the bed making and errand running and water hauling and wood chopping for the sorcerer. He got very tired of it, too, for it did seem that with all the magic under the sorcerer's tall hat, he should be able to find easier ways of doing the housework.

"If I had that magic hat, I'd never work again!" Mickey thought enviously as he watched the sorcerer weaving magic spells one day. Mickey, at the time, was busy filling the big tub in the middle of the cavern with bucketfuls of water from the well outside. As soon as he rested for a moment to watch the magic, he felt the sorcerer's stern gaze upon him, and he hurried off to fill his buckets. But when he came back again, Mickey found the cavern empty. The sorcerer had gone off to visit a neighboring magician. And he had left his magic hat behind!

This was the moment Mickey had been waiting for. Very cautiously he tip-toed over to the table, picked up the magic hat, and set it on his own head. It fitted perfectly. Being a magic hat, it would fit anyone who wore it, but Mickey did not know that.

"Gee," he thought happily, "I guess probably I was born to be a magician."

Now to test the hat's powers! As Mickey glanced around the gloomy cavern, he spied the old broom leaning against the wall.

"That will do," he thought.

Looking as stern and masterful as he could, Mickey pointed his fingers at the broom.

The broom quivered. Then, while Mickey's eyes grew bigger and rounder with pleased surprise, it jumped away from the wall and began to waddle across the room toward him.

"I'm a sorcerer!" Mickey thought proudly.

"With this magic hat I can do anything my master can. No more housework for me! I'll let the broom do my water carrying!"

"Broom!" he ordered in his sternest tones. "Fill this tub for me!"

The broom bobbed forward in a little nod. Then, as Mickey watched, wide-eyed, it waddled out of the cavern, up the stone steps, to the well, and was soon back with two buckets full of water. Into the tub went the water, and away waddled the broom for more.

This was wonderful. Mickey capered around the room in a gleeful dance, to celebrate his freedom from toil. Then he sank into the sorcerer's armchair and leaned back to dream of all the marvelous things he would do, now that he could make magic.

He smiled with satisfaction at the steady swish of the broom going about its work. Then his head...nodded...and Mickey... dropped off to sleep.

In his dream, Mickey was standing on a great, high cliff overlooking the whole world. Around him the stars and planets wheeled and danced at his every nod and gesture. Far below the ocean roared, and when he beckoned the waves rose up and bowed before him. Higher and higher dashed the

waves, until one broke at his very feet . . . and Mickey awoke with a start.

Water was lapping at his toes. The sorcerer's chair in which he sat was bouncing on a little sea. The whole cavern was flooded! While Mickey slept the broom had worked on, filling the tub to overflowing and finally flooding the whole great room. And here it came now, waddling down the steps to empty two more buckets onto the flood!

"Stop!" cried Mickey. "Stop, broom. Stop, I say!"

He waved his arms. He pointed trembling fingers. He tried every trick and gesture he had seen the sorcerer use, as far as he could

remember, but the broom went sturdily on about its work.

Mickey tried to snatch away the buckets, but still the broom would not be stopped. Then he thought of the ax. With a mighty blow he smashed through the broom's wood handle. Then chop, chop, chop! He hacked it into a hundred bits.

"Well, that's done!" Mickey said to himself with a great sigh as he sank down on the

steps to rest for a moment. "Now to get rid of all this water."

But what was this? Before Mickey's horrified eyes each splinter of wood became a full-sized broom, armed with two water buckets. Now a hundred brooms were hauling water into the cavern which one had filled to flooding!

"No! No! Go back!" he cried, holding out his arms to stop the march of brooms. But on they came, pushing Mickey into the water as they marched with terrible steadiness to the tub, dumped their buckets, then started back to the well.

Poor Mickey! As he floundered in the swirling waters, the sorcerer's book of wisdom floated past, and he snatched at it as his last hope. Pulling it up to a dry step, Mickey began paging through the thick, water-soaked pages in a desperate search for the words that would make everything right again. He was so intent on his search that he did not even notice when a dark shadow fell over the cavern. The sorcerer had returned!

One glance was enough to tell the magic master what had happened.

He lifted his arms in a commanding gesture—and the waters vanished! Mickey could

scarcely believe his eyes, but it was true. The floor of the cavern was dry, the broom leaned lazily against the wall, the tub of water stood waiting, still just half full, with the empty buckets beside it. Everything was just as it had been when the sorcerer had left—all but one small thing. The magic hat was still on Mickey's head.

With a sheepish grin, Mickey handed the hat to the sorcerer. Then without a word he picked up the buckets and raced up the stairs to the well.

"At least," Mickey told himself as he trudged back toward the cavern, a moment later, with the heavy buckets sloshing at his sides, "at least at this job I know how to stop when it's finished!"

PERRI

From the Walt Disney Motion Picture of Felix Salten's Original Story

ONCE UPON A SPRINGTIME, deep in a forest, a little squirrel was born. The mother named her little squirrel, Perri.

Perri's home was in the hollow of an oak tree whose top had long ago been torn away in a storm. The nest was softly lined with grass and it was warm and dark.

The baby squirrel enjoyed the warmth, as she lay cuddled beside her brothers. At first, Perri did not even know that it was dark. Like many other new-born creatures, she could not see. Then one day, when her mother had gone from the nest for food, Perri opened her eyes. She could see!

Through a small window in back of the nest, sunlight appeared. Perri crawled over to the window and looked out for the first time on a bright world. She saw the earth and trees and a blue sky. She saw her mother picking brown seeds from a pine cone. She saw her father watching, sharp-eyed, from his nest in a pine.

Then suddenly, across the earth, a shadow fell—the long, slinky shadow of the marten. The marten was not so large and fierce an animal as other enemies of the squirrel. But he was more dangerous, because he could climb a tree as well as any squirrel.

"Save the babies! Quick!" warned Perri's father, as the mother leaped for the hollow tree. "I'll head the fellow off!"

The father squirrel was quick, but he was not quick enough. The marten pounced. . . .

"How brave your father was!" Perri's mother mourned. "He saved us this time, but the marten will be back. We must leave."

One by one, she carried her children to the nest the father had left in the high branch of the pine tree. Perri was the last of the baby squirrels to be moved.

"Let me climb to the nest by myself," she begged her mother.

"Nonsense!" her mother scolded gently. "A little thing like you! Don't think you are grown up because you've opened your eyes on the world!"

"It's a very lovely world," Perri said, staring around her.

"It is," the mother sighed. "Yes, it's a lovely world, but not an easy one. We will never see your father again."

Perri had many neighbors in the pine tree nest. At the tip of the branch, a hummingbird's family raised hungry beaks for the seeds their mother brought. In a nearby oak, a raccoon was coaxing her brood down to the ground. And not far away, some young skunks were taking their first wobbly steps.

"It's time you children learned to get about," Perri's mother announced.

How far away the ground looked when Perri made her first journey to the tip of the limb! But in a week she could run along the branch from her home to the hummingbird's nest. She could hang by her tail, too. Still, her mother said she was not old enough or strong enough to venture down to the ground and out into the world.

One evening, the frisky little adventurer pranced out to the hummingbird's nest and peered inside. Perri meant no harm to the hummingbird, but the mother bird darted forward on whirring wings.

Perri felt herself falling. Down, down, down she fell to the soft spongy earth.

"So this is what falling feels like," Perri

said, not at all alarmed. "I'll just explore a bit before I climb back to the nest."

She frisked and danced along the warm earth, until she came to the bank of a swift stream. Perri had heard of this creek, where all the grown-ups came to drink.

I think I will have a sip of cool water myself," said Perri.

Just then a woodpecker called a sharp warning: "The marten!"

Perri started for a tree, but the marten was close on her trail. What should she do?

"Jump in the creek, you silly little squirrel," cawed a blue jay. "You can swim if you try. Martens can't!"

Perri plunged boldly into the swift water. The marten stood on the bank and watched her swim. How furious he was when he saw her reach the opposite bank!

Perri was safe, but wet and forlorn. She

longed to go home, but not for anything in the world would she risk the journey alone. She was wondering what to do when a warning squirrel bark came to her ears.

Close by, his great paw lifted to pounce, was a giant creature, more terrible than a marten. Perri leaped up a tree and sat trembling on a slippery branch.

"I'll give that wildcat a chase," a voice said, as a young boy squirrel swung down by his tail. "Watch me. I'm Porro!"

Perri was too frightened to watch. She closed her eyes, shivering, until she heard the hungry wildcat slink off.

"He's gone," Porro called. "Come down and we'll have a feast."

Proudly, he led the way to a hollow log half burried in pine needles. He showed Perri his store of pine cones and seeds.

"Is this where you and your family live?" Perri asked in surprise. After all, the proper place for a home was in a tree.

"Don't have a family. Can't be bothered with a nest," Porro answered. "At night I just sleep on the branch of my pine tree."

"Everybody has to have a home," Perri said. "I intend to build one at once."

But finding a place for a home was not easy. Perri discovered a hole in a nearby tree, but when she looked, an old bearded flying squirrel drove her away with a flick of his tail. She found a lovely rotted stump, but a family of woodpeckers lived inside.

At last she found a hole in an aspen tree. She lined it neatly with grass and leaves, then popped her head out and looked around. Darkness was creeping over the forest. But Perri was safe. She curled up inside her new nest and went to sleep.

The heat of summer covered the forest before Porro decided to build a nest for himself. He threw a few twigs and bits of bark together and invited Perri and their bird neighbors to see his fine new home. The jay looked at it and screeched:

"Haw, haw! Even the magpie builds a better nest than that!"

Porro paid no attention to the blue jay. Up the tree he went, and into the nest. Then he fell right through the bottom and tumbled back down to the ground.

Even after the nest was mended, Porro was too venturesome to stay in it. On a midsummer's eve, when the moon was high, Perri looked out from her nest to see an owl perched on a limb. He was eyeing Porro, who had decided just then to get a drink of water.

"Danger!" Perri called.

The owl swooped down, and Porro barely had time to escape into his hollow log. There he stayed, until the owl flew away.

Perri and Porro frolicked and played together through the long summer days. They stored acorns and fresh pine cones in the hollow log, without exactly knowing why.

The flying squirrel was hoarding, too; and grumpy old Scarface, the black squirrel.

59

The birds began to talk of making journeys. Perri and Porro hardly listened. They danced about through the red and gold autumn leaves, their little jaws bulging with nuts to store in the hollow log.

Suddenly, one evening, Perri was startled by a loud noise she had never heard before. Porro was leaning against an oak, just as surprised and frightened as she was.

"Did you hear that Perri? I wonder what it could be," said Porro.

Then they heard the noise again. The jays and crows—the only birds left in the forest —fluttered and screamed. A light flashed, followed by a louder noise than before.

Porro dashed for his hollow log and Perri scrambled after him. There was another peal of thunder, and Perri saw her tree house bright with flame.

The fire spread, and all the animals began running from the smoke and flame. Smoke tickled Perri's nose, and she and Porro followed the other animals to the creek. They plunged into the water and swam to a log.

A weasel and a raccoon were clinging to the log. The wildcat floated by. They paid no attention to the squirrels. Enemies and friends huddled together against the enemy of them all—fire.

At last it began to rain. The fire died away. But, all night, Perri clung to the log in the creek. At dawn she crept to the land and to her burnt-out nest. Porro's nest was gone, too, and he refused to make another. The hollow log was good enough.

But Perri was a neat housekeeper. With twigs and brown, rustling autumn leaves, she bravely began to build again.

The days grew short, the nights grew long and cold. One morning, as the sun came up, Perri was awakened by Porro.

"Come, look!" he called to Perri. "The beaver is making a dam! He's got his whole family working with him. Let's watch the beavers build their bridge over the Big Water, from one bank to the other!"

All day the two squirrels watched the beavers at their work. But as the short day ended and the shadows of night came, Perri saw a frightening thing. The marten stood on the opposite bank, eyeing her hungrily.

"Danger! Danger!" Porro called.

Perri was too terrified to move.

The marten began to cross the bridge the beavers had built. Carefully he moved, putting down first one paw and then another. Soon he would reach the opposite bank.

Suddenly the beaver dived underneath the dam. The twigs and branches heaved and swayed, and the marten tumbled into the swift current of the stream.

Perri found her voice again.

"He can't swim! Martens can't swim! He will drown!" she cried, and she leaped into the tree beside Porro.

The squirrels raced from treetop to treetop, feeling the joy of being safe. But their delight lasted only a few days. One morning, Perri woke to see fat, white flakes falling softly in front of her door. The whole forest was white, piled high with snow. The only creatures she could see stirring were the rabbits and the deer.

"Will the world stay like this?" Perri wondered, as she sat there shivering.

She called Porro, but he did not answer. She was too sleepy to go down and find him. "Later," she said to herself. "Now I'll just take a little nap."

And she rolled up in her tail and slept. Through the long winter, Perri slept, or woke drowsily to eat and sleep again. Sometimes she dreamed that she was frisking in the trees with, her friend, Porro.

Porro was asleep, too, in his hollow log— and so were the raccoons and skunks and

badgers. All winter these animals slept, while the other animals, the rabbits and the deer ran swiftly over the silent snow.

There came a day when the sound of bird song filled the forest. Perri opened her eyes and stretched. As she heard the song, she yawned, and looked out at the world. The snow was almost gone, and here and there little green things were sprouting. The sun was warm. It was spring.

She heard a call. Porro's voice! There he was, hanging by his tail from the limb of his pine tree. With a leap and a bound, Perri was in the treetop. Porro raced after her. From branch to branch, from tree to tree, she darted to the edge of the creek.

Across the water, all green and gold in the spring sunlight, was the home of her childhood. She danced across the beaver's bridge, running straight to the tree where she was

born. Her family was no longer there, but it did not seem to matter. Perri was grown up now, and Porro was with her.

They found a store of nuts which Perri's mother had left behind in her nest, and they both ate hungrily.

"We must get busy at once and build a nest," Perri said.

"Whatever for?" Porro asked.

"Whatever for?" Perri scolded happily. "For babies, of course! I shall take this hollow tree. I'll line it with grass and leaves.

Porro folded his paws across his chest. "Build away, Perri," he said. "I'll keep intruders away from the nest."

He looked around at the greening earth. "It's a lovely world," Porro said.

"Yes, it's a lovely world, but not an easy one," Perri answered, just as her mother had, a whole long year ago.

The Grasshopper and the Ants

*"Oh, the world owes me a living,
    Tra la la lalala la."*

THE grasshopper was singing his song as he jumped through the fields. He almost jumped on top of some ants who were pulling a grain of corn up an ant hill.

Said the grasshopper to the ants:

*"Why are you working
    All through the day?
    A summer day
    Is a time to play!"*

"We can't play," said the ants. "Winter will soon be here."

The busy little ants did not have time to feel the warm summer sun, or to run and jump just for fun. From the beginning of day till the end, they were busy hauling the corn away. Winter was coming. They had no time to play.

All summer the grasshopper danced his grasshopper dances in the grasses. When he was hungry, he reached out and ate.

And the grasshopper sang:

"The good book says:
'The world provides.
There's food on every tree.'
Why should anyone have to work?
Not me!
Oh, the world owes me a living,
*   Tra la la lalala la."*

With that he took a big swig of honey from a blue harebell that grew above his head. Then he spit a big wet spit of grasshopper tobacco juice. It nearly landed on a little ant who was dragging a load of cherries to store in the ant house for the winter.

Said the grasshopper to the ant:

"The other ants can work all day.
Why not try the grasshopper's way?
Come on, let's sing and dance and play!
Oh, the world owes me a living,
*   Tra la la lalala la."*

The little ant was so charmed by the music that he dropped his heavy load and started to dance. Then came the queen, The Queen of All the Ants.

And The Queen of All the Ants frowned on the dancing ant so that he picked up his cherries and went back to the other busy ants. Then The Queen of All the Ants spoke sober words to the grasshopper:

"You'll change your tune
When winter comes
And the ground is white with snow."

The grasshopper made only a courtly bow.

"Winter is a long way off," he said. "Do you dance? Let's go."

"Oh, the world owes me a living,
*   Tra la la lalala la.*
The other ants can work all day.
Why not try the grasshopper's way.
Come on, let's sing and dance and play!"

But even as he sang and danced and played on his fiddle, The Queen of All the Ants hurried away. She, like the other ants, had no time to play.

All through the long lazy summer months the grasshopper went on singing:

"Oh, the world owes me a living,
Tra la la lalala la.
Why are you working
All through the day?
A summer day
Is a time to play!"

There was not tomorrow. There was only today, and the sleet and the snow seemed far away. But the little ants worked harder than ever. As long as the sun was in the sky, they went back and forth carrying the foods from the fields into their ant houses.

Then the winter wind began to blow. It blew the leaves off all the trees. The ants ran into their ant houses and closed the door, and you didn't see them in the fields any more. Every day the winds would blow. And then one day, SNOW.

The grasshopper was freezing. He couldn't find any leaves to eat. All he had was his fiddle and his bow. And he wandered along, lost in the snow. He had nothing to eat and nowhere to go. Then far off he saw one leaf still clinging to a tree.

"Food! Food!" cried the hungry grasshopper, and he leaned against the wind and pushed on toward the tree. But just as he got there the wind blew the last dry leaf away. It fluttered away among the snowflakes. The grasshopper dropped his fiddle and watched the last leaf go. It fluttered away through the white snowflakes. It drifted slowly away. It was gone.

And then the grasshopper came to the house of the busy ants and their Queen. He could hear them inside there having a dance. They had worked hard all summer, and now they could enjoy the winter.

The grasshopper was too cold to go on. The wind blew him over, and he lay there where he fell. His long green jumping and dancing legs were nearly frozen. Then very slowly he pulled himself through the snow to the house of the ants and knocked.

When the ants came to the door, they found him there, half frozen. And ten of the kind and busy ants came out and carried the poor grasshopper into their house. They gave him warm corn soup. And they hurried about, making him warm.

Then The Queen of All the Ants came to him. And the grasshopper was afraid, and he begged of her:

> "Oh, Madam Queen,
> Wisest of ants,
> Please, please,
> Give me another chance."

The Queen of All the Ants looked at the poor, thin, frozen grasshopper as he lay shivering there. Then she spoke these words:

> "With ants, just those
> Who work may stay.
> So take your fiddle—
> and PLAY!"

The grasshopper was so happy that his foot began beating out the time in the old way, and he took up his fiddle and sang:

> "I owe the world a living,
>   Tra la la lalala la.
> I've been a fool
> The whole year long.
> Now, I'm singing
> A different song.
> You were right,
> I was wrong.
>   Tra la la lalala la."

Then all the ants began to dance, even The Queen of All the Ants.

And the grasshopper sang:

> "Now I'm singing
> A different song.
> I owe the world a living,
>   Tra la la lalala la."

The Adventures of Mr. Toad

From the original story "The Wind in the Willows"
by Kenneth Grahame

Tucked away among the willows, deep in the peaceful countryside, lie the homes of three good friends.

In his cozy house in the river bank lives Mr. Water Rat—his friends call him Ratty. Close by lives Mole, as kindly and gentle a soul as ever drew a breath.

And in a great mansion set in its own spacious park lives Toady—the madcap, the reckless, extravagant, the fabulous Mr. Toad.

Why, you may ask, do we call him the reckless, extravagant Toad? Well, Toady, you see, is a speed demon. As a boy he went from the fastest tricycle to the fastest bicycle to the speediest boat on the river.

And even after he was quite grown up, he still was always in trouble.

He would knock down old ladies on his speeding bicycle. He would upset picnic parties with his speedy boat. There were always lawsuits threatening and damages to pay.

His good friends Ratty and Mole worried constantly about him. And poor old Mac-Badger, who managed Toad's money, could scarcely keep up with his tremendous bills.

It is no wonder Toad's friends were delighted when news came that Toad had reformed. Ratty told Mole as they sipped their tea one afternoon.

"MacBadger has had a very firm talk with Toad, and he has promised to mend his ways," said Ratty.

"Splendid," said Mole with a happy smile. And he sighed a happy sigh. "It seems almost too good to be true!" said he.

Alas, it was too good to be true! At that moment there came a knock on the door. It was the postman with a special delivery for Mr. Water Rat.

"Come at once to Toad Hall!" it said, and it was signed "A. MacBadger."

"Oh, dear!" said Ratty, with a shake of his head. "This means trouble."

But friends are friends through thick and thin, so off they started, snatching a last nibble of toasted muffin as they went.

At Toad Hall they found poor MacBadger pacing up and down.

"Ah, lads!" said he. "You've come at last! I'm close to being a nervous wreck!"

"What seems to be the trouble, MacBadger?" asked Mr. Rat.

"It's Toad," groaned MacBadger. "This time he's gone too far!"

"But he promised—" said Mole.

"Oh, yes, he's given up fast bicycles and speedy boats, it's true," said MacBadger. "But now he's rampaging about the country in a canary-colored gypsy cart."

"A gypsy cart!" echoed Rat and Mole.

71

And it was true, too true.

Rat and Mole had just turned down the road toward home, after a long talk with Mac-Badger, when a great cloud of dust came rolling toward them. Out of the dust a voice called. And the voice was the voice of Toad.

"Hello, you fellows!" cried Toad. "You're the very animals I was coming to see."

"We want to have a talk with you," said Mr. Rat severely.

"A visit?" cried Toad. "Splendid."

But a visit was not what Ratty had in mind.

"Really, Toad," Ratty said solemnly, "this has gone far enough—too far, in fact. Your reckless pranks are giving us animals a bad name. And you will soon have thrown away all your money and will have nothing to live on. You must give up your horse and cart."

"My horse and cart! Give them up? Nonsense!" cried Toad. He cracked his whip and away he went, down the road in a cloud of dust. Suddenly a strange sound filled the air. Honk, honk! it went. Honk! Honk!

Up went the horse's heels in fright. And over they went, horse, Toad, cart and all.

The motor car, which had caused it all, went chugging off out of sight. And Mole and Rat hurried over to pick up their fallen friend.

"Well, Toady, this should be a lesson to you," said Ratty. "You can see that speed brings nothing but trouble. I hope you are through now with that horse and cart."

"Horse and cart?" Toad repeated. There was a strange far-off look in his eyes. "Oh, yes, I'm through with gypsy carts forever. I'm going to get a motor car!" Think of that!

Well, Rat and Mole managed to get Toad safely home, and they put him straight to bed. They locked him in, too, for he was raving noisily about his motor car. And they sat themselves down in the hall.

But they did not know Toad! Stone walls could not make a prison for Toad. He knotted a rope of twisted sheets and slipped down it to the ground.

"A motor car! A motor car! I've got to have a motor car!" he panted as he trudged away down the moonlit road. "I'll have one, too, if I have to beg or borrow it!"

Rat and Mole were shocked by Toad's wild excitement. But imagine how much more shocked they were next morning. They were still on guard at the bedroom door when they saw the headlines in the local paper.

"TOAD ARRESTED — STEALS CAR!" screamed the headlines.

"Toad!" cried his friends. "It can't be! He's safe in bed!"

They quickly unlocked the door and flung it open. The rope of sheets still hung out the open window. And Toad indeed was gone.

Yes, it was just as the paper had said. Toad was in jail for stealing a car.

On the day of the trial, Rat and Mole and MacBadger sat in the courtroom, feeling sad indeed.

But not Toad. He was as gay as you please. He explained to the court that he had not stolen the car at all. He had bought it from some weasels, and in exchange he had given them the deed to Toad Hall.

"The deed to Toad Hall!" the words swept through the crowded courtroom. "He traded his home for a motor car?"

No one could believe it, no one but Toady's own friends. They knew how strong his longing for speed could be.

The judge and jury did not believe it. Especially since the weasels lied and said it was not so.

So Toad was found guilty and sent to jail— to jail for 99 years!

Poor Toad! He thought everyone had forgotten him. Months passed, and he sat huddled in his dreary cell. But his mind was not idle—not Toad! And on Christmas Eve he slipped past the jailer and made his escape.

Of course the jailer was not fooled for long, but by the time he knew what had happened, Toady was on his way. Disguised as a stout little old lady, he was speeding through the night.

And where did he go? Why, straight back to that quiet spot beneath the river willows, where Ratty and Mole were spending a sad and lonely Christmas Eve.

When Toad appeared in the doorway, he found that Ratty and Mole had another caller. MacBadger was there, talking excitedly.

"We've made a great mistake, lads!" he was saying. "Toad did trade Toad Hall for a motor car. And the weasels are living there now. We must go and get the deed from them, so Toady's name will be cleared!"

With this good news, they were glad indeed to welcome the runaway Toad.

It was midnight when the four friends rowed silently up a secret tunnel that led back from the river to Toad Hall. Then up the back stairway they crept to the great hall where the weasels were, all sound asleep.

They woke up, alas, just as Mole was making off with the deed. And then the fight was on.

Oh, what a fight it was, too! Wham, slam, crash, bam! Our friends were outnumbered, but they fought like heroes, and at last they won.

So Toad was cleared of the charges, and better still, he promised to give up motor cars.

"What a happy day!" said Ratty, when it was all settled.

"Isn't it wonderful?" said Mole.

"Come, lads," said MacBadger. "Let's drink a toast. To the New Year! And to the New Toad!"

Crash! The sound of falling bricks broke in on their toast. And from outside the window a voice called to them.

"Come on, you fellows!" called the voice, and they knew at once it was Toad. "This is the life! Travel—adventure—excitement! And the sky is the limit!"

They ran to the window and looked out. There was Toad, waving to them from a brand-new airplane!

Yes, life went on peacefully there beneath the willows. But peace and quiet were never enough for Toad.

"Well, lads," said MacBadger after a moment, with a thoughtful shake of his head, "here's a toast nonetheless—to our jolly, charming madcap—the fabulous Mr. Toad!"

The Orphan Kittens

Told by Margaret Wise Brown

THREE LITTLE KITTENS were once born into the world. One was black. One was white. One was a calico kitten. And when they felt the warmth of their own little bodies, they all began to purr. For they thought the world was wonderful.

They even thought that the mean old farmer who owned them was wonderful. And just as soon as they could crawl, they crawled all over his house. But the farmer did not like the kittens.

"One cat on a farm is enough," he said. "Get rid of those kittens. Throw them away."

So the farmer's son put the kittens in an old gunny sack and started for the river to drown them.

But the kittens thought the old gunny sack was wonderful, too. They rolled about in the darkness of the sack and wrestled and hugged each other. Then they curled up in a warm pile of fur and went to sleep.

They did not hear the farmer's son stop when he came to the river. They did not hear him say, "These little kittens might find a home if I carried them in to the town. I

don't want to throw them into the river to drown. The river is too cold."

The three little kittens only woke up when they were dumped from the sack into a snowy garden. And that was wonderful, too. They had never before felt the snow under the cushions of their little kitten feet. They did not see the hand that held the gunny sack disappear over the wall. They did not know that they had been thrown away into the white snow.

All that they knew was that the white snow was wonderful. They went creeping across it. Their bright little kitten eyes were shining like the stars in the night. The snow began to fall softly in the empty garden. The little black kitten batted it with his paw. And the other two kittens went pouncing after the soft snowflakes as they drifted toward the ground.

It was the little black kitten who found the cellar door open. With long leaps through the snow, the other two kittens followed him in through the open door. First they came into exciting black darkness.

The little black kitten blinked his bright green eyes in the darkness. The little white kitten blinked two little yellow eyes, and the little calico kitten blinked his great big blue eyes. For kittens can see in the dark.

The three little kittens crept ahead until they came to some steps. The steps were steep and hard to climb. But, one by one, each little kitten pulled himself up—step by step.

At the top of the steps was a long crack of light. That was where the little kittens were going. Beyond was a kitchen full of good cooking smells.

Three little kitten heads came peeking

through the door. And there was the most wonderful thing of all, to kittens. Milk! There was a full saucer of it, warm from the warmth of the room. The little kittens drank it so fast, they spattered it all over their faces.

They were sitting under the stove, licking each other clean and dry, when they heard the big feet coming. They were great big feet, the biggest feet the kittens had ever seen. The feet came nearer. Two hands put a pie on the kitchen table. Then the feet went away.

It didn't take the three kittens long to climb right up on the table and sniff around the pie. Then the little black kitten pounced right into the middle of the pie, and squirted the red juice of it into the white kitten's eye. The little calico kitten just stood on the other side of the pie and waited, with his eyes shining. And when the little black kitten crawled out of the pie and onto the table, they grabbed him. They grabbed the black kitten and gave him a good cat-scrubbing with their tongues.

Then the little black kitten went pouncing too near the edge of the table cloth, and fell. Down, down, he went, pulling the whole table cloth with him. Plates and pans came crashing down. The little white kitten slid down the table cloth like a shoot-the-chute. And the pie landed right on top of him.

The kittens liked the noise of the crash. It was such a big exciting noise. Then they licked themselves clean once more, and went off to explore the house.

In the dining room, they saw a feather blowing about in the air. The black kitten began a dance with it. He jumped in the air and smacked it with his paw. The calico kitten danced, too. But it was the white kitten who discovered the hot air coming up through the grate in the floor. He put his paw in it. But the air blew right past him. He couldn't see what it was, but he knew that it was warm and soft and wonderful. He waved his paw in it back and forth, back and forth.

Then they discovered the piano. Ping pang! ping pang!—Kitten on the keys. The black kitten danced on the high notes, and the white kitten danced on the low notes.

In came the two big feet and they chased the three little kittens all around the house.

Finally, the kittens ran upstairs and hid in the little girl's room. They hid in her closet, and each little kitten climbed into a shoe and went to sleep.

The little black kitten climbed into a soft red slipper and went to sleep. The other two kittens climbed into a pair of sneakers and went to sleep.

There they were when the little girl found them. They were all curled up in her shoes— three sleepy little soft angel kittens. And the little girl loved them and kept them forever. And the kittens thought the little girl was wonderful. Even the cook, who owned the big feet, grew to love the three little kittens.

Pilgrim's Party

LET'S HAVE a real New England Thanksgiving dinner," suggested Minnie.

"Splendid!" Mickey exclaimed. "Turkey and cranberry sauce and pumpkin pie! It makes me hungry just to think of it!"

As they drove though the states of Connecticut and Massachusetts, yellow pumpkins lay on the ground among shocks of corn that looked like Indian tepees.

"They are just ready for pumpkin pies," said Minnie, with delight.

Everywhere that Minnie went in New England she asked the same question: "What will be the best place for Thanksgiving dinner? Which state makes the best pies?"

Whether she was on the coast of Maine or in the farming country of New Hampshire, in the dairy country of Vermont or the rolling hills of Massachusetts, the answer was always the same: "You'd better stay right here! We make the best pies!"

It was hard to decide what to do until Mickey had a good idea. "Let's go to Plymouth and have Thanksgiving where the first one was held," he suggested.

"Just the thing!" the others agreed.

So Mickey turned the car toward Plymouth. The last red and yellow leaves were falling from the sugar maples. The harvests were in, and winter was coming upon the land. There was a frosty crispness in the air.

The road led through the city of Boston, and Mickey stopped to see the sights of the town. The streets in the old part of the city were very narrow. Mickey had trouble in driving through them, but he found the Old North Church where Paul Revere had seen the lantern, and they saw Boston Common and the Bunker Hill Monument. Then they left the city behind and drove through Massachusetts. Minnie was very much surprised to see big shipyards where huge ships were being built. She was amazed to see big cotton mills and shoe factories.

"Why, I thought that the only boat the Pilgrims had was the Mayflower," she said. "I thought the Pilgrims had to spin their own thread and make their own shoes. That's what the history books say!"

"That was a long time ago," Mickey explained. "There have been a great many changes around here since the Pilgrims came." It was too much for Minnie to understand, so Mickey changed the subject. "But you're going to see just how the Pilgrims lived and how they dressed. Every year in Plymouth the people dress up like the Pilgrims and have a big dinner. We're invited!"

"May we dress up?" asked Minnie.

"Yes, we may," said Mickey. "Who do you want to be?"

Minnie decided to be Priscilla, and Mickey decided to go to the Thanksgiving dinner as Elder Brewster. Donald could not make up his mind whether to be Massasoit or Miles Standish. It was growing cold, so he decided to be Miles Standish.

"What can Pluto be?" asked Minnie.

"I've heard that there was a dog on the Mayflower," Mickey replied. "It was a spaniel. Let Pluto be the spaniel of old Plymouth."

On Thanksgiving morning Mickey and Minnie and Donald, with Pluto behind them, marched with the other Pilgrims to the big hall. The room was beautifully decorated with colored leaves, cornstalks, and pumpkins. A delicious odor of roasting turkey filled the air. Pluto began to sniff much too loudly. But just

then a band of Indian braves came into the room. They had feathers in their hair and paint on their bronze faces. Pluto disappeared under a table. He began to bark.

"They're only make-believe Indians who don't mind the cold," whispered Donald in too loud a voice.

"If you don't behave, you'll have to go outside," warned Mickey. Pluto quieted down, but Mickey sat down near him.

All the people were delighted to see Mickey and Minnie and Donald. They gave the travelers a warm welcome. Then in came one of the Pilgrim mothers. She was carrying a big turkey, and she put it down in front of Mickey. She asked him to carve.

Mickey looked at the turkey doubtfully. It was very big. He took up the carving knife.

"Don't cut yourself," warned Minnie.

Mickey couldn't reach the turkey, so he had to stand up in his chair. As he did so, Pluto put his head out from under the table and began to sniff loudly. Mickey tried to kick Pluto and put the fork into the turkey at the

same time. His hand slipped. The turkey shot off the table and onto the floor.

"Oh, I'm so sorry!" cried Mickey, but Pluto was not sorry. In an instant he had the turkey in his mouth and was rushing headlong out the open door.

"Catch him!" shouted Mickey as he jumped from the chair and darted after Pluto.

The Indians leaped forward, but Pluto dodged between their bare legs. Out into the street he ran, with Mickey and the red men after him. Pluto glanced back once and saw them.

Now the Indians were good runners, but they could not catch Pluto. At last they were tired out, and they stopped. Mickey joined them. They turned back toward the hall.

"I can't tell you how ashamed I am of Pluto," said Mickey, but the Pilgrim mothers assured him that there were plenty more turkeys in the kitchen.

"Let Donald carve the next one," suggested Mickey.

Donald rose in his place when the turkey

was brought in. He made a speech, and everyone clapped and cheered. Then he carved the turkey with his sword.

When the day was over Minnie sighed with pleasure. "The Pilgrims are charming people," she said. "I thought they were very stiff and sober. They're not. They're lots of fun. The history books have everything wrong again."

It was late in the evening before Mickey and Donald found Pluto. He was curled up beside Plymouth Rock sound asleep!

The day after Thanksgiving, Mickey, Minnie, Donald, and Pluto started south. As they went through Rhode Island the factories in and around Providence were as busy as they could be, but all the summer homes were closed. Snow was already drifting across the tobacco fields in the Connecticut Valley.

"Don't you think we ought to see Yale University before we leave New England?" asked Mickey.

But Donald had never done well in school. He couldn't spell.

He thought it best to keep away from colleges.

They crossed the Hudson River and drove across the state of New Jersey. "There are a great many factories, homes, and market gardens in New Jersey," said Mickey.

Then their road took them through the states of Delaware and Maryland. They stopped to visit the shipyards at Wilmington and Baltimore. Minnie christened a ship while she was in Baltimore. She meant to name it Minnie, but Donald whispered "Ha Ha" right after it so the boat was named Minnehaha by mistake.

Minnie was furious, but Mickey comforted her.

"Minnehaha is a nice name, anyway," he said. "You know it was the name of a beautiful Indian maiden. So don't you mind."

BEN AND ME

From the Motion Picture "Ben and Me" based on the book by Robert Lawson

IF YOU should ever visit the fair city of Philadelphia, Pennsylvania, very likely you will see a fine statue to the memory of Benjamin Franklin. He was one of our country's first great leaders. Benjamin Franklin was a philosopher, an inventor, and a patriot.

If you are fortunate enough to have a good view of the crown of the statue's broad-brimmed hat, you may see there a tiny statue to one of our country's unsung great, a chap by the name of Amos Mouse.

It was Amos, you see, who was really responsible for many of the great deeds credited to Franklin. And here is the story in his own words:

I was born and raised in Philadelphia, in the old church on Second Street. Our home was in the vestry, behind the paneling.

There were twenty-six children in the family. With that many mouths to feed, we were naturally poor. In fact, we were as poor as church mice.

Since I was the oldest, I decided to set out into the world and make my own way. If I were successful, I could help the others; but in any case, it left one less mouse to feed.

It was the winter of 1745. Those were difficult times. Jobs were scarce, especially for a mouse. All day I tramped through the snow, dodging icicles, brooms, and cats. By

God helps Thofe who help themfelves

nightfall I did not know where to turn. If I didn't find shelter soon I'd be done for.

My last hope was an old run-down shop out near the edge of town. A sign just over the door read, "Benjamin Franklin, Printer & Bookbinder."

Somehow that sounded promising. So I found my way inside. The place was full of strange contraptions, brass rods, tangles of wire and such. It was about as cold inside as out. Back in the shadows sat a round-faced man, trying to write by candlelight.

As I watched the little man, he began to shiver with cold. Then came a mighty sneeze —Ah—ah—choo! Off flew his glasses, and they crashed on the floor!

"Oh dear! Don't tell me!" cried the little man. "My last pair! Now what will I do? I'll never get my paper out. And if I don't pay my rent in twenty-four hours, the men I owe money to will take my press and my furniture and throw me out!"

"Twenty-four hours?" I said thoughtfully. "It isn't much."

"It's hopeless," said the little man.

"But you can't give up!" I told him. "Nothing ventured, nothing gained, Mr. Franklin!"

"My name's Ben," he said. "Plain Ben. And what would you do, whatever your name is?"

"My name's Amos," I told him. "One of the church mice from over on Second Street. And the first thing I'd do is figure out a way to heat this place."

I suggested a fire box in the middle of the room, so the heat didn't go up the chimney. Of course it had to be made of iron, with a pipe to the chimney, to carry off the smoke. It sure wasn't much to look at, when he got it made, but—

"It works, Amos!" he had to admit. "Say, I wonder if we couldn't make these and sell them. Call them Franklin stoves!"

If you know your history, of course you know they did make those stoves.

Well, while Ben had been fooling around with the stove, I'd been at work on his eyeglasses. He'd broken both his outdoors and his reading pair; the only thing left was to make one pair out of the two, fitting the glass together as best I could.

"Will they do?" I asked Ben Franklin, when he tried them on.

"Will they do?" he echoed. "Why, Amos, they're great! Two-way glasses! By George—

bifocals, we'll call them." And to my surprise they became famous, too—even more so than the Franklin stoves.

We were ready then to get to work on the paper, and when I took a look at it, I found it really needed work. *Poor Richard's Almanac*, it was called—poor indeed, I thought. There wasn't a real bit of news in the whole sheet.

"What would you suggest?" Ben said.

"First I'd give it a new name—something

snappy like—ah—the *Gazette*—*the Pennsylvania Gazette*. That's what I'd call it! Then I'd give them some news, real news."

"But where will I get news at this hour?" Ben Franklin wanted to know.

So of course I had to go out and get it for him. I found a big fire on Chestnut Street; I came upon some fellows plotting to cheat the city. I filled my pocket notebook full of news. Then I raced back to Benjamin Franklin and helped him set the story of the fire and the plot to cheat the city in type and print off the sheets on his hand printing press.

It was a long night's work, but I'm here to state it was worth it. By evening of the next day, everyone in Philadelphia was reading the *Gazette*. Ben Franklin was a success.

From then on I went everywhere with Ben, riding conveniently on his hat so I could lean down and give him pointers now and then.

Well, the years went by quickly, and Ben's reputation grew. Letters poured in from all over the colonies, asking Ben's advice on all kinds of things. It took most of my spare time to answer them.

Meanwhile Ben was puttering around with his experiments. And it was one of them that led us at last to the parting of our ways.

Ben took up kite flying. That was the beginning. And to the framework of his largest kite he fastened a small box just for me.

I was so thrilled by flying — seeing the whole countryside spread out like a story-book below—that I failed to notice a sharp pointed wire fastened to the kite.

The first hint I had that anything was wrong was when the sky darkened with thunderclouds and a mean rain wind began to blow. The kite spun and shivered, but Ben would not pull me in!

I screamed myself hoarse. I tugged at the rope. Now lightning was flashing along the horizon. Thunder rolled. The storm was moving our way.

Suddenly with a blast that seemed to split the world, lightning struck my kite! The shock went through me and almost tore the kite to ribbons.

I thought my end had surely come. Now—too late—Ben began to wind his rope. The kite and I, in tatters both, came staggering down the wind and landed in a tree.

When Ben found us there, he scooped me up in one hand.

"Amos! Amos! Speak to me!" he cried. I could almost forgive him for what I had suffered, he seemed so deeply upset.

Shakily I managed to open one eye.

"Amos!" he cried again. "Was it electricity?"

I had been the victim of a plot! All he cared about was whether or not the sizzle in a lightning bolt was the same as electricity! That was the end for me!

"Good-by!" I said. And though he pleaded with me to change my mind, I left Ben then and went back to my family.

The years that followed were troubled ones. Restless crowds filled the streets. There were riots, and loud talk against the stamp tax and other outrages of the king.

It was during this crisis that Ben was chosen to go to England and lay our case before the king. The colonies eagerly awaited his return. But Ben's mission was a failure. The king would not listen.

It seemed as if war must surely come. But the people had no clear statement of their cause to hold them together through a long, bitter fight. Poor old Ben was worried.

I couldn't help feeling sorry for the little man. It was a heavy responsibility he had—more than he could carry. I could help him—

I knew I could. But no! I could not go back to work for Benjamin Franklin. After all, a mouse has his pride!

One night in the summer of 1776 I was awakened by a voice calling my name.

Who could it be at that hour? I wondered.

Sleepily I staggered out of bed and through the mousehole in the vestry paneling.

There on his knees was the great man, Ben Franklin himself.

"Amos, I've come to ask you to come back," he said, as humbly as you please.

I was pleased and touched, but I could not let him see it. "Out of the question," I said, and turned to go.

"Please, Amos. Consider your country," he begged. "I have many big decisions to make, and I can't make them alone. You just must come back, Amos."

"On my own terms?" I asked. "If I draw up an agreement, will you sign it?"

"I'll sign it, Amos. I'll sign any agreement you draw up," he vowed.

So I went back, having spent the night writing out our agreement by candlelight.

Ben was glad to see me the next morning, you may be sure. He took my hat and coat.

He made me some tea. But I was not to be put off my course. I gave him, at once, my agreement to sign.

"Of course, of course," he said. "Do you mind if I read it?"

"If you wish," I said.

That was when the knocking came at the door. It was Thomas Jefferson—"Red," Ben called him. And he was in a terrible state. You see, he was one of the leaders of the colonies, too. And he was supposed to write for them all a statement of what they believed—a Declaration of Independence, you might say. But he could not get the beginning right, struggle as he would.

"The time has come when we the people of these colonies—" he began to read, but then he broke off and shook his head. "No,

Ben, it isn't right. The time is at hand—no—"

"Psst, Ben!" I said, when I saw how upset the poor Thomas Jefferson was. "How about our contract?"

"Shh!" said Ben. "Just a minute."

"No," I insisted. "Now!"

So Ben got out his magnifying glass and began to read it aloud:

"When, in the Course of human events, it becomes necessary—"

"Ben!" cried Red Jefferson, perking up. "That's it! That's it!"

So that's how it happened that I supplied the beginning for the Declaration of Independence. Oh, I didn't get public credit, of course. But fame doesn't matter to a mouse. I have my memories—wonderful ones—of the good old days and Ben and me.

GOLIATH II

Story and Pictures
by Bill Peet

ONCE upon a time in a far-away jungle, there lived a tiny elephant. His name was Goliath the Second, and he was just barely five inches tall. He was so small he couldn't even pull up a daisy.

"I'll never grow up," said little Goliath sadly. "I'll never be a giant elephant like my father."

His father, great Goliath the First, was the biggest tusker in the whole jungle, and leader of the elephant herd. He was so huge and powerful he could uproot the biggest tree without even trying.

"It's not fair," he grumbled. "Why should I

have a little bit of a son who can't even pull up a daisy?"

But Goliath's mother, like most mothers, was proud of her little son no matter what. She didn't care one whit about uprooting trees or pulling up daisies.

"Don't worry, Goliath," she said, "brute strength isn't everything. You'll amount to something one day, just wait and see."

Raising such a tiny son in the dense and savage jungle was a big problem.

Mother Goliath's number one problem was Raja, a crafty old tiger who could hardly take his greedy eyes off little Goliath.

"I've always been curious to taste an elephant," said old Raja, "and now at last I've found one just bite size."

But Goliath's mother wasn't taking any chances. She kept a sharp eye on her little son every minute of the day. And at night she tucked him safely into bed in an empty bird's nest high on a tree limb.

Each day the elephants took a dip in the river. And little Goliath was left on the bank

90

to splash and play in one of his mother's huge footprints.

"Now stay right here where I can see you," she warned. "Don't you dare leave your pond. Now I mean it."

Goliath was getting tired of being treated like a baby.

"I'm nearly eight years old," he said. "I'm old enough to look out for myself."

One day when his mother wasn't looking, Goliath left his footprint pond and wandered off down the elephant trail.

It was a perfect day for running away. The jungle was sunny and warm and very, very quiet. There was only the gentle whisper of

the breeze and the sound of footsteps — soft, velvety footsteps. And they weren't Goliath's.

Suddenly he saw two pale yellow eyes peering through the grass. It was old Raja!

Goliath tried to run but he tripped on his trunk and fell flat on his face. Raja sprang into the air. But he never came down!

Something had old Raja by the tail. It was Goliath's mother — and she was furious!

"You bloodthirsty old scoundrel!" she screamed. She swung him round and round like a yoyo until his head was spinning.

Then with all her strength, Goliath's mother sent that old tiger flying high over the treetops, and all the way across the river to the far end of the jungle.

That was the end of old Raja. At least the old tiger was never seen again in that part of the jungle.

But that wasn't the end of little Goliath's

troubles. For one thing, his mother gave him a good sound spanking with a blade of grass.

This didn't hurt Goliath half as much as one scornful look from his father, great Goliath the First.

Goliath had broken one of the first laws of the herd. A runaway elephant is called a rogue and a traitor and treated as a criminal. Little Goliath had never felt quite so small in all his life. As an elephant, he was a failure.

One afternoon, as big Goliath led the herd down the elephant trail toward the river, something happened. A most terrifying thing. There in the path was a fuzzy little creature with black beady eyes and a string tail.

"Mouse!" cried big Goliath. "It's a mouse! Run—run for your lives!"

The herd went crashing off through the jungle in a wild stampede, and leaped into the river.

There they stayed, trembling with terror, and with only the tips of their trunks sticking out of the water.

Only little Goliath stood his ground. He didn't move a muscle or blink an eye.

"What's the trouble, Buster?" said the mouse. "Are you scared stiff?"

"I'm not scared at all," said Goliath. "I'm just as big as you are."

"That's not the point. I'm a mouse and you're an elephant. And elephants are afraid of mice."

"Why?" asked Goliath.

"I'll show you why!" said the mouse. In a flash he seized Goliath by the trunk, whirled him into the air and slammed him to the ground. Then the mouse jumped up and down on Goliath's head and pinned him to the ground by his ears.

"Do you give up, Jumbo?"

"Never," said Goliath.

And with a wild kick he sent them both tumbling in the grass.

They rolled over and over and came closer to the edge of a steep cliff. Down below an old crocodile was waiting for someone to drop in for dinner—just anyone.

The mouse pushed Goliath toward the edge.

"Over you go, Buster!" he said.

But Goliath saw the crocodile. Desperately, he grabbed for the mouse's tail, and seized it in his trunk. Then with a sudden jerk he swung the mouse out over the cliff, right over the wide open jaws of the crocodile.

"Please don't let me down," cried the mouse. "I give up! You win, ole pal, ole pal! Okay?"

"Okay," said Goliath, and the battle was over.

As a reward for his great victory, Goliath was given the very highest position in the elephant herd—a place of honor on his proud father's head.

And the whole herd kept a kindly eye on little Goliath—for they didn't want to lose him.

Happiest of all was Goliath's mother. "I always knew you'd amount to something one day," she said proudly.

The Lonely Little Colt

Told by Margaret Wise Brown

WHEN DAWN came in the barnyard, the little colt was still asleep. His mother nudged him with her nose until she had him on his feet.

The colt shook himself and looked out of the window. But he shook himself too hard. He hadn't been in the world long enough to know how hard a colt should shake himself. His legs were not yet very strong. So down he went on his knees. But soon he was on his feet again and giving stiff little jumps on his brand new legs. His mother watched him with pride and joy.

He ran with his mother out of the barn and into the fields. Once around the field they galloped. Twice around the field they galloped.

Then the farmer came to the field. He whistled to the mother horse. "It is time for you to go back to work," he said. "You have galloped around with your baby long enough. Now you must help me cut a field of clover to make some hay."

Then the farmer took the mother horse away from the field. The little colt was left there all by himself.

At first the little colt wasn't very happy. He had never been left by himself before. And he did not like it. He galloped around close to the fence and neighed for his mother. Then he just galloped around the field faster and faster.

After a while he began to enjoy himself. He felt the warm sunshine. He smelled the green

grass. He went to the fence and watched some geese march by. He wished the geese were big enough to play with. But he couldn't gallop around the field with a goose.

Then the old gray dog came dashing across the field.

"The dog can run with me," thought the little colt. With a kick of his heels, he galloped after the dog.

But the dog would not wait to play that day. He ran right across the field and under the fence where the little colt couldn't go. The old gray dog was going to the hill to take care of the sheep. He didn't have time to play with a little colt.

Then the little colt saw a little pig running down the road. He ran over to the fence and neighed to the little pig. But the little pig only squealed and ran away. He was looking for something a little pig could eat. He did not want to play with a little colt.

Then the colt saw a sleepy little calf looking over the fence. The little colt ran over to the calf and stopped. Here was an animal his own size. They rubbed noses.

The little colt kicked up his heels.

The little calf kicked up his heels.

Then the little colt neighed.

Then the little calf mooed.

The little colt stiffened his legs and jumped.

The little calf stiffened his legs and jumped.

After that they seemed to feel that they knew each other. So they ran up and down beside the fence.

The calf ran up and down on his side of the fence.

And the colt ran up and down on his side of the fence.

Then a little boy came and opened the gate, and the colt rushed into the field with the calf. Soon they found another gate open. So they both ran into the farmyard and jumped over everything they saw.

They jumped over a chicken.

They jumped over a cat.

They jumped over a pig.

And they jumped over the bull.

They jumped and they jumped and they jumped.

And then when evening came, the mother horse whinnied and the colt ran home.

And the mother cow mooed and the calf ran home.

All this happened the day the colt and the calf came to know each other. After that the little colt was not lonely any more.

DUMBO
of the Circus

THE CIRCUS ANIMALS paced back and forth in their cages nervously. They sniffed the air for the first smells of spring and peered at the skies anxiously.

Everyone in the circus was eager for spring to come. After long months at winter quarters in Florida, the clowns, the ringmaster, the musicians, the acrobats and the animal trainers were restless.

The trapeze artists were limbering up their muscles for their dare-devil tricks. The circus train's locomotive, Casey Jr., was exercising his piston rods, and the calliope was practicing a few toots on his pipes. Before long, Casey Jr. would take the circus on tour.

They all stopped occasionally to look at the sky. They were expecting something!

Finally it came—a great flock of storks

Suggested by the story "Dumbo, the Flying Elephant," by Helen Aberson and Harold Pearl, Copyright 1939 by Roll-A-Book Publishers, Inc.

carrying big bundles in their beaks. The messenger birds zoomed low over the circus and dropped their packages. Parachutes blossomed forth, and the eagerly awaited bundles floated gently to earth.

When each bundle had been delivered safely, the circus animals were happy!

Leo Lion and his wife had four of the cutest cubs anyone had ever seen—

Mrs. Chimpanzee had a baby chimpanzee to dandle on her knees—

There was a tiny hippopotamus weighing only three hundred pounds—

An infant seal had come, as long as your hand and as bright as a cricket—

There was a baby tiger who loved to have his mother, Mrs. Tiger, polish his fur with her clean, soft tongue—

And two miniature zebras had come, complete with stripes—

But for Mrs. Jumbo, the elephant, who had been waiting so patiently, there was *nothing!* She scanned the sky for one of the messenger birds. As she waited, Mrs. Jumbo stamped nervously in her stall. Her elephant friends tried to comfort her, as much as possible. But it was difficult, for they were almost as disappointed as she was.

"Maybe the messenger's just a little late," one of the elephants said to Mrs. Jumbo. Even a baby elephant is a heavy bundle for a stork, you know."

Mrs. Jumbo did not give up hope until the circus train pulled up on the loading platform and the animals marched into their cars. It was a happy time for everyone but the elephants. They did not want to go on tour without a baby elephant!

Casey Jr., the circus train locomotive, was not worrying about baby elephants. He blinked his lamps, stretched his piston rods to get the cramps out of them, blew the rust out of his whistle and a few experimental smoke rings out of his stack, and looked back to see how far the loading of the circus train had progressed. He whistled impatiently and shot a hiss of steam from his boiler to let everyone know he was ready.

"All aboard!" called the circus boss.

"All aboard!" whistled Casey, as he crouched low, pushed his wheels against the tracks, and pulled forward. The cars jerked into movement behind him, and he puffed away from the winter quarters, gaining speed and rolling along more and more easily.

Casey Jr. let out a long, high whistle. It was good to feel the cool fresh air rushing past him as he sped northward. He tooted a greeting to some birds who flew alongside him. He whistled to the cows in a field, who looked up and mooed to him, as they did every spring, when Casey Jr. passed.

As he rattled across the plains, the young colts in the pastures challenged him to races. Casey Jr. purposely slowed down to let them beat him in order not to hurt their feelings. This pleased the colts' mothers, who looked on proudly and decided that Casey Jr. was a grand fellow.

On and on the little locomotive chugged,

tooting at steamboats when he ran alongside rivers, and at factories when he passed through cities. They whistled back, for they were all old friends of Casey Jr. Casey had serious responsibilities, too. In the mountains, when he saw a tunnel ahead, he had to toot a warning to the giraffes to pull their necks down. And there was one particular long, dark tunnel where he wasn't exactly afraid, but it somehow kept up his courage to whistle to himself a little.

In the train behind him, clowns sang in time to the clickety-clack of the wheels, and the animals rocked their babies to sleep with the swaying motion of their cars. But in the elephant car, Mrs. Jumbo stayed alone in her compartment, and her friends stood together without chattering and gossiping as they usually did.

Mrs. Jumbo would have been much happier if she had known who was sitting on a cloud not far away.

It was a special delivery stork! He had detoured around a bad thunderstorm and had lost his way. But here he was at last, on the trail of Mrs. Jumbo. Far below, he could see the circus train crawling across the country.

"Look out below!" he cried, as he picked up his bundle and descended in a power dive.

"Mrs. Jumbo? Where's Mrs. Jumbo?" he called as he came up to the two giraffes, who pointed to the elephant car ahead.

"Oh, Mrs. Jumbo!" sang the stork.

"In here!" cried the elephants. "In here! This way, please!"

The stork flew through the opening in the roof into the car where Mrs. Jumbo was so eagerly waiting for him.

"Mrs. Jumbo?" the stork said, tipping his cap politely, and putting his bundle on the floor beside her.

Mrs. Jumbo started at once to untie it, but the messenger insisted that Mrs. Jumbo sign the receipt for one elephant before she opened the package. Then he tipped his hat

and flew away, as all the other elephants gathered round excitedly.

"Quick, open the bundle, Mrs. Jumbo!" cried one of the elephants.

"I'm on pins and needles!" cooed another.

"This is a proud, proud day for us elephants," said a third.

And when Mrs. Jumbo's trembling trunk had at last unfastened the bundle, there lay a little elephant all curled up asleep.

"Isn't he a darling?" cooed one of the elephants to the others.

"Just too sweet for words," said another.

Mrs. Jumbo just beamed at the little fellow.

"What are you going to name him?" asked the first elephant.

"Little Jumbo," said the mother proudly.

"Kootchie, kootchie, kootchie!" went one elephant, as she tickled the baby playfully.

That made him sneeze! And when the baby sneezed, his ears, which had been hidden, flapped forward.

The elephants jumped back in amazement! Those were the most enormous ears anyone

had ever seen on an elephant. They were larger by far than the ears on all the grown-up elephants! They could not help staring at the baby elephant. Even Mrs. Jumbo looked startled and amazed.

The baby elephant looked up and smiled. His ears dropped back down again and dragged on the floor. One of the big elephants tittered.

"Isn't he silly-looking?" she whispered to the elephant next to her, but in a whisper so loud that everyone heard.

"Simply ridiculous!" said the other. "Why, he's just a freak elephant, that's all."

Mrs. Jumbo glared at them, and beamed at her baby. When he grew into those ears he would be the biggest and most magnificent elephant in the world.

"I think you'd better change his name," said the oldest elephant, trying to make her voice sound especially sweet. "Jumbo won't quite fit, I think *Dumbo* is what you mean."

All the other elephants giggled and laughed merrily over this clever joke. But Mrs. Jumbo could stand it no longer. She slammed her compartment door in their faces.

Through the walls, the mother elephant heard the others laughing and joking. She lay down and took her little baby in her arms, caressing him gently with her trunk. The baby elephant made small contented noises and gradually fell asleep.

Everyone in the circus called the baby elephant Dumbo. His big ears became the great joke of the circus. Every time the train went through a tunnel, a clown said he hoped Dumbo had pulled his ears in first. When the wind blew strongly, the big elephants tried to act worried, saying that if the wind caught Dumbo's ears, it would pick up the whole train and blow it away.

Dumbo just smiled when he heard these things. He was just a little bewildered that others were not more friendly with him. He even laughed at some of the jokes himself. He thought that the idea of flying away in the wind was fine—it sounded like fun.

Mrs. Jumbo stayed in her own compartment almost all the time, and kept little Dumbo with her. Her temper grew worse, and she began to brood and worry. And it is not good for elephants to brood and worry.

An evening finally came when everyone forgot about Dumbo. That was when Casey Jr. puffed wearily to a stop in the city where the first show was to be given. It had been a long pull for Casey Jr., but despite his fatigue he was excited, too. Even the storm that was raging could not dampen the spirits of the members of the circus. They set to work in the driving rain to raise the tents and get everything ready for the first show, which was to be given the next day.

The roustabouts opened the doors of the freight cars and began to unload the tents and the ropes. The animal keepers led out the elephants and set them to work. The big animals lifted the tent poles in their trunks and carried them to the middle of the open lot. They pushed the circus wagons off the flat cars and pulled the heavy loads that men could not possibly handle. And all the time they worked, the rain poured down on them and the thunder boomed.

When the lightning flashed, Dumbo could see short glimpses of the hurried work going on all around him. When the thunder rumbled he just grasped his mother's tail a little more firmly and kept on trudging behind her. Wherever she went, lifting, pulling, and hauling, he tagged along.

As the sun rose in the morning, the clouds were chased from the sky by a fresh wind, and in the open field the circus, all set and ready for the first show, glistened in the bright morning light.

After breakfast, everyone got ready for the big parade. The clowns put on their wigs and make-up and costumes. The horses were brushed until they shone, and bright ribbons were put on their manes and tails. The animals marched into their cage-wagons, and the elephants got in line, tail and trunk, tail and trunk. The calliope brought up the rear, his shining pipes uttering little toots of impatience. This first parade of the season was his first chance to play those tunes that delighted the children lining the streets.

Finally the parade began. Bright flags were flying and hundreds of cheering people lined the streets. Boys and girls, men and women, grandmothers and grandfathers and babies in their mother's arms, were all there, cheering as the beautiful white horses appeared at the head of the parade. Everyone cried with pleasure as the well-trained animals pranced and reared back gracefully.

Next came the first group of clowns, jumping and leaping and running in circles. Then the big cage-wagons with the wild animals rolled into view, followed by more clowns. In the distance people could hear the shrieking song of the calliope, and they knew that the end of the circus was approaching. But first came the elephants, marching majestically down the center of the street. They kept perfect step as they walked along, each elephant holding with his trunk the tail of the elephant in front of him. At the very end of the line came Dumbo. He had a hard time reaching up with his trunk to the tail of his mother in front of him. And he could not keep step, no matter how hard he tried.

At first glance people thought Dumbo was cute. But when they saw his floppy ears dragging on the ground, they tittered and giggled and some laughed out loud. The people laughed at Dumbo more than they had at the monkeys or the clowns. Monkeys and clowns are supposed to be laughed at, but elephants are dignified and majestic creatures. You can say "Oh!" or "Ah!" or "How big!" or "How strong!" about an elephant, but you just can't laugh at him.

Poor Mrs. Jumbo's ears burned to hear all the laughter over her little son. She glared furiously at the people on the sidewalks. She was glad when the parade was ended. But she did not know that even worse was in store for her and for Dumbo.

Back in the tent, Mrs. Jumbo gave Dumbo a bath so that he would look fine for the first show that afternoon. She scrubbed him with her trunk until he laughed and said it tickled. He splashed in his tub and made his own shower bath by taking water in his trunk and spouting it into the air over him.

When Mrs. Jumbo had carefully wrung out Dumbo's big ears and he had shaken himself dry, they ate their lunch and then went to their stalls in the menagerie. The other animals had taken their places, the performers were all ready, and the ringmaster had shined up his black top hat. Outside the big tent, the barkers were shouting to the first of the crowd, telling of the wonderful sights to be seen inside—the fat lady, the thin man, Stretcho the india-rubber man, the man who swallowed sharp swords, the man who ate fire, the lions, the tigers, the acrobats, the clowns, and the elephants.

Soon the crowd was streaming through the tents. A group of boys gathered near the rope in front of Mrs. Jumbo's stall. They pointed at Dumbo and laughed. Dumbo, trying to be

friendly, walked toward them, but at the very first step he tripped on one ear and rolled on the ground. The little boys roared with laughter, and a bigger crowd gathered.

"What a wonderful sailboat he'd make," yelled one boy.

Another boy opened his coat and held it far out from his body.

"Look! Here's Dumbo!" he cried, as he wiggled his coat and everyone laughed.

Mrs. Jumbo could stand no more. She reached out quickly and grabbed one boy—who had just been sticking out his tongue at Dumbo. Then she spanked him soundly! The other boys screamed and ran away, and the keepers came running as fast as they could.

"Wild elephant!" someone yelled, and the crowd began to run for the exits.

When the first of the animals' keepers tried to push Mrs. Jumbo back into the corner of her stall, she picked him up with her trunk and tossed him into a pile of hay. The ringmaster came with a whip, and Mrs. Jumbo threw him into a big tub of water.

More keepers came running with their long, spiked poles. They poked Mrs. Jumbo, trying to force her back in her stall, where they could tie her fast. But now the mother elephant knew that they wanted to lock her up, away from her little Dumbo. She lifted her trunk and bellowed loudly. She knocked down the keepers in front of her.

But a man slipped behind her and quickly put a chain around her rear leg. Then other men rushed forward and bound her.

"Take her to the prison car!" cried the dripping ringmaster. "She's dangerous!"

So Mrs. Jumbo was led away to prison and Dumbo was left all alone. He didn't have anybody at all.

That night in the elephant tent, all the big animals were gathered around a pile of hay for dinner. They were busy eating and talking about the terrible things that had happened that day.

"I used to think he was funny," one of them said. "But now I think he's a disgrace. Mrs. Jumbo was a fine, decent, and respectable elephant until he came along."

"Dumbo is not just a disgrace to his mother," said another. "He's a disgrace to all elephants the world over."

On the other side of the pile of hay was a very tiny creature who listened wonderingly to their conversation. It was Timothy, the circus mouse. He had smoothed out a comfortable bed for himself, and was lying there wondering how soon he should step out and scare the elephants. As long as he lived, he never stopped getting a thrill out of scaring elephants. Whoever it was that arranged things so that elephants were frightened of mice had a great idea.

When Timothy was feeling a little blue, whenever he had a bad day—he could always make himself feel fine and important again just by scaring a bunch of elephants.

But today Timothy cocked his head on one side and listened carefully to the chatter of the big animals. Ordinarily the elephants didn't talk much while they were eating. Now they muttered and whispered in shocked tones, and Timothy guessed that they were really enjoying the whole affair even though they pretended to be horrified.

Something exciting had happened, anyway, Timothy concluded. Too bad he had missed it, whatever it was. It must have occurred while he was away searching for furniture for the new house he was building under the floor of the ringmaster's car. He

stuck his head out of the hay to hear what the elephants were saying.

Then Dumbo came in, looking for something to eat. He smiled cheerfully up at the big elephants, for he was very lonesome. But when they saw him, they stopped talking at once, turned their backs on him, and closed the space around the pile of hay. The smile faded from Dumbo's face, tears came to his eyes, and he turned slowly away.

Now Timothy Mouse knew what the elephants were talking about. And when he saw Dumbo's ears he knew why.

"They can't do that to a little fellow," he muttered, "no matter who he is."

He brushed off his little red jacket, set his red bandmaster's cap at a jaunty angle, and leaped among the elephants.

"Boo!" he yelled, just as loudly as he could.

The elephants jumped back, looked at the tiny mouse with terror in their eyes. Then the tent became a mass of rushing elephants, bellowing, running, stamping, and squealing. One elephant ran up a ladder, and two of them even scurried up the tent poles. When they were all just as far from the mouse as they could get, Timothy stood in the middle of the floor, put his hands on his hips, and glared around at them all.

"Pick on a little fellow, will you?" he cried. "You ought to be ashamed of yourselves! With all those big bodies you've got, you'd

think there'd be a little heart in them. But no, not you! Just appetite and gossip, that's all. You wouldn't even let the little guy have something to eat. You made fun of him and called him names. You probably did the same thing to his mother and drove her wild. And why? Just because he was born a little different from you, that's all. Sure, I can figure it out. He's got big ears. So what of it? I'll bet he's got a heart inside of him, and that counts. It's more than you've got."

He paused for breath and looked around at the cowering elephants.

"Boo!" Timothy Mouse yelled again. "Boo! Boo! Get out of here!"

With a yell of fright, the terrified elephants dashed out of the tent.

Timothy knew it would be at least a half hour before they were all rounded up and brought back again. He smiled to himself and looked around for Dumbo.

"Hey, little fellow, where are you? Where are you, Dumbo?" he called.

Then he saw the tip end of a little trunk waving from under a bale of hay. Timothy walked over and patted the end of the trunk.

"No need to be afraid, Dumbo," he said. "Come on out. That's just an act I put on for those big fellows."

But Dumbo was afraid. But when he had listened to Timothy Mouse telling those great big elephants how mean they were, when he heard the mouse telling them all it didn't make any difference just because he had big ears, Dumbo's heart had been warmed as never before. He lay under the pile of hay and smiled.

"It's lucky for you I came along," said Timothy, "because I'm the one to help you out of your troubles. You leave all your troubles to Timothy Q. Mouse."

Dumbo crept out from under the pile of hay and stood beside Timothy Mouse who looked him over very carefully.

"Pretty big ears, all right—" he said, al-most to himself. But when he saw Dumbo look sad again he added, "But that's all right. No, it's better than all right. See, you're different from all other elephants. That's something. What if you were just like the rest of them? What would that get you? Not a thing. But you're different. You're a little elephant with big ears, so you ought to figure out something you can do that no other elephant can do. Then they'd all look up to you."

Timothy began to pace back and forth across the floor, thinking hard. Dumbo grabbed the mouse's tiny tail in his trunk and walked up and down behind him, just the way he did with his mother. Somehow, Dumbo felt safe and secure with Timothy.

"I've got it!" Timothy shouted, whirling around, "If you could just be a big success in the circus, they'd let your mother out of prison. And all the elephants would admire you, and so your mother would be happy and everything would be all right."

Dumbo nodded. Everything sounded so sure and easy when Timothy talked about it.

"So we must figure out an act of some kind," Timothy muttered. "An act just made for you. Say—you know that big elephant balancing act at the end of the performance?"

Dumbo nodded eagerly.

"Well," said Timothy, "just picture this. The elephants have finished building their pyramid. Then you rush out, with a flag in your trunk. See?"

Dumbo nodded again.

"You run across the ring," said Timothy Mouse, "to that springboard the acrobats use. Now remember Dumbo, the springboard is always pulled to one side of the ring before the elephant act. Well, you run and jump on the springboard and leap right up to the very top of that pile of elephants! Then you wave the flag! The audience applauds! and you're the hit of the show!"

Dumbo was very excited. But he shook his head wonderingly.

"Sure, you can do it!" cried Timothy. "I'll help you. We'll sneak out and practice at night for a while. We'll show 'em!"

With an affectionate pat on Dumbo's trunk he scampered away. Dumbo started eating the hay, paying no attention to the other elephants when they returned, still nervous and worried about the mouse. Dumbo smiled when he thought how Timothy frightened them so much and at the same time was such a good friend of his.

Later that night, Dumbo was sound asleep in his stall. He felt a tiny tapping against his trunk, and there was Timothy.

"Come on, Dumbo," he whispered. "We've got to practice the act."

It was not an easy job. Dumbo ran up to the springboard all right. He bounced on it hard and flew into the air. But then he lost all control. Sometimes he landed on his back, sometimes on his tail, sometimes on his trunk, sometimes on his head.

Once in a while Dumbo just bounced up and down on the springboard. He said that bouncing up and down made him feel as if he were flying. He would have liked to bounce up and down for hours, but Timothy always made him get back to work.

After several nights of practice, Dumbo improved. He could land on his feet, even when he jumped from the springboard to a stand ten feet high, then fifteen feet high, then twenty feet high.

Then Timothy decided Dumbo was ready for his big act. The next day, the performance went on as it always did. But little did the elephants or the ringmaster know what Timothy and Dumbo were planning to do.

Dumbo was as nervous as he could be. So much depended on his doing everything right. He clutched his little flag tightly.

The great moment finally came! The pyramid of balancing elephants was swaying in the ring. The audience was applauding loudly.

"Now!" cried Timothy.

Before he knew it, Dumbo was running toward the springboard.

THEN IT HAPPENED!

Dumbo tripped over his ears!

A gasp rose from the audience as Dumbo fell and rolled trunk over tail, trunk over tail straight for the springboard. He hurtled the length of the board, bounced into the air, and crashed right against the big ball on which the bottom elephant was balancing. The ball started to roll, and desperately the bottom elephant fought to control it while the pyramid above him swayed and rocked crazily in and out of balance.

"Run for your lives!" screamed someone in the audience, and there was a rush for the exits. Round and round, back and forth, the tottering mountain rolled. It crashed into circus apparatus, tore away ropes and poles, knocked the trapeze artists off their perches, and drove panicky clowns before it. The ringmaster tore his hair, jumped on his hat, and beat his breast.

Little Dumbo, confused, dazed, and scarcely knowing what he was doing, stumbled after the reeling pyramid, waving his flag in his trunk with a pathetic hope that he might still get to the top where he belonged.

But now the top elephant seized the center pole of the tent with his trunk. He clung to it even when it swayed and creaked and the ropes snapped. The great tent sagged and then, with a crash, the pole toppled to the ground and the whole structure gave way. Amid yells and screams and roars and bellows, the tent settled to the ground.

From the wreckage, the trunk of a little elephant waved a tiny flag.

It was night. Casey Jr. had pulled the circus train out of town far behind schedule because of the wreck caused by Dumbo's fall, which had disgraced the entire circus.

The elephant car looked like a hospital. Old Rajah stood with a sling supporting his heavily bandaged trunk. "Sixty years I've been

in the circus," he moaned, "but never have I seen anything like that."

Another elephant with big lumps on his head, cried, "Yes, and it was that ridiculous little son of Mrs. Jumbo that did it, too."

"He's a disgrace to our race," said another elephant. "I think we should disown him as an elephant!"

"Yes! You're right!" they all cried.

"It's a real shame," Old Rajah said to the elephants. "But I suppose it's the only thing to do. We can't ever admit to anyone that an elephant became a clown."

"A clown?" gasped others in horror.

"Yes, that's his punishment," Rajah said. "The ringmaster has decided to turn him over to the clowns."

The elephants all agreed that this was indeed the worst punishment that could have been found for an elephant.

At the next town the circus equipment was repaired and the clowns prepared for their new act with Dumbo. They fastened a bright yellow ruff around his neck. They powdered his head a clownish white, and on his sad face they painted a big crimson grin. A pointed dunce cap topped off the silly make-up.

Dumbo was the saddest little elephant in the whole world.

Oh, it was fine for the crowds, who had never seen anything so funny. It was fine for the ringmaster, who at last could figure on some profit from his ridiculous little elephant. It was fine for everyone but Dumbo, who cried himself to sleep every night, and for his mother, who wanted more than ever to be with her little son to comfort him and care for him, and for Timothy, who felt that it was really all his fault because his idea had turned out so badly.

Timothy tried to smile and make Dumbo feel good. He said he would have another idea, a better one that would surely work. But he knew the clowns would never let Dumbo go, that no one would ever give him a chance again.

The new act was the hit of the show. The clowns built, right in the middle of the big tent, a three-story building. Of course, it was only a false front, like a movie set. Suddenly flames and smoke belched from the windows and the clowns rushed in dressed like firemen. Their buckets were sieves and their hoses squirted just a drop of water at a time, and the audience roared at their antics.

Suddenly, at the topmost window, Dumbo appeared. Wearing a golden wig and dressed in a pink nightgown, he was frantically waving a white handkerchief in his trunk. A clown rushed into the tent—crying to the firemen to save her darling child. The fire fighters brought out a large round safety net and cried, "Jump! Jump!"

Then Dumbo jumped. Down, down, down he hurtled as the crowd howled in excitement. Dumbo hit the net hard—and crashed right through it, landing in a large tub of white plaster underneath.

The audience roared with laughter and the clowns took their bows. It was the biggest success of the circus!

Yes, Dumbo was now the great climax of

a big success. But it brought him no happiness. He trudged out of the tent, dripping wet plaster behind him, having fun poked at him all the way. As he passed the other elephants they turned their backs to him, and even the monkeys looked the other way.

But back in his stall there was Timothy. Timothy was smiling bravely, telling Dumbo there was still a little plaster behind his ears as he washed himself, trying to make jokes and see Dumbo laugh. But it was no use. Dumbo wouldn't smile. He wouldn't eat, even when Timothy brought him a few peanuts he had saved for him.

Timothy did not know what to say as they settled down to sleep. He climbed up Dumbo's trunk and found a comfortable bed in the brim of Dumbo's little pointed hat.

"Dumbo," he said.

Dumbo just nodded slowly to show Timothy he was listening.

"Dumbo, I'm going to figure out something so that this clown business stops, so your mother will be free, and so you'll be a success. Now just go to sleep and stop worrying. Pretty soon you'll be a great success, you'll be happy, you'll be flying high!"

Dumbo smiled. Timothy was a good friend, even if his ideas didn't work. He dropped off to sleep, smiling over Timothy's idea that soon he would be flying high. That reminded him of the times he used to jump from the springboard. How good that felt!

Dumbo fell asleep, dreaming of that one great chance, which had turned into such failure, and now in his dream it became a great success. He waited at the entrance, sped gracefully toward the springboard, and bounced high into the air. Up and up he soared, gliding into the air with such ease that it seemed no effort at all.

It was a wonderful dream, and it seemed very real to Dumbo.

The morning sun rose on a perfectly natural landscape. There were trees and grass and a brook and a road. But there was something wrong about the scene. It was not at all according to Nature or Nature's laws that a certain tree should bear, high up in its branches, the form of a sleeping elephant.

The elephant was comfortably cradled in a forked limb, lying on its back with its ears and legs dangling loosely. The ears were unmistakable. It was Dumbo! And in the brim of his hat lay Timothy, still sleeping soundly.

A noisy group of birds had gathered around them, chattering their disapproval and scolding shrilly. Timothy stirred, disturbed by the insistent racket, and opened his eyes sleepily. He blinked, and a pair of eyes not a foot away blinked right back at him. A large, rusty-looking crow, evidently the leader of the birds, was glaring at him. Timothy shifted uncomfortably under the crow's stern look.

"What are you doing down here?" he finally asked irritably.

"What are *you* doing up *here*?" the crow snapped back.

"Oh, go away!" said Timothy, who didn't like to be bothered before he was fully awake. He closed his eyes and settled down for another nap, since Dumbo was still asleep. "I'm here because I belong here," he muttered to the crow. "I live here!"

"So do we!" cawed the crow.

This made Timothy blink again. These birds were getting more and more annoying.

"Oh, stop talking nonsense," Timothy said. "Run along and mind your own business."

"Haw!" cawed the crow loudly. "That's good! I suppose it's not my business when an elephant comes flying in here at midnight! And it's not my business when you knock my nest to pieces and scare my whole family out of their feather beds! Say, do you have any idea where you are?"

"Sure," replied Timothy, rubbing his eyes. "I'm right where I belong, in the circus. And what are you and your friends doing around this tent, I'd like to know."

Screams of laughter burst from the circle of birds. Timothy sat bolt upright and peered down to look at Dumbo, whose eyelids were beginning to flicker. Then he gazed at the canopy of leaves overhead, the trunk, the bark, and the branches of what certainly was a tree. And then he looked down—far, far down—at the ground.

They really *were* up in a tree!

"Dumbo!" he cried. "Dumbo! Take a look down—down there!" But just as Dumbo, who was still sprawled out on his back, started to turn his head, Timothy thought better of it. "NO, DON'T! DON'T LOOK!"

Dumbo had already glanced down. For one long minute he looked. Then he scrambled to his feet. Trying to balance in the wobbly fork of the tree, he teetered back and forth like a tightrope walker in a high wind.

Dumbo lost his hold and fell to the branch below. Timothy clutched the elephant's hat brim and shut his eyes. The second branch broke, and Dumbo fell. He clutched at the lowest branch, and it seemed that it might save him. But elephants were never meant to cling to branches. Dumbo fell!

He landed in a shallow brook that flowed under the tree, and Timothy fell into the water beside him. Dripping wet, the two sat in the stream while raucous shouts of laughter poured down on them. The hoarse voice of the crow rasped through the branches.

"Now, try to keep your feet on the ground," he cawed. "It's not right for elephants to fly."

Dumbo and Timothy picked themselves up without a word and trudged off into the woods. They were bewildered and confused. Where were they? Dumbo could not imagine what had happened.

Timothy was speechless. He plodded along, hands clasped behind his back, his face a mask of puzzlement. Thoughts popped in his mind like firecrackers. "It's not right for elephants to fly? I wonder what that old crow meant. How did we ever get up into that tree? Dumbo can't fly. He hasn't got any wings. The only thing he has are those big—*say*, that gives me an idea!"

He stopped and turned to Dumbo. "Did you fly last night?"

Dumbo shook his head and smiled at Timothy as if he were a little crazy. Then he stopped with a startled expression on his face.

"What is it?" Timothy asked impatiently. "Come on, tell me!"

Dumbo told Timothy Mouse about his

dream the night before—how he had jumped on the springboard, sailed into the air, and flown away.

"If dreams could only come true, Dumbo!" Timothy said. "Well, I guess there's nothing to that flying idea."

They walked on aimlessly. But the same thought kept running through Timothy's head. "We got up into that tree somehow, dream or no dream. And people have walked in their sleep—so why couldn't they fly in their sleep?"

Timothy Mouse stopped and put his hands on his hips. "That just must be the answer! Dumbo flew in his sleep, and that's how we got up in that tree. And if Dumbo hasn't got wings, then the only thing he could fly with are his ears!"

He turned to Dumbo. "Listen, Dumbo. You can fly. You were right! You flew last night. You are going to fly again! Come on over here and we'll practice."

Dumbo followed Timothy obediently. But he remembered the many bad falls he had taken when he practiced on the springboard, and he remembered how that idea had finally turned out. This would be even worse. But he could think of nothing else to do, so he put himself in Timothy's hands.

In the field, they set to work. Timothy told Dumbo to flap his ears up and down vigorously, going faster and faster.

"One! Two! One! Two! Up! Down! Up! Down! Faster! Faster!" Timothy Mouse shouted at the little elephant.

Dumbo flapped his ears in time and a cloud of dust arose around them. Birds and small animals of the woods gathered around this strange sight in curious wonder. Then the flapping became slower and slower and ceased altogether, and out of the dust staggered the two grimy and choking partners.

From the trees around them came a chorus of laughs and jeers from their audience, chiefly from the crows who had followed them through the woods.

"Get a balloon!" shrieked the leader of the crows, and the others cackled loudly at his clever joke.

Timothy Mouse gritted his teeth, pulled his hat way down over his ears, and began with Dumbo again.

Dumbo galloped in a circle, and about every fifth step his flapping ears lifted him off the ground a few inches. The birds thought this was the funniest thing they'd ever seen, and they fluttered along beside him, imitating his clumsy efforts. Dumbo, confused and excited, didn't look where he was going and ran into a tree. He lay sprawled on the ground while the birds gathered round and jeered.

"Happy landings!" the big crow cackled, and the other crows cawed their approval. Even Dumbo thought it was funny, much to Timothy's disgust.

"Don't pay any attention to them," he said to Dumbo. "They probably laughed at the Wright brothers, too. You're doing fine. Now let's go over to this little hill and take off from there."

Dumbo took off from the little hill, all right, but he landed, too—in a mudhole. And Timothy, who made the trip in Dumbo's hat, bore his share of the crack-up.

The crows followed Timothy and Dumbo and laughed louder than ever.

Timothy could stand it no longer.

"Wait a minute!" Timothy shouted at them in a voice hoarse with rage.

The birds cocked their heads wonderingly.

"I want to ask you something. Is there a single one among you who has a heart?"

Timothy looked around at them all. The little mouse stared at them hard in the sudden silence. They all felt a little embarrassed and stirred uneasily.

"If there is," the mouse went on, more calmly, "I want to tell you a sad story. I want to tell you about somebody who had the misfortune of being born different from others —somebody who, just because he *was* different, and through no fault of his own, brought sorrow to himself and his poor old mother. This little fellow tried to hold his head up and smile, to be a success. But then came the cruelest blow of all. They made him a CLOWN!"

A chorus of sympathetic noises came from the birds and animals.

Then Timothy drove home his point.

"Here I am trying to help my friend Dumbo be a success, and what do *you* do? You sit on your perches and laugh at us—yes, you laugh at us!"

The birds hung their heads guiltily. There was a silence, and then the big crow spoke.

"Well, you see," he said apologetically, "we didn't understand. We'll do whatever we can to help, won't we, fellows?"

There was a loud cawing of approval as the birds flew down and gathered around Dumbo and Timothy.

The old crow took Timothy to one side. "Listen," he said, "the only reason Dumbo can't fly is that he hasn't any confidence. He

a thing, but then he felt Dumbo moving beneath him. Then, as the dust cleared away, he looked over the brim of the hat. Dumbo was FLYING!

"Look, Dumbo, look!" Timothy shouted, and for the first time Dumbo opened his eyes. When he saw himself heading for a treetop, he almost fainted and fell, but he clutched the feather, flapped his ears, and banked gently in a curve around the tree. The crows flew around him, cheering encouragingly. Dumbo flew more and more gracefully, sailing through the air with ease.

It was wonderful! It was even more wonderful than his dream!

Slowly he leveled off to come to a landing. For his first attempt, it was pretty good. He bumped a little and nosed over on his trunk, spilling Timothy out on the ground. But the two partners did not mind at all. They got up laughing and shouting with glee as the birds circled around them, cawing their applause.

For the next few hours, Dumbo practiced. The crows taught him how to bank and turn and soar and glide and loop. In a short while Dumbo was making smooth three-point landings every time.

Timothy now saw that the sun was sinking; it was late.

"Say, we must be getting back to the circus," he said to Dumbo. "We're going to surprise them in that show tonight. We'll have to think of some story to explain where we've been all day."

The old crow told them how to get to the circus grounds, a few miles away, and with a dipping salute to his friends the crows, Dumbo flew away.

Timothy made him land on the edge of town and walk into the circus grounds. He had a carefully laid plan for the evening performance, and he didn't want Dumbo to give away their secret until exactly the right moment. Dumbo promised not to say a word or act differently in any way.

just thinks he can't. We have the same trouble with our young ones. They don't want to try it at first, either. They're scared when they look out of the nest. So we give them a feather—any old feather—and tell them it's a magic feather from Persia and that anyone who holds it in his beak can fly. It always works. Here's a feather. Go on Timothy —try it on Dumbo."

Timothy took the feather from the old crow and ran joyfully back to Dumbo. The little elephant looked doubtful, but Timothy was so happy, so certain, so confident, that he began to believe him. When he took the feather in his trunk, he seemed to feel a new strength flowing into him.

Timothy climbed into Dumbo's hat, and the little elephant scampered up the hill once more. The birds gathered around expectantly, no longer making fun. There was silence as Dumbo stood on the crest of the hill and began to flap his ears. He closed his eyes, clutched the magic feather, and flapped his ears faster and faster.

Timothy held on to his hat. He closed his eyes to keep out the dust. He could not see

And so the two partners came back home to the circus. Timothy scampered off to his house under the ringmaster's tent, and Dumbo brought joy to the clowns by his return. They had been afraid that the funny animal which was the climax of their act had disappeared forever.

Dumbo sat patiently while the clowns put on his make-up and his costume for the evening performance. And when the time came for him to climb up behind the window of the fake building, Timothy joined him and jumped into his hat.

"Our big moment has come, Dumbo!" Timothy whispered excitedly. "Just wait until after this act, and the whole world will be eating out of our hands."

Dumbo just nodded and smiled. Inside he was trembling, but he tried to act calm and serene. He didn't want Timothy to know that he was afraid. Dumbo looked confidently at the little black feather, which he clutched in the end of his trunk.

The clown act began. Smoke and flames poured from the windows of the building. The clowns rushed in with their sieve-buckets and waterless hoses. Dumbo stood at the window, the spotlight on him. Below he saw

the clowns with the life-saving net spread out above the tub of wet plaster.

No more plaster for him! he thought. And he jumped. But at that moment, the black feather slipped from his trunk and floated away. Dumbo stared in horror, and his heart sank in fear. Was he to fail once again?

Timothy saw the feather go, too, and realized what effect this would have on Dumbo. As they plunged down, down, toward the ground, Timothy shouted to Dumbo, pleading with him to spread his ears and fly. But Dumbo seemed not to hear. He had closed his eyes and decided that once more his high hopes would be dashed. In a flash, Timothy jumped from the hat and, holding on tightly, scampered down Dumbo's trunk and looked him in the eye.

"Dumbo!" he shouted frantically. "Dumbo! You *can* fly! That feather didn't mean a thing. It was fake. You can fly without it. You *can* fly! *You can fly!*"

Timothy's insistent words reached Dumbo's ears. He opened his eyes and saw the firemen's net just below him. "YOU CAN FLY!" screamed Timothy, as Dumbo spread his ears wide and swooped up into the air when he was not two feet above the net!

One mighty gasp arose from the great audience! They rubbed their eyes! They pinched themselves! They knew it couldn't be, but it was happening!

Dumbo was flying!

Timothy, who had braced himself for the crash, slowly opened his eyes and pulled himself back up to the hat brim. When he got his breath back, he looked over the edge and gloried in the sight of the wildly applauding crowd below him.

"Dumbo, you're wonderful!" he shouted. "Marvelous! The greatest thing on earth! Dumbo, look at them shouting for you! The audience is shouting for you, Dumbo!"

Dumbo swooped up to the highest point in the tent and then plunged down, down,

DOWN, and not until the very last instant did he level off and sail gently over the heads of the audience, which was in a state of utter collapse from the sheer excitement of it all.

Then Dumbo repeated his power dive. He flew upside down, barrel-rolled back to level flight, and did loops, spins, and falling leafs. He swooped down to pick up peanuts and squirted a trunkful of water on the clowns. The crowd roared.

The news spread like wildfire. The town was aroused and came rushing to the circus.

All the animals in the circus, too, heard

what was going on. And the animal keepers quickly brought Mrs. Jumbo from her prison car so she could watch her son thrilling the crowds. Dumbo dipped in salute to her as she came into the tent, and the crowd roared its applause for the mother of this flying marvel.

Dumbo flew for a full hour, and when he finally came to a beautiful landing by the side of his mother, everyone was exhausted from the excitement, hoarse from shouting. With dignity, Dumbo escorted his mother to their stall, as Timothy held back the crowds that surged around.

"Stand back, everyone," he shouted. "Give the star a chance to rest. Give the great Dumbo, the Flying Elephant, an opportunity to have a little time alone with his dear mother. No conferences until tomorrow morning," cried Timothy Mouse.

And so Timothy became Dumbo's manager. And he saw to it that Dumbo got a wonderful contract, with a big salary, a pension for his mother, and a special streamlined car on the circus train. Dumbo flew in great aviation contests, made a good-will tour of South America, broke all altitude records, and helped the Army and Navy in their aviation training programs.

And through it all he remained the simple, kind little fellow that he had always been. He didn't forget his old friends the crows, who frequently went on private flying parties with him. He bought some shiny new whistles for Casey Jr. He saw to it that Timothy had always on hand a supply of every known type of cheese.

And now, as the circus train puffed across the country, Casey Jr. tooted his bright new whistles happily. In the elephant car, the big elephants stood on boxes, flapping their ears. They jumped, hoping they would fly even a few feet. But each one of them crashed and gave up.

At last all the elephants, even Old Rajah, agreed that there could be only one Dumbo, the Flying Elephant.

In the special streamlined car at the rear of the train Dumbo sat snuggled close to his mother, Mrs. Jumbo, whose trunk was curled about him affectionately. Nearby sat Timothy Mouse nibbling contentedly on a piece of fine cheese and humming a tune.

Thus the circus train with "Dumbo's Flying Circus" sped across the country toward the bright lights of Hollywood, where new triumphs awaited Timothy Mouse and Dumbo, the one and only Flying Elephant.

PAUL REVERE

THERE WAS once a man named Paul Revere who rode under the midnight moon. He knew he might never return. But he went riding, ridding, riding for liberty—because he wanted a country without a king, a country where all men could be free.

Paul Revere was a silversmith in old Boston town. If anything could be made of silver, Paul Revere could make it. In his shop on Fish Street he made teapots and cream pots, buckles and bowls, and spoons and jugs and cups.

But on this April night he left his shop. He walked quickly through the streets, keeping away from the King's soldiers in their red coats.

Robert Newman was waiting for him, almost hidden by the shadow of Christ Church.

"The King's soldiers march tonight," Paul Revere said. "They want to capture our guns and gunpowder, and some of our men. I am riding to Lexington to give the warning, but the redcoats may stop me. We are to tell our men with lanterns how the British go—one if by land, and two if by sea."

Robert Newman nodded. "I know the plan. I will show the lanterns from the tower of the church."

"Show two lanterns. The redcoats are going by sea," said Paul Revere.

While Robert Newman started up the tower, Paul Revere hurried home. He put on his boots and riding-coat, and said good-bye to his wife and children.

"Good luck, father," said young Paul, his oldest son.

"Thank you, son," Paul Revere said. "Now it's up to you to take care of things here, for there is no telling when I will return home."

Once again Paul Revere went out into the night. With two friends he went to the river bank, where he had hidden a rowboat.

"My spurs!" he said. "I've forgotten my spurs! How can I ride without them?"

Then he saw that his dog had followed him. Writing a note to Mrs. Revere, he tied it to the dog.

"Home, boy!" he said. "Home—as fast as you can!"

The dog was back in a few minutes—and tied around his neck were the spurs.

"Ah, that's better," said Paul Revere.

Getting into the boat, Paul Revere and his friends began to row across the river. Floating on the water was the ship *Somerset*. It was a big ship, the King's ship, and it had sixty-four cannons. Its lanterns shone out in the darkness like staring eyes.

Paul Revere kept listening for the roar of cannon, or the shout of a ship's officer. But he could hear nothing, and at last the boat touched shore.

"We did it!" Paul Revere said. "We did it! Right under their noses!"

Not far from shore, Paul Revere met some men. They led him to Deacon Larkin's house and gave him a horse.

"You must be careful, sir," said one of the men. "There are redcoats on the road."

"I will," Paul Revere said, as he got into the saddle. "Well, gentlemen, I must be off."

And Paul Revere began riding, riding, riding for liberty. Past fields and meadows, past orchards and farms, he rode. Brooks and streams flashed by in the moonlight. And in all the world there was no sound but the rush of wind, and the thud of the horse's hoofs on the road.

Then, ahead of him, he saw two men on horseback. Their pistols gleamed in the moonlight.

"Soldiers!" Paul Revere said. "Redcoats!"

One of the soldiers galloped toward him, and Paul Revere cut across a field. Near a swamp he suddenly turned aside. He smiled as the horse behind him crashed into the swamp, its hoofs sinking in the mud.

Spurring on his horse, Paul Revere raced to another road. Riding, riding, riding, he came to the village of Medford. He stopped at a house and pounded on the door.

"Wake up!" he shouted. "The redcoats are coming."

At every house, all the way to Lexington, Paul Revere shouted his warning:

"To arms! To arms! The redcoats are coming."

And everywhere, men reached for their rifles. They were Minute Men, ready to fight in a minute. Women ran to the swamps with their children. Church bells rang, and drums rolled. For the redcoats were coming, and the time had come to fight for liberty.

And when the redcoats marched into Lexington, the Minute Men were there before them. A shot was fired, and the battle started. And the battle was the start of a great war.

For years the war went on. And when the war was over, there was a new country—the United States of America. It was a country without a king, where all men could be free.

And Americans have never forgotten Paul Revere, who rode under the midnight moon— riding, riding, riding for liberty.

Alice in Wonderland

MEETS THE WHITE RABBIT

*Adapted from the Motion Picture based on the
story by Lewis Carroll*

Do you know where Wonderland is? It is the place you visit in your dreams, the strange and wondrous place where nothing is as it seems. It was in Wonderland that Alice met the White Rabbit.

He was hurrying across the meadow, looking at his pocket watch and saying to himself: "I'm late, I'm late, for a very important date.

"I'm in a rabbit stew, oh oh! Can't even say good-by—hello! I'm late, I'm late, I'm late!"

He hopped across the brook and disappeared into a hollow tree.

"That's curious," said Alice. "A rabbit who wears a waistcoat, and carries a watch, and can talk!

"He's in such a hurry, he must be going to a party. I surely would like to go, too."

So Alice followed him.

"What a peculiar place to give a party," she thought as she pushed her way into the hollow tree.

But before she could think any more, she began to slide on some slippery white pebbles inside. And then she began to fall!

"Curious and curiouser!" said Alice as she floated slowly down, past cupboards and lamps, a rocking chair, past clocks and mirrors she met in mid-air.

By the time she reached the bottom the White Rabbit was disappearing through a little door, too small for Alice to follow him.

Poor Alice! She was all alone in Wonderland, where nothing was just what it seemed. (You know how things are in dreams!)

Whenever she ate a bite of cake or took a sip to drink, she would shoot up tall or grow so tiny she was sometimes afraid she would vanish quite away.

She met other animals, yes, indeed, strange talking animals, too. They tried to be as helpful as they could. But they couldn't help her find the White Rabbit.

"And I really must find him," Alice thought, though she wasn't sure just why.

So on she wandered through Wonderland, all by her lonely self.

At last she reached a neat little house in the woods, with pink shutters and a little front door that opened and—out came the White Rabbit!

"Oh, my twitching whiskers!" he was saying to himself. He seemed very much upset. Then he looked up and saw Alice standing there.

"Mary Ann!" he said sharply. "Why, Mary Ann, what are you doing here? Well, don't just do something, stand there! No, go get my gloves. I'm very late!"

"But late for what? Alice began to ask.

"My gloves!" said the White Rabbit firmly. And Alice dutifully went to look for them, though she knew she wasn't Mary Ann!

When she came back, the White Rabbit was just disappearing through the woods again.

So off went Alice, trying to follow him through that strange, mixed-up Wonderland.

She met Tweedledee and Tweedledum, a funny little pair.

She joined a mad tea party with the Mad Hatter and the March Hare.

She met a Cheshire cat who faded in and out of sight. And one strange creature—Jabberwock—whose eyes flamed in the night.

They all were very kind, but they could not show Alice the way, until:

"There *is* a short cut," she heard the Cheshire cat say. So Alice took it.

The short cut led into a garden where gardeners were busy painting roses red.

"We must hurry," they said, "for the Queen is coming!"

And sure enough, a trumpet blew, and a voice called:

"Make way for the Queen of Hearts!"

Then out came a grand procession. And who should be the royal trumpeter for the cross-looking Queen but the White Rabbit.

"Well!" said Alice. "So this is why he was hurrying so!"

"Who are you?" snapped the Queen. "Do you play croquet?"

"I'm Alice. And I'm just on my way home. Thank you for the invitation, but I really mustn't stay."

"So!" cried the Queen. "So she won't play! Off with her head then!"

But Alice was tired of Wonderland now, and all its nonsensical ways.

"Pooh!" she said. "I'm not frightened of you. You're nothing but a pack of cards."

And with that she ran back through that land of dreams, back to the river bank where she had fallen asleep.

"Hm," she said, as she rubbed her eyes. "I'm glad to be back where things are what they seem. I've had quite enough for now of Wonderland!"

Donald Duck
PRIZE DRIVER

WELL, what did you learn in school today, boys?" Donald Duck asked his nephews one evening.

"We're studying safe driving, Uncle Donald," said Huey, Louie, and Dewey Duck.

"Good idea," said Donald. "That's what this country needs. You boys just watch your Uncle Donald. You'll see what safe driving is!"

"How did you bash your fender, Uncle Donald?" asked Huey.

"We noticed it outside," said Louie.

"Now there was a stupid driver," said Donald. "Turned right out in front of me. I was coming along at a good clip, minding my own business. Boy, was I burned up! I told him a thing or two."

The nephews nodded at one another.

"Driving too fast in traffic is bad," said Dewey.

"Anger causes accidents," said Louie.

"Always figure the other driver is not as smart as you are," said Huey. "Be ready for him to make a mistake."

"Now listen, you fellows," said Donald. "I was driving a car before you were born. You don't have to teach me! I'm going over to call for Daisy now. Do you want to trust my driving and come along or not?"

"Sure, Uncle Donald. We'll come," said the boys. They all hopped into the back seat. And they got out pencils and papers.

As Donald flipped the starter, he glanced at his watch.

"Gosh, we're late!" he said. "Have to make up a little time."

The first stop light turned yellow as they came up, but Donald sneaked on through. One, two, three, the boys made notes on their pads! But Donald did not see that.

When he tried to turn onto the busy highway, traffic was racing by. No one would wait for him.

"Doggone these drivers," Donald fumed. "They never think of the other guy." And at last he stamped his foot on the gas and swung out in front of an oncoming car so it had to slam on its brakes. "That'll show him," Donald said. The boys' pencils all went back to their pads.

"Now," said Donald, "we can make some time." So down the busy highway he zoomed, swishing from one lane to another, back and forth across the road. The boys had to hang onto each other.

"Wow! This is too fast!" they cried.

"So you want to go slow," cried Donald in

disgust. They were in the left lane now, the fast lane, but Donald crept along. Cars lined up behind them. Drivers tried to swing out around them. What a traffic jam he caused!

Z-z-zing! came a siren. It was a police car.

"Sorry, sir," said the policeman. "This lane is for faster traffic. If you want to drive slowly, please keep to the right on busy highways."

He saluted and went back to his car.

"Well!" said Donald Duck, surprised. With a sheepish smile, he started up again. And they went on to meet Daisy Duck.

Back home the three boys went into a huddle.

"Sure looks bad," they said.

"Why all the gloom, boys?" Donald asked.

"Well, we entered you in a contest at school for the most courteous driver in town," said Huey.

"You did?" said Donald. "Say, that's great!"

"Yes, but look at your record on this trip," said Louie.

"Sneaked through a yellow stop light," Dewey pointed out.

"Took a chance because you were angry," Huey added.

"Wove from lane to lane on a busy highway," said Louie. "And jammed up traffic by driving too slow in the fast lane."

"You have all the answers, don't you?" Donald snapped. "But take a look at the things I do right. I keep my brakes adjusted and my lights working right. And I don't pass on hills and curves."

"Yes, we know, Uncle Donald," the nephews sighed. "But for us to win the contest, you have to be the most courteous driver in the PTA. And you're a long way from that."

"Oh, I am, am I?" cried Donald. "Well, I'll show you! I'll show the whole PTA!"

Next day, as Donald was driving the boys home from school, he saw some cars waiting to turn onto the busy highway. So he slowed down and let some of them in.

He drove at the speed of the rest of the traffic, staying in one lane most of the time.

He was careful in parking to get close to the curb, and not to slide over the line into the next parking space.

And when he parked the car on a hill, he turned the wheels in toward the curb so the car would not start to roll back down the hill.

"Courtesy doesn't take much time," the boys were quick to point out. Donald politely opened the door and bowed as they stepped down out of the car.

And as the days went by, Donald found it was fun to be polite. He liked to see the ladies smile when he stopped to let them cross the street.

He liked to see the truck drivers wave in salute when he had let them make a left turn.

When he saw cars waiting to turn, as he was coming toward them, he stopped to let them go.

He always signaled carefully when he was going to turn or stop or slow down.

Soon along came a meeting of the PTA.

The boys took part in a safety drill while Donald watched from the audience.

"By golly," Donald whispered to Daisy at his side, "those kids are the best of the lot!"

Next the school principal introduced Police Chief Horsecollar.

"The Chief will award the prizes in the courteous-driving contest we've been running here in town," the principal explained.

"It's a pleasure to be here," said the Chief. "I guess you can see it's been some time since I was here learning my three R's. But folks, we're never too old to learn. And the biggest lesson we need to learn today is: In driving, it pays to take time to be polite.

"Tonight it is my pleasure to award the prize for the most courteous driver in town to—"

Donald smoothed his hair and straightened his tie, all ready to stand up.

"—Mr. Mac Turner, father of Sandy Turner of this school."

"Thanks," said Mr. Turner from the platform. "I drive a truck for a living. And anyone who drives all the time can tell you it pays—really pays—to take time to be polite."

"Now," said the Chief, "we have another prize to award. An even more important one, because it proves we can keep on learning, even when we're grown up. The prize for the driver who has *improved* most in driving courtesy goes to the uncle of Huey, Louie, and Dewey Duck—Mr. Donald Duck!"

"Folks," said Donald from the platform, "I used to think it was smart to be speedy. But I've learned it's a lot more fun, and smarter, too, to take time to be polite. The credit really belongs to my teachers, though. They did all the work. Huey, Louie, and Dewey, come and take a bow."

Huey, Louie, and Dewey came to the platform. And they took it—one, two, three!

GOOFY
MOVIE STAR

ONCE UPON A TIME there was a wonderful place called Hollywood.

It was the center of Movie Land.

Everyone in Hollywood, it seemed, wanted to be a Movie Star.

Every waitress was waiting to be discovered, so she could be a Starlet for a Movie Studio.

Every young man working in a filling station planned to grow up to be a Movie Star.

They were all waiting for a Talent Scout to happen along. For a Talent Scout is a man,

you know, who finds most new Movie Stars.

Driving down the streets of Hollywood, you knew at once you were in Movie Land. You almost wanted to be a Movie Star, too.

There was just one person in Hollywood, it seemed, who didn't care to be a Movie Star.

His name was Dippy Dog. And he was a happy soul.

Dippy liked the movies, of course. He liked to sit in the balcony with a bag of popcorn and settle down to see a picture show.

"Yuk yuk yuk!" he would laugh his merry laugh. And everyone around would laugh with him.

One night some Talent Scouts heard Dippy laugh.

"Who is that laughing?" they cried. "He has the makings of a Movie Star!"

And when they found it was Dippy Dog, the Talent Scouts hustled him off to a Movie Studio. They didn't even wait for Dippy to see the rest of the show. Talent Scouts waste no time!

Soon Dippy was signing a contract to be a Movie Star.

"What's your name, son?" said the producer. "Dippy Dog? That will never do!

"We need a name that breathes romance—Dandy—Daffy—Goofy! That's it!"

So Goofy signed his new name to the contract. And then he was a Movie Star.

Now Goofy had to dress like a Movie Star. He had whole closets full of clothes.

And he had to have some shiny new cars—not one new car but four!

He had to move from his little house to a mansion worthy of a Star.

It had a swimming pool for each day of the week. And there was a special pool for Saturdays.

Goofy had to have his picture taken, of course. He had his picture taken waking up, eating his breakfast—and even when he was brushing his teeth.

He had his picture taken dressed for golf—and tennis and hopscotch and polo.

Goofy was so busy having pictures taken for newspapers and magazines and television shows, that he never had time really to play anymore.

He even had pictures taken for a Movie. He was the Star, of course.

Now whenever he went to eat in a restaurant, Movie Fans waited at the door, to see him walk in and out.

The night his Movie opened, all the pretty girls and handsome young men who wanted to be Movie Stars too lined up outside the theater.

"Isn't he wonderful?" they said.

Then along came a famous newspaper writer to interview the new Star.

"What is the secret of your success?" she asked.

"Yuk yuk yuk!" laughed Goofy—the laugh that made him famous. "I guess I just have fun, that's all."

And that is the story of how Goofy became a Movie Star in Hollywood, once upon a time.

Babes in Toyland

Based on the Motion Picture "Babes in Toyland"

"LOOK, MARY!" said Tom. "There's a bridge. I wonder if that is the one."

Mary read, " To find the Toymaker, who will decide your fate: First go down the ridge. Then you'll find a bridge."

"Oh, it must be," she said. "It fits the directions just perfectly."

"Yeah! Hooray!" shouted all the children, who were Mary's little brothers and sisters.

"I'm glad that we got lost in Toyland," said Little Boy Blue. "And I'm glad that the kind trees captured us, and that we never have to leave."

"Hurry! Let's go see the Toymaker!" said Bo-Peep.

On the other side of the bridge there was a tall building with candy-cane columns and ice-cream domes.

Little tin soldiers stood by the gates, and a floppy-eared dog slept on the steps.

Tom knocked on the door. He rang the doorbell. And three times he called, "Anyone home?" Then Mary pointed to a sign above a window.

The sign said:

TOYLAND TOY FACTORY
Closed for Alterations
business is not as usual
Genius at Work Inside

Tom, Mary and the children all crowded around the window. They could see two men. One of them had a sweet, gentle face.

"That must be the Toymaker," said Tom.

The other man was pointing excitedly at a huge object covered with blue velvet.

"I've got it! I've really got it this time," said Grumio, the Toymaker's helper.

"Got what?" asked the Toymaker.

"The greatest invention in the world," answered Grumio. "A toy-making machine!"

"All I know," said the Toymaker, "is that you have got to get to work. Do you know what time it is?"

"Half past October," answered Grumio. "That leaves us two and a half months before the Christmas deadline. And with my invention, we don't need half the time."

Grumio unveiled his machine.

"There!" he said. "Isn't it magnificent?"

"If it works," replied the Toymaker.

Sadly he thought of Grumio's other inventions, all lying at the bottom of the Toyland scrap heap.

"Watch," said Grumio. He started putting things into the machine, singing as he did:

"A touch of sugar, a dash of spice;
Add a pinch of everything nice.
Cheeks of pink, eyes of blue;
Now add a ribbon, a bow or two—
And I'm through."

He pulled the lever marked *Start*.
Lights flashed.
Buzzers buzzed.
Wheels spinned.
Churns churned and dials turned.

In less time than it takes to say "Toyland," a beautiful doll fell out of the slot marked *Finish*.

"Amazing!" said the Toymaker.

"And that's not all," said Grumio. He showed the Toymaker how his machine could make:

doll houses,
and squeaky mouses,
and balls
and baseball bats,
puzzle parts,
and party hats,
alphabets,
and rocket jets,
and toys
not even thought of yet!

"Wonderful!" said the Toymaker. "But we need millions of dolls and millions of alphabets not just one or two."

"I know," said Grumio proudly. "And my machine *can* make millions of toys at a time."

"Bravo!" cried the Toymaker. He quickly pinned some medals on Grumio.

Then the happy Toymaker started pressing buttons all over the machine.

He pulled all the levers for all kinds of toys, the ones marked *Girls* and the ones marked *Boys*.

"Stop!" cried Grumio. "The machine will

make millions of toys at a time. But it can only make *one kind at a time*."

The warning came too late. Grumio couldn't move fast enough to stop the Toymaker.

The machine began to hum: Chug a chug, blub a blub, bim a bam a BOOM! Chug a chug, zub a zub, zim a zam a ZOOM!

Then it began to quiver.

Then it began to quake.

Then it really began to shake.

Then the smoke blew.

And the sparks flew.

A sign flashed that said:

QUITS

And the toy machine gave a great big groan, and smashed in a million bits.

"Oh, oh, oh!" cried the Toymaker. "Now I'm really ruined."

"If only you had listened to me," groaned Grumio.

"Won't somebody please listen to me," said Tom, coming into the Toyshop. "My name is Tom Piper, and this is Mary. The trees told us to turn ourselves in to you. We and the children have been trying..."

"Children!" cried the Toymaker. "Don't you know the first rule of Toyland? *Children are never allowed to see the toys before Christmas*."

"But there won't be any toys this Christmas," sighed Grumio.

"Oh yes there will," said Tom. "We'll all help. That is, if you agree, Mr. Toymaker."

"I not only agree," said the delighted Toymaker, "I sentence it as your fate."

And a very happy fate it was for everyone.

All the children were given tasks working on their favorite toys.

Little Boy Blue put the button eyes on teddy bears.

And Wee Willie Winkie put the rockers on rocking chairs.

And Bo-Peep made bean bags shaped like pears.

Tom put the finished toys in boxes.

Then Mary wrapped everything in yards of ribbon and tissue paper.

And the happy Toymaker put on the Don't-Open-Till-Christmas stickers.

Even Grumio helped. He gave up making toy machines and discovered one that would make pink lemonade instead.

And everyone thought him a truly great genius because he made the best pink lemonade in Toyland.

FOREST FRIENDS

Based on "Snow White and the Seven Dwarfs"

NOTHING is so contagious as a secret. You can't see it, you can't smell it, you can't taste it but just the same it's very catching.

Clusters of toadstools bent their heads together. Even the leaves on the trees whispered to one another and the branches hummed as busily as telegraph wires.

The squirrels and the bunnies and the chipmunks tittered and squeaked among themselves and then settled back on their haunches in a most tantalizing manner as

much as to say, "Oh, yes, I know, but I won't tell YOU!"

And the look of all of them put together said just as plain,

"It's a SECRET!"

Everybody in the whole forest seemed to be catching it—everything and everybody except the Little Red Squirrel.

"Oh me, oh my!" he said to himself. "It won't do at all if I let them see that I don't know. I'll just pretend I'm wise!"

So off he went, with a leap, over to Mama Chipmunk.

"Lovely morning, isn't it?" he said. "Have you heard the news? Everyone is full of it!"

"Full of what?" asked Mama Chipmunk as cool as a cucumber.

But the Little Red Squirrel kept on pretending, although he knew it was no use.

Swishing his bushy tail and trying to look mysterious, he said, "Oh, well, if you don't know. . . . ."

"Ha! ha! ha!" laughed Johnny Chipmunk sitting on a toadstool.

While his sister shut her mouth so tightly it almost looked as if she couldn't trust it.

"Oh me, oh my," sighed the Little Red Squirrel when he was alone again, and flattened himself out along the branch of an old oak tree.

Above and all around him the birds were twittering and tattling among themselves as though there were a fire in the tree next door.

"Tweet-tweet-tweet!"

And every minute it grew harder for the Little Red Squirrel to go on pretending he knew what it was all about. So, when he was sure no one saw him, the smile disappeared and a terrible pout took its place.

The birds were far too busy and important to even notice. They fluttered and chirped and flew back and forth spreading the secret.

But not one of them came down to whisper into the ear of the Little Red Squirrel.

"Oh me, oh my," he sighed again and began to run up and down the branches and take flying leaps to the ground, but no one paid the slightest attention.

And then he had a bright idea! A capital idea! And off he went as though he had wings to ask the squirrel who lived in his tree, one flight up. She was such a chatterbox he felt perfectly certain he could count on her to tell him what all this fuss was about.

One-two-three, he leaped from branch to branch until he was just below her door and could hear her high-pitched voice running

along even faster than usual. But at the sight of Little Red Squirrel she stopped right in the middle of what she was saying and didn't even bother to close her mouth. Her eyes fairly danced and her furry tail twitched with excitement.

He didn't quite know what to do so he just turned around and went down to his own house and closed the door.

But no sooner was he inside than he wanted to come out. As quiet as a mouse, he turned the knob and very, very slowly opened the door again.

If someone had suddenly said, "BOO!" behind him, he would probably have jumped up right out of his skin, he was in such a state.

And small wonder, with the goings-on all around him! Even the raccoons were washing and brushing themselves. Mama Raccoon made her little ones sit perfectly still while she inspected them from head to foot—or rather, we should say, to the tip of their fuzzy striped tails.

Everyone was in a holiday mood. The squirrels, too, were busy fluffing out their tails. They slicked their coats, and their little paws flew back and forth over their faces until they almost didn't look real anymore.

The pheasants puffed out their plumed chests and strutted around.

The bunnies appeared as white as fresh-fallen snow with a touch of soft pink inside each long ear to match their eyes.

They all seemed to be vying with one another to see which one could look the most beautiful. Perhaps it was the SECRET that made their eyes shine and dance with mischief and their little feet move so fast they hardly touched the ground.

But, whatever it was, it worked like magic!

The morning was gone before it had begun—as mornings have a way of doing when something is afoot.

Presently, a little breeze as light as a whisper arose, and traveled around from leaf to leaf, from one animal to another, even stirring the feathers of the little birds.

It was a signal!

Out of the bushes, up from holes in the ground, down from the sky, far and near, they started to arrive.

"Oh me, oh my!" gasped the Little Red Squirrel when he saw them coming in his direction. He darted down the trunk of his tree as fast as he could go.

Of all things! He was going to hide. He scurried this way and that, looking for a likely place, and finally ducked down under an enormous toadstool. It spread above him like a parasol.

But, though he tried to make himself as small as possible, there he was for everyone to see without even stooping down.

First came the bunnies, grinning from ear to ear, followed by the chipmunks and the squirrels, while overhead the birds swooped dizzily back and forth.

From all directions the animals came, chatting and laughing and twittering. It was a gay procession. On and on it came and didn't stop until it reached the very toadstool where the Little Red Squirrel was hiding.

He grew so nervous and excited, he

jumped up and down. He couldn't bear it another minute, and standing on his hind legs he popped up over the edge of the parasol toadstool. His eyes almost jumped out of his head when he saw all the animals gathered there. Even the youngest little deer were there.

There were animals to the right of him, animals to the left of him, animals behind and in front of him, animals all around him.

He pursed his mouth and gave a low long whistle of astonishment.

From all directions, as far as he could see, more and more animals were arriving in groups of twos and threes.

"Jiminy Christmas!" he said at last and his tongue was so dry it stuck to the roof of his mouth. He didn't know what to think!

And you wouldn't either if your head were crammed as full of great big question-marks as the Little Red Squirrel's was. He didn't know what to think and if he had it wouldn't have done him any good because he was completely numb from head to foot. It wasn't exactly stage-fright, but almost.

Well, the old mud turtle was the last to

arrive, as everyone expected. He was huffing and puffing and grunting to himself as he waddled behind the rest. Some little birds flew out to shoo him along faster.

"Tweet-tweet! You're holding up the whole party—hurry up!"

And there it was at last, that fagell-dagell-magical word:

PARTY!

The animals couldn't wait until the old turtle reached the edge of the circle before they all began to sing at the top of their voices:

"Happy Birthday to you!
Happy Birthday to you!
Happy Birthday Little Red Squirrel!
Happy Birthday to YOU!"

Poor Little Red Squirrel! He was SO surprised he could hardly stand up and if he hadn't been leaning on the old toadstool, he most certainly would have fallen down. He just grinned and grinned at all of the animals and they could see how happy he was. The birds sang: "Surprise! Surprise!"

The excited squirrels chattered shrilly in their glee.

A couple of baby chipmunks, who had never been to a party before, were all eyes and they nestled up close to the Little Red Squirrel because they weren't at all sure what would happen next.

What did happen was the most fun of all.

Scattering in different directions, all the animals began to scratch and dig up the ground. Everyone was busy as could be. It was almost like a Treasure Hunt except that each one knew exactly where to dig and what he was digging for, because only a few hours earlier he had buried it there himself.

And what treasures there were when the feast was spread—assorted nuts and berries and tender green shoots, and all kinds of delicious crunchy little bugs. There was a special treat to tickle the palate of every one of them.

Little Red Squirrel ran happily from group to group. He ate and he laughed and he chatted. He told them all how he had tried to find out what the secret was. He even told how he had pretended to Mama Chipmunk that he knew. All the animals laughed and laughed at that.

The bunnies and the little raccoons ate and ate until their tummies looked like toy balloons, only they didn't feel a bit like floating up to the sky. In fact it was very difficult to move at all. So they just sat and talked about wheel-barrows and how much fun it would be if one would suddenly appear so they could all ride home in it.

Altogether it was the happiest, liveliest party you can imagine, and the liveliest, happiest one of them all was the Little Red Squirrel. He could hardly contain his joy. In his whole life he had never been so happy as this, and here he was—two years old today!

All this fun was for him, all the little forest people had come to *his* party!

When the shadows crept farther and farther over the ground, mama deers called their young ones to go home.

"Please, not yet," they begged, "we're having such a good time."

And they looked as sweet and adorable as they knew how—it had always worked before. Each one of them knew, even before she spoke, that her mother would say:

"Well then, just a little while longer."

Meanwhile, the mischievous chipmunks were up to all sorts of tricks, setting a shocking example for their little brothers and sisters. And the worst of it all was that the other animals never suspected the chipmunks of tweaking their ears or pulling their tails, because when they turned around there sat Johnny Chipmunk or his sister, who was just as bad as he was, looking as sweet and innocent as if they had just come out of church.

"Naughty little squirrels!" everyone scolded instead.

And indeed the squirrels did have a guilty look, always scampering off and swinging from the highest branches, as much as to say: "Catch me if you can!"

Over in the clearing two little bunnies played Hide-and-Seek with a young deer. While he stood with his back against a tree, counting slowly up to seven, the cottontails scurried off to hide.

Lying in the tall grass, still as still, they cocked their ears to listen, but all they could hear was the bump-bump-bump of their own little hearts, pounding away like trip-hammers.

Four long ears peeped above the grass like four tiny church steeples. Anybody at all could have seen them—even a baby deer. But each time they were discovered, the little bunnies laughed and laughed. They thought it was the most amazing thing!

"Tweet-tweet," chirped a messenger-bird flying low over the heads of the playful young deer. "Your mother wants you RIGHT AWAY. It's time to go home!"

All the little shadows joined hands as the sun slipped slowly down behind the trees. It was getting late; time for all the little woodland creatures to go to bed.

The party was over.

And all the sleepy forest friends trooped off home to dream of the good time they had had.

Johnny Chipmunk, the little raccoon boy and the chattering squirrel were the last to leave.

Swinging on a low branch of his tree the Little Red Squirrel was loathe to turn in.

"Oh me, oh my," he sighed to himself. "I wonder how long it takes to make another birthday?"

The Flying Mouse

Told by Margaret Wise Brown

THERE WAS once a mouse who longed for wings, great big wonderful flying things. He wanted to fly away through the sky on great big wings that would carry him high. He wanted to be a flying mouse and fly over everybody's house. He was tired of being a little ground mouse.

And then one time in the middle of the night there came a bright light into his room. And a small voice said, "Little mouse, little mouse, get up and go to the place where the brook flows into the river. And from the second branch of the smallest tree pick two green leaves."

So the little mouse combed his whiskers and ran down to the place where the brook flows into the river. There was a little beech tree that grew there. And from the second branch the little mouse picked two green leaves.

"Now," said the mouse, "I have two green leaves. But what can a little mouse do with these?"

Then came the bright light again, all over the river. And a small voice said:

"Little mouse, little mouse. Take the leaves you have there. Put them under your arms and fly through the air!"

And, lo and behold, the little mouse took the two green leaves and flew through the air.

And as he flew, the leaves became wings, great big wonderful flying things. And the little mouse began to fly. He flew over the houses of the other mice.

He flew along with his wings up there. And he flew, and he flew, and he flew through the air. He flew over the treetops and everywhere.

Then he came down out of the air to play with the other mice. But when they saw him, they ran away. They were all afraid and would not play with a flying mouse.

Then the little mouse went to tease the cat. And the cat said, "Goodness! What is that?" And electricity flew out of his hair. "I can't chase a mouse up in the air."

The cat switched his tail like a lion in its lair. Who ever saw a mouse flying through the air! He would not play with a flying mouse.

Then the mouse went to a rat to ask for some cheese. And the rat looked at his wings and said, "What are these? And why should I give a flying mouse cheese? I have no cheese for a flying mouse. Get out of my house!"

Then the mouse went calling on the birds in the air. He waved his wings and flew up there. And the birds all fluttered, and one bird sang: "Little flying mouse, you may have wings. But we only play with feathered things. We cannot play with a flying mouse."

And then came on the dark black night. The places he knew were out of sight. And

then, in the darkness, he heard an awful hiss.

"Heavens!" said the mouse. "Now what is this?"

And there in the air, flying everywhere, were terrible bats. They looked like great black flying rats. Bats!

The bats were glad to see the mouse, and they flew with him into a darkened house.

But the mouse was not very pleased at that. A mouse will never be pleased with a

bat. The mouse was not happy there in the dark with the snarling bats, and the hiss and the squeak and the other sounds that black bats speak.

When morning came and he looked around, the bats were sleeping upside down. So the little mouse flew down to the ground. He flew to the ground and he ran to the brook. And

there in a pool of the water—he took one look!

"Oh, dear me! Now what is that?"

For the flying mouse looked like a little fat bat. And the little mouse did not like that.

Then the little mouse began to shiver, and he ran and he ran and he ran to the river. He sat down under the little beech tree. And he wondered and wondered what on earth he could be.

There was no place on earth for a flying mouse. He didn't want to live in the Black Bat House. And no one would play with a flying mouse.

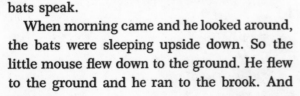

"Oh dear me," said the little mouse. "How I wish I were like other mice!"

And, lo and behold, the light came back all over the river. The mouse's wings began to quiver. His wings flew back to be leaves on the tree. And the little mouse danced and cried with glee, "I am ME!"

And the small voice said, "Little mouse, little mouse. Go back to your house and be a mouse!"

THROUGH THE PICTURE FRAME

Adapted from the Hans Christian Andersen story, "Ole Lukoie"

It was Hialmar's bedtime. He gathered up all his toys and put them neatly away in the big cupboard. Then he yawned sleepily and hopped into bed.

Hardly had he closed his eyes when the window was pushed slowly open and a funny little old man, with long white whiskers and spindly legs, came into the room. He carried an enormous umbrella.

He tiptoed over to Hialmar's bed and peered at him over the edge of the covers.

"Hmmm," he muttered, "everything's in order. He's asleep on time and his room's neat and tidy."

Hialmar opened one eye. "Who are you?" he said wonderingly.

"I'm Ole Lukoie," the little old man answered in a small rusty voice. "Get ready, if you want to go!"

Hialmar was wide awake now. He began to understand. Ole had come to take him on an adventure. "Where are we going?" he cried excitedly.

Ole Lukoie looked around the room. On the wall, in a gilt frame, was a picture of tall trees and a winding river that ran through green meadows.

"That will do," said the little old man. Then

As Hialmar stepped into the boat it glided noiselessly away over the smooth water.

Gaily colored birds flew above him. They flapped their wings so close to him that the breeze helped fill the sails, and the boat sped along even faster.

Hialmar looked down into the water. There were hundreds of fishes, with scales of silver and gold, swimming after him. They were the most beautiful fishes he had ever seen. They would leap right out of the water, turn a fancy somersault, then dive back in again. They seemed to enjoy it.

While Hialmar was watching all these wonderful things a mermaid came shimmering to the surface and clung to the side of the boat. She swished her tail gracefully and smiled up at him. In her hand she held a garland of seaweed. She reached over and dropped it around Hialmar's neck. Hialmar blushed. He tried to thank her, but somehow the words just wouldn't come out.

Other mermaids were swimming around

he flipped open his umbrella and held the handle towards Hialmar. "Hang on!" he cried.

No sooner had Hialmar gripped the handle than he found himself being whisked across the room, through the frame, and into the middle of the picture. He was standing in the meadow. A warm breeze rustled the top of the tall trees, and a little red boat with silver sails bobbed up and down at the water's edge.

the boat now. One of them sang a soft note, and suddenly the air was filled with music so sweet that the nightingales in the far-off woods stopped to listen.

Past mossy banks speckled with primroses and violets, under the shady boughs of drooping willows, then out into the open again and over a gleaming waterfall sailed the little boat.

There were tiny islands dotted about, glowing with brilliantly colored flowers.

Here and there tall castles rose up, reflecting their beauty in the water. They were made of glass and burnished gold.

Just as Hialmar passed under a golden bridge he noticed a lonely gray tower standing at the water's edge. "I wonder who lives there," he thought.

"If you're really interested I could tell you," whispered a small voice behind him. Hialmar looked round and saw a funny little green and yellow frog sitting in the stern of the boat. "But it wouldn't do you any good to know," the frog went on. "And it wouldn't do me any good to tell you either, because if the Black Horseman found out that I had given away his secret he would turn me into a stone." With that he let out a frightened croak, hopped back into the water and disappeared.

Now, locked up in a room in the top of the tower was a beautiful Princess. Her only companion was a snow-white pigeon. Day after

day the Princess sat weeping and waiting for someone to rescue her from the Black Horseman who held her captive.

She looked through the bars of her little window and saw Hialmar. He was gazing up in her direction.

The Princess hastily scribbled a note and gave it to the pigeon. "Deliver this to him at once," she whispered hopefully. "He may be the Prince who has come to save me."

In a twinkling the snow-white pigeon was winging its way down towards Hialmar, far below. It dropped the message at his feet. Hialmar picked it up and read it. "A Princess in distress!" he exclaimed. "I must go to her rescue!"

"It won't be at all easy," said the pigeon, who had perched itself beside him. "As a matter of fact it's against all the rules for anyone but a real Prince to rescue a Princess."

"What does it matter who rescues her?" said Hialmar. "A maiden in distress is a maiden in distress."

"Well, now that you put it like that," said the pigeon, "I'm inclined to agree with you. If you are really quite sure you want to go on this adventure, I think I can manage the details."

"Of course I'm sure," answered Hialmar bravely.

Then the snow-white pigeon muttered some magic words and Hialmar was suddenly surprised to see that he was dressed like a Prince. A sword hung from his waist. Before he could say a word he found himself mounted on a noble horse, charging full tilt towards the tower. Straight through the heavy walls plunged horse and rider. Hialmar shut his eyes as massive stones came tumbling down all around him.

It was dark inside the tower. But Hialmar wasn't a bit afraid. He rode in and out of the big halls, searching for the staircase that led up to the Princess' prison room. The clatter of his horse's hoofs on the marble floors echoed like claps of thunder throughout the tower.

"There must be some way to get to the top of the tower," thought Hialmar.

At one end of a long hall hung with ornaments made of spun gold, Hialmar came to a door. It was studded with precious gems, so dazzling that he could hardly bear to look at it. The door was as high as the ceiling and as thick as the heavy stones on which it was hinged. Hialmar dismounted, drew his trusty sword, and struck at the door with all his

might. Immediately it flew open. The sparkling jewels changed into bluebirds and flew happily around Hialmar's head, singing songs of the forest.

"I must have broken the spell that held them prisoners," Hialmar thought. "Now I will find the Princess and release her."

He walked towards a narrow winding stairway that led up to the top of the tower. A loud hissing noise came from somewhere behind him. The air became hot and smelled of strong sulphur.

"Ah, I've been expecting you," wheezed a low, hollow voice.

Hialmar turned quickly and saw that he was face to face with a terrible Dragon. It was snorting with rage.

Hialmar drew his sword and rushed at the Dragon.

Down came the sword. There was a blinding flash, followed by a great puff of white smoke.

When the smoke cleared away the Dragon was sitting down, purring like a kitten and smiling.

"I feel so much better now—thanks to you," the Dragon said. "Won't you have something to eat?"

Popcorn popped out of his nostrils into a basket filled with butter which was hung around his neck. Huge slices of chocolate cake and dishes of ice cream were stacked in shelves along his back. Ice-cold lemonade poured out of his ears.

"Help yourself," said the Dragon. "It's all free."

Hialmar was tempted to stop and eat. But he thought of the little Princess locked in the tower.

"I can't stop now," Hialmar said. "I have to rescue the Princess."

He ran up the winding stairway. At the top he saw the fearsome Black Horseman, his spear raised high.

Hialmar bravely grabbed the spear with one hand and pulled the Horseman to the ground.

With a terrific crash the Black Horseman broke into a thousand little pieces on the stone floor.

Hialmar rushed past him into the tower room. The happy Princess flung herself into his arms.

"We must get out of here at once," Hialmar said.

He seated the Princess on his horse, leaped into the saddle, and dashed away. Out into the night flew the gallant charger. Over the treetops, over the roofs of houses they sailed.

"At last, I am rescued," the Princess said joyfully.

"Hold on tightly!" cried Hialmar over his shoulder. "I will return you safely to your father, the King."

Hialmar reined up his horse as he saw the royal palace, like a tiny speck, far below.

Down, down, down they sailed until the horse finally came to a stop right outside the palace gates.

The Captain of the Guard came out to meet them.

"Halt! Who goes there?" he demanded curtly.

When Hialmar told him who he was, and that he had rescued the King's daughter, all the soldiers threw their hats in the air and cheered. Then they formed a guard of honor and marched with Hialmar and the Princess into the palace and right up to the throne where the King sat.

As soon as the King saw the Princess he rushed up to her and embraced her fondly, weeping with joy. He was so happy that he proclaimed a day of national rejoicing, and ordered all the flags in the kingdom to be flown for a whole week.

The King turned to Hialmar. "You shall be justly rewarded for your brave deed," he said. Taking out his brightly jewelled sword, he tapped Hialmar gently upon each shoulder and said, "I dub thee knight. Arise, Sir Hialmar!"

Then followed the royal celebration in Hialmar's honor. The circus grounds were ablaze with colored lanterns. Merry-go-rounds whirled. Bands played. Everybody sang and danced to the stirring music. The Princess danced with Hialmar.

On came the parade! There were clowns, performing elephants, jugglers, cowboys! Never was there such excitement.

Afterward Hialmar rode back to the palace between the King and the Princess in a golden coach.

The King stood in the palace doorway and clapped his hands. Instantly a hundred cooks appeared.

"They are yours to command," the King told Hialmar.

"Please bake me the largest cake you've ever baked, with frosting six inches deep," Hialmar said.

And so Hialmar feasted in the royal banquet hall. He sat next to the Princess. He had such a wonderful time that he hoped it would never end.

But it was getting late. Hialmar's boat was waiting for him at the dock. He thanked the King and kissed the Princess on the cheek, then started back.

Along canals he sailed, between houses that were fast asleep. Some of them were snoring heavily in great, gusty breaths. With each snore they blew the little boat along faster until it left behind it a trail of white foam.

Suddenly the white foam turned into soft, billowy clouds, and the bubbles became stars. Hialmar was sailing through the sky. As he drew near to one big star he heard music coming from within.

Three little angels were singing out of hymn books.

Hialmar thought they were the sweetest voices he had ever heard.

He looked over at the bright moon that hung like a huge yellow lantern in the sky. Someone was standing on a ladder, polishing its face. Hialmar walked over toward it to see who it could be.

It was Ole Lukoie!

"I didn't expect to see you here," said Hialmar.

"I'm always here at this time of night," replied Ole. "If I didn't keep the moon and the stars polished nobody would ever see them at all. They get rusty so quickly out in the damp night air."

"There must be millions of stars in the sky," Hialmar said. "I wonder you have time to finish them all before morning."

"It keeps me pretty busy," Ole agreed. "The stars aren't so bad; I can do them two at a time. But polishing this moon is hard work. Sometimes when I get a little behind, I don't have time to finish it all. That's why you often see only part of it shining."

Hialmar stepped back to admire the brilliant shine Ole was putting on the moon's face. As he did so his foot slipped off the edge of the cloud and he tumbled headlong into space.

Down through layer upon layer of fleecy clouds he fell. He saw the top of his house coming up at him. He braced himself. Then, crash!

Hialmar sat up. He was right back in the middle of the picture frame. He looked into the room. Ole was already there. He was arguing with the portrait of Hialmar's great-grandfather on the wall.

"Disgraceful, I call it!" his great-grandfather was saying, wagging his finger angrily at Ole. "You're old enough to know better than to take a little boy out of his bed and keep him away most of the night."

"And you're old enough to know that every little boy in the world loves to come with me on an adventure," Ole shot back. With that he snatched up his umbrella and stalked out of the window.

Hialmar was so sleepy, as he sat dangling his legs over the edge of the picture frame, that he paid little attention to the argument. He yawned, then climbed out of the frame and slipped quietly back into bed. In two minutes he was sound asleep.

THE RUNAWAY LAMB

From the Walt Disney Motion Picture "So Dear To My Heart"

DANNY WAS a little lamb, black all over— as black as midnight. He was in a pen in a great big barn full of mooing cows, ba-a-ing sheep, and grunting pigs.

Danny's master, Jeremiah, patted Danny on the head. "Now, you wait here, Danny," said Jeremiah. "I'm going to look around at the Fair. You be a good little lamb, and maybe we'll win a prize later on, you and I."

Then Jeremiah went away.

"So this is the County Fair," said Danny Lamb to himself. "Ba-a-a, Ba-a-a, I don't like it one bit! I don't like being shut up in a stuffy little pen like this! I want to find Jeremiah and see the Fair with him."

So Danny put his black head down and began to butt against the bars of his pen.

Although Danny was just a little lamb, he was good at butting. Soon a bar was broken and Danny was free! There was an open door ahead that led right into the Fairgrounds.

It was noisy out there in the Fair, and there were more people than Danny had ever seen in his whole life.

They pushed Danny Lamb this way. They shoved him that way.

"Ba-a-a! Ba-a-a! How can I ever find Jeremiah in this big crowd of people?" said Danny Lamb, as he looked around the Fairgrounds.

But on went Danny Lamb, looking for Jeremiah. In and out of the horse barn. In and out of the poultry barn. Past rows of farm machines, shiny and red in the sunlight.

A little boy blew a toy horn next to Danny's ear. "Ba-a-a, Ba-a-a," said Danny Lamb, and he scampered away.

But not a sign of Jeremiah did Danny Lamb see. Danny followed the crowd into another big building.

It was as big as the barns. But there was something different about this building.

It was full of wonderful smells that tickled Danny's little black nose.

There were stacks of golden pumpkins, there were heaped-up apples, pears, and grapes. There were jars of jam and pickles, and plates of tasty homemade pie.

Right before Danny was the plate that held the prize pie. Danny reached for a bite. But a woman spied him.

"Down, doggy!" she cried, with a slap at Danny Lamb's little black nose.

Danny skipped away before she took a second look. Lucky Danny! For if she had seen that he was a runaway lamb, his adventure would have ended right then and there!

On went Danny. He saw prize-winning oats and wheat and some blue-ribbon corn. It made him hungry, just to look.

"Ba-a-a, Ba-a-a," he said.

"What was that?" said a man. "It sounded like a lamb."

But Danny was behind the man, and the man didn't see him. "Ba-a-a," said Danny, and skipped away.

All around the Fair went Danny, looking for Jeremiah. His eyes went wide at the sights he saw. His nose and ears tingled with the strange smells and sounds.

Danny listened to the music of the merry-go-round, to the bells that rang, and to the ticket-seller's shouts.

Danny smelled the taffy apples, and the sizzling hot dogs, and the spun sugar candy in twisted paper cones. Oh, how hungry he was!

The little black lamb's empty tummy told him it was feeding time, but he did not know the way back to his pen in the barn.

Danny's tummy was right. It *was* feeding time. At that very moment, Jeremiah, with a cane and a cowboy hat and a pinwheel he had won, ran to the barn to give his pet lamb his noonday mash.

But when Jeremiah got there, the pen was empty!

"He's gone!" cried Jeremiah. "My little black lamb has run away!"

"Well, you'd better find him soon," said a

man near by. "They're going to pick the prize lamb in a few minutes now."

"Oh, dear," cried Jeremiah. "Where can he be?"

So off ran Jeremiah to hunt for his lamb.

It was a little boy who spied Danny first.

"See the black lamb, Mommy," he cried. "May I take him home?"

"Lamb?" said his mother. "Why, it's a runaway lamb!" People turned to look.

"A runaway lamb!" the cry went up.

The shouts frightened Danny, and he ran. He did not watch where he was going. He just put down his head and ran as fast as he could.

So it happened that he did not see the balloon man ahead, with his big bunch of gaily colored balloons.

The next thing Danny knew, he was all tangled up in those balloon strings, and the gas balloons were carrying him up, up toward the sky—above the reaching hands, above the whole big Fair!

"There he goes! Catch him, someone!" the people cried.

But Danny had floated far out of reach and was bobbing along on the breeze.

"Get a ladder!" a man shouted.

So they brought a tall ladder, and they set it up in Danny's path. Then a tall man climbed way up on top of the ladder, and waited for Danny to come flying by. But a playful breeze turned the balloons aside. The man came down with empty hands, and Danny sailed merrily on.

"The Ferris wheel!" cried someone else. "He's headed that way."

So folks crowded onto the Ferris wheel, just as Jeremiah came along. He had been looking everywhere for his lost lamb.

"Time to pick the prize lamb," called a far-

off voice. "Bring your lambs to the judging ring."

"Oh, dear," cried Jeremiah, "now Danny won't have a chance to win!"

"We'll do our best to get him for you," cried the people on the Ferris wheel.

But someone else reached Danny first.

It was a red-headed woodpecker, flying over the Fair to take a look at the sights below.

He spied the balloons, and his eyes danced.

"This looks like good pecking," he said to himself. And he dove at the first balloon with a rat-a-tat of his sharp little bill.

Ping! went the red balloon. It vanished before the woodpecker's eyes. Ping! went the blue balloon and it vanished too.

Down the bird circled, picking off balloons— Ping! Ping! Ping!

Down flew the woodpecker, and down came Danny, without the balloons to help him fly.

Down he came, and landed right in the judging ring!

"And for the Grand Special Award—" the judge was saying, when Danny dropped down beside him. The judge looked startled, but went on with a laugh—"how can we help giving the Grand Special Award to Danny, the Flying Lamb?"

How the people cheered and shouted! And they lifted Jeremiah into the ring to receive the purple ribbon for his very famous lamb.

"Now aren't you glad you came?" Jeremiah asked his lamb. "Don't you like the County Fair now?"

"Ba-a-a," said Danny Lamb happily. "Ba-a-a, ba-a-a, ba-a-a."

GRANDPA BUNNY

From the motion picture "Funny Little Bunnies"

DEEP IN THE WOODS where the brier bushes grow, lies Bunnyville, a busy little bunny rabbit town.

And in the very center of that busy little town stands a cottage, a neat twig cottage, with a neat brown roof, which is known to all as the very own home of Great Grandpa Bunny Bunny.

Great Grandpa Bunny Bunny, as every bunny knows, was the ancestral founder of the town, which is a very fine thing to be.

He liked to tell the young bunnies who always gathered around how he and Mrs. Bunny Bunny, when they were very young, had found that very brier patch and built themselves that very same little twig house.

It was a happy life they lived there, deep in the woods, bringing up their bunny family in that little house of twigs.

And of course Daddy Bunny Bunny, as he was called then, was busy at his job, decorating Easter eggs.

As the children grew up, they helped paint Easter eggs. And soon the children were all grown up, with families of their own. And they built a ring of houses all around their parents' home.

By and by they had a town there, and they called it Bunnyville.

Now Grandpa Bunny Bunny had lots of help painting Easter eggs—so much that he began to look for other jobs to do.

He taught some of the young folks to paint flowers in the woods.

They tried out some new shades of green on mosses and on ferns.

They made those woods so beautiful that People who went walking there marveled at the wonderful colors as they talked among themselves.

"The soil must be especially rich," they said, "or the rainfall especially wet."

And the bunnies would hear them and silently laugh. For they knew it was all their Grandpa Bunny Bunny's doing.

Years went by. Now there were still more families in Bunnyville. And Grandpa Bunny Bunny had grown to be Great Grandpa Bunny Bunny. For that is how things go. He still supervised all the Easter egg painting, and the work on the flowers every spring.

But he had *so* much help that between times he looked around for other jobs to do.

He taught some of the bunnies to paint the autumn leaves—purple for the gum trees, yellow for the elms, patterns in scarlet for the

sugar maple trees. Through the woods they scampered with their brushes and their pails.

And the people who went walking there would say among themselves, "Never has there been such color in these woods. The nights, in these woods, must have been especially frosty."

And the bunnies would hear them and silently laugh. For they knew that it was all their Great Grandpa's plan.

And so it went, as the seasons rolled around. There were constantly more bunnies in that busy Bunnyville.

And Great Grandpa was busy finding jobs for them to do.

He taught them in winter to paint shadows on the snow and pictures in frost on wintry window panes and to polish up the diamond lights on glittering icicles.

And between times he told stories to each crop of bunny young, around the cozy fire in his neat little twig home. The bunny children loved him and his funny bunny tales. And they loved the new and different things he found for them to do.

But at last it did seem as if he'd thought of everything! He had crews of bunnies trained to paint the first tiny buds of spring.

He had teams who waited beside cocoons to touch up the wings of new butterflies.

Some specialized in beetles, some in creeping, crawling things.

They had painted up that whole wild wood till it sparkled and it gleamed.

And now, the bunnies wondered, what would he think of next? Well, Great Grandpa stayed at home a lot those days, and thought and thought and thought.

And at last he told a secret to that season's bunny boys and girls.

"Children," Great Grandpa Bunny Bunny said, "I am going to go away. And I'll tell you what my next job will be, if you'll promise not to say."

So the bunny children promised. And Great Grandpa went away. The older bunnies missed him, and often they looked sad. But the bunny children only smiled and looked extremely wise. For they knew a secret they had promised not to tell.

Then one day a windy rainstorm pelted down on Bunnyville. Everyone scampered speedily home and stayed cozy and dry in their cottages.

After a while the rain slowed down to single dripping drops.

Then every front door opened, and out the bunny children ran.

"Oh, it's true!" those bunnies shouted. And they did a bunny dance. "Great Grandpa Bunny Bunny has been at work again. Come see what he has done!"

And the people walking out that day looked up in pleased surprise.

"Have you ever," they cried, "simply *ever* seen a sunset so gorgeously bright?"

The little bunnies heard them and they chuckled silently. For they knew that it was the secret. It was all Great Grandpa Bunny Bunny's plan.

The Ugly Duckling

ONE BEAUTIFUL spring morning, a mother duck sat on her nest. Under her, very warm and snug, lay five round eggs. The mother duck was very still, as she sat waiting for her five eggs to hatch.

At last she gave a quack of joy and sprang off the nest. The eggs, in the nest, were moving around and from inside them came the sound of pecking and scratching. The mother duck bent her head to watch.

Then one egg shell after another cracked open. Out tumbled one! two! Three! FOUR! ducklings, as yellow as butter, as soft as down, with eyes as bright as black cherries.

With soft little peeps they climbed out of the nest and waddled into the tall grass.

"What a beautiful family!" thought the mother, as she looked at her four ducklings.

But then she looked sadly back at the nest and shook her head. For there lay the fifth and biggest egg, which had not yet hatched. It was a dull, white egg—not at all like the others—but she sat down again and waited.

In a moment a strong bill broke through the shell. Then a head appeared. But the duckling that stumbled out of the egg shell was not small and yellow and downy as its brothers had been. Instead it was big, and white, and clumsy!

"Honk!" said the new duckling, eager to be liked by the mother duck.

"Goodness!" said the mother duck in horror. "This little duckling does not sound like any child of mine."

"Peep!" said the other ducklings. "He's funny looking. We don't want to play with him." And they waddled after their mother down the path to the pond.

The Ugly Duckling couldn't understand why no one would play with him or why they called him ugly. He wanted to be friends, so he followed the others down to the pond.

There was the mother duck swimming in the clear water. On her back sat the four little ducklings having a lovely ride.

"Honk!" called the Ugly Duckling in his friendliest voice, hoping for a ride, too.

But the mother duck just scolded at him and told him to go away.

The poor Ugly Duckling sat alone on the bank of the pond.

"Why won't they play with me?" he wondered sadly. "Why do they call me ugly?" And big tears filled his eyes and dropped into the water below him.

He watched the rings they made as they fell. Suddenly he saw a strange and frightening sight. There, all blurred and twisted with the ripples, was his own reflection!

"Oh dear!" cried the Ugly Duckling. "I am indeed ugly. I will run and hide where no one will have to look at me." So he turned away from the sunny pond and started into the dark forest.

How frightened and lonely he felt there in the deep forest! Silent shadows swayed gloomily beneath the trees as a chilly wind moved their branches to and fro.

Suddenly there was a rush of wings overhead and into the woods flew a whole family of young pheasants.

"Oh," thought the Ugly Duckling, "perhaps they will play with me." And he started towards them hesitantly, hoping that they would not scold him and leave him. But the birds in the bushes flew up as he approached and disappeared between the trees.

"That is because I am so ugly," thought the Ugly Duckling, and he shut his eyes to keep back the tears.

And so it went on the first day, and the second day, and for many days after that.

Once, as he swam alone through the rushes, he met a duck who smiled at him and bobbed pleasantly on the green water.

"At last!" thought the Ugly Duckling happily. "I have found a friend." And he swam up to the new duck and spoke to him timidly. But the new duck only kept smiling and would not answer.

The Ugly Duckling did not guess that his new friend was only a painted toy duck some children had set on the water and allowed to float away.

It was lonely having no one to talk to, but a toy duck was better than none, and so the Ugly Duckling played with him.

But one day, when the water on the pond was ruffled with waves that the wind made, the toy duck turned suddenly with the current and struck the Ugly Duckling sharply on the head with his painted bill.

Weakly the Ugly Duckling swam to shore and rested on the bank. He watched his smiling friend bob off across the water until he was out of sight. He suddenly understood that the little toy duck had no heart at all and therefore could never love him.

The pain in his head was great but the pain in his heart was greater still. The Ugly Duckling could no longer keep back his tears and he cried and cried.

Spring turned into summer, summer into fall, and after fall came the cold snows. The Ugly Duckling grew bigger and bigger. During the long winter he had to work hard to stay alive, for food was scarce. Still he was alone and he grew very sad.

Then one day, when the trees around the pond were soft with new green leaves and the forest was alive with spring, something wonderful happened!

The Ugly Duckling was swimming among the rushes at the edge of the pond, when there flew over the water the most beautiful bird he had even seen. After it came another and another. The Ugly Duckling hardly dared to breathe for fear these new creatures would see him and fly away.

"What can they be?" he wondered, enchanted, as he watched them drop on the clear surface. "Surely they are the Kings of Birds, for they are the most beautiful creatures I have ever seen."

Drawn by their grace, hardly realizing what he was doing, the Ugly Duckling swam nearer and nearer.

Suddenly one of the great birds raised its little neck and looked right at him. The Ugly Duckling quickly turned his head to hide. He could not bear to have these beautiful creatures see how ugly he was.

But the great swan (for that was what he was), cried to the others:

"Here's a new one!"

And all the other swans gathered around the Ugly Duckling saying,

"A new one, and the most beautiful of us all!" and they bowed their heads before him.

Glancing into the smooth water the Ugly Duckling, or the King of the Swans as we must call him now, saw his own beautiful reflection. How he had changed! His neck had grown curved and graceful, his feathers sleek and white, and his head was marked with handsome black lines. Yes, he was beautiful indeed.

As he floated across the water with his new friends, the mother duck said to her ducklings, "Who is that lovely bird? How beautiful he is!"

The family of pheasants said to each other, "How wonderful it would be to be so graceful and so strong!"

Even the little painted duck looked impressed as the swan sailed past.

The Ugly Duckling was very happy now that he had friends, and he kindly forgave the ducks, and the pheasants, and even the little painted duck for the way they had treated him. And as for them—they had learned that you never know when you may meet a King in disguise.

UNCLE REMUS

Retold from the original "Uncle Remus" story by Joel Chandler Harris
Adapted from the Motion Picture "Song of the South"

Johnny and Uncle Remus were friends. Johnny's hair was brown, his skin was fair, and he was not quite nine. Uncle Remus' hair was white, his skin was black, and no one knew how old he was.

The house where Johnny lived had everything—big rooms, big doors, big doorknobs, big chairs, big windows that looked out on the family's fields of cotton, tobacco, and corn. The cabin where Uncle Remus lived had almost nothing at all, just one little room where Uncle Remus slept and cooked and smoked his corncob pipe. His only window looked out through the trees toward a swamp.

The reason Johnny loved Uncle Remus so much was the wonderful things that he knew.

He knew everything there was to know about the birds, the animals, and all the creatures. He even understood the language they used when they spoke; he understood what the Screech-Owl said to the Hoot-Owl in the tree outside his cabin; he understood *I-doom-er-ker-kum-mer-ker*, the Turtle talk, that bubbled up from the bottom of the creek.

Johnny liked to hear Uncle Remus tell stories about what the creatures were doing, and he liked the funny old-fashioned way he spoke. Every evening before supper, he and his friend Ginny went down to Uncle Remus' cabin to listen. All Uncle Remus had to do was to take one puff on his pipe, and a story would just start rolling out with the smoke.

Material based in part on "Told by Uncle Remus," copyright 1905 by Joel Chandler Harris, Copyright renewed 1932 by Esther La Rose Harris.

It might be a story about a Lion, an Elephant, or a Bullfrog; but most of the stories were about that smartest of all little creatures, Brer Rabbit, and the tricks that he played on Brer Fox and Brer Bear.

"An der will never be an end ter de stories about Brer Rabbit," said Uncle Remus to Ginny, "cause he's always up ter somethin' new. Brer Rabbit, he ain't very big; he ain't very strong; but when dat thinkin' machine of his starts cookin' up devilment, he's de smartest creetur on dis earf."

DE TAR BABY

One day, Brer Fox and Brer Bear wuz sittin' round in de woods, talkin' about de way Brer Rabbit wuz always cuttin' up capers an actin' so fresh.

"Brer Rabbit's gettin' much too sassy," say Brer Fox to de Brer Bear.

"Brer Rabbit's gettin' much too bossy," say Brer Bear to de Brer Fox.

"Brer Rabbit don't mind his own bizness," say Brer Fox.

"Brer Rabbit talk much too biggity," say Brer Bear to de Brer Fox.

"I don't like de way Brer Rabbit go prancin' *lippity clippity lippity clippity* down de road," say Brer Bear.

"Some day I'm goin' ter ketch Brer Rabbit an pull out his mustarshes, *pripp! propp! pripp! propp!*" say Brer Fox.

"Some day I'm goin' ter ketch Brer Rabbit an knock his head clean off, *blim, blam! blim, blam!*" say Brer Bear.

Right den, Brer Fox get a powerful big idea. "I'm goin' ter ketch Brer Rabbit *now*."

Well suh, Brer Fox went straight ter wurk. First, he got some tar. Den, he make it inter a shape, sorter like a baby, wid arms and legs, a stummock, an a head. "Now," he say, "we got ter make dis Tar-Baby look real." Wid dat, he pull some hairs, *plip! plip!* right outer Brer Bear's back, and stick um on de Tar-Baby's head. He snatch off Brer Bear's yellow hat an his own blue coat, an he put um on de Tar-Baby. "Come now, Brer Bear, help me carry dis Tar-Baby ter de big road wher Brer Rabbit's sure ter come."

Dey took de Tar-Baby, and dey sot nim

down under a tree at de side of de road, sorter like he mighter been restin'. Den, Brer Fox and Brer Bear lay down in de bushes ter wait fer Brer Rabbit.

Dey didn't have ter wait long. Purty soon, dey heard a whistlin' an a hummin', an along come Brer Rabbit prancin' *lippity clippity*, sassy ez a mockin' bird. All 't once, he spy de Tar-Baby.

"Howdy!" sing out Brer Rabbit.

De Tar-Baby, he say nothin', an Brer Fox an Brer Bear, dey lay low in de bushes an dey say nothin'.

Brer Rabbit wait fer de Tar-Baby ter answer. Den he say, louder dan before, "What's de matter wid you? I said *howdy do*. Is you deaf? If you is, I can holler louder."

De Tar-Baby, he say nothin', an Brer Fox an Brer Bear, dey lay low.

Den Brer Rabbit holler real loud, at de Tar-Baby, loud ez he can. "Wher's your politeness? Ain't you goin' ter say *howdy do* like respectubble folks say when dey meet up on de road?"

De Tar-baby, he say nothin', an Brer Fox an Brer Bear, dey lay low.

Now Brer Rabbit sorter mad. He clinch

his fist and he walk right up close ter de Tar-Baby. "If you don't say *howdy do* by de time I count three, I'm goin' ter *blip* you in de nose." Now de Brer Rabbit he start countin', "One, two, . . ."

But de Tar-Baby, he say nothin', an Brer Fox and Brer Bear, dey just wink der eyes an grin an dey lay low.

"Three!" yell Brer Rabbit. Now he mighty mad. He draw back his right fist, and *blip!* he hit de Tar-Baby smack in de nose. But Brer Rabbit's right fist stuck der in de tar. Brer Rabbit he can't pull it loose.

Now Brer Rabbit turrible mad. "Let go my fist!" he holler. Wid dat, he draw back his other fist, and *blip!* again he hit de Tar-Baby smack in de nose. But dis fist stuck der in de tar too. He can't pull it loose.

De Tar-Baby, he say nothin', an Brer Fox an Brer Bear dey sorter chuckle in der stummocks an dey lay low.

"If you don't let go my fists," holler Brer Rabbit, "I'm goin' ter kick your teef right outer your mouf!"

Well suh, Brer Rabbit kicked. First he pull back one behind foot, an *pow!* he hit de Tar-Baby in de jaw. But Brer Rabbit's behind foot

stuck der in de tar. Den he pull back de other behind foot. Den, *pow!* Brer Rabbit hit de Tar-Baby in de stummock wid de behind foot. Dis foot stuck der in de tar too.

"If you don't let go my behind foots," squall out Brer Rabbit to de Tar-Baby, "I'm goin' ter butt you wid my head till you ain't got no bref left in your body!"

Brer Rabbit butted, but his head stuck der in de tar. Now Brer Rabbit's two fists, his two behind foots, an his head wuz all stuck in de Tar-Baby. He push an he pull, but de more he try ter get unstuck-up, de stucker-up he got. Soon Brer Rabbit is so stuck up he can't skacely move his eyeballs.

Now Brer Fox an Brer Bear come outer de bushes, an dey feel mighty good. Dey dance round an round Brer Rabbit, laffin' and hollerin' fit ter kill.

"We sure ketched you dis time, Brer Rabbit," say Brer Bear.

"You better say your prayers, Brer Rabbit,"

say Brer Fox to him, "cause dis is de very last day of your life."

Brer Rabbit, he shiver an trimble, cause he wuz in a mighty bad fix, an he wuz mighty skeered of de Brer Fox an de Brer Bear. But right den Brer Rabbit set his mind aworkin' how ter get hisself outer dat fix real quick.

"Brer Rabbit," say Brer Bear, "you been bouncin' round dis neighborhood bossin' everybody fer a long time. Now I'm de boss, an I'm goin' ter knock your head clean off."

"No," say Brer Fox. "Dat's too easy an too quick. We got ter make him suffer."

"Brer Rabbit," he say, "you been sassin' me, stickin' your head inter my bizness fer years an years. Now I got you. I'm goin' ter fix up a great big fire. Den, when it's good an hot, I'm goin' ter drop you in an roast you, right here dis very day."

Now Brer Rabbit ain't really skeered any more, cause he got an idea how he goin' ter get loose. But he talk like he's de most skeered rabbit in all dis wurld. "I don't care what you do wid me," he say, pretendin' ter shake an quake all over, "just so you don't fling me over dese bushes into dat brier-patch. Roast me just ez hot ez you please, but don't fling me in dat brier-patch!"

"Hold on a minute," say Brer Bear, tappin' Brer Fox on de shoulder. "It's goin' ter be a lot of trouble ter roast Brer Rabbit. Furst, we'll have ter fetch a big pile of kindlin' wood. Den we'll have ter make de big fire."

Brer Fox scratch his head. "Dat's so. Well den, Brer Rabbit, I'm goin' ter hang you."

"Hang me just ez high ez you please," say Brer Rabbit to Brer Fox, "but please don't fling me in dat brier-patch!"

"It's goin' ter be a lot of trouble ter hang Brer Rabbit," say Brer Bear. "Furst, we'll have ter fetch a big long rope."

"Dat's so," say Brer Fox. "Well den, Brer Rabbit, Im goin' ter drown you."

"Drown me just ez deep ez you please," say Brer Rabbit, "but please, *please* don't fling me in dat brier-patch!"

"It's goin' ter be a lot of trouble ter drown Brer Rabbit," say Brer Bear. "Furst, we'll have ter carry him way down to de river."

"Dat's so," say Brer Fox. "Well, Brer Rabbit, I expect de best way is ter skin you. Come on, Brer Bear, let's get started."

"Skin me," say Brer Rabbit, "pull out my ears, snatch off my legs an chop off my tail, but please, *please*, PLEASE, Brer Fox an Brer Bear, don't fling me in dat brier-patch!"

Now Brer Bear sorter grumble. "Wait a minute, Brer Fox. It ain't goin' ter be much fun ter skin Brer Rabbit, cause he ain't skeered of bein' skinned."

"But he sure is skeered of dat brier-patch!" say Brer Fox. "An dat's just wher he's goin' ter go! Dis is de end of Brer Rabbit!" Wid dat, he yank Brer Rabbit off de Tar-Baby an he fling him, *kerblam!* right inter de middle of de brier-patch.

Well suh, der wuz a considerabul flutter in de place where Brer Rabbit struck dose brier-bushes. "*Ooo! Oow! Ouch!*" he yell. He screech an he squall! De ruckus an de hulla-baloo wuz awful. Den, by-m-by, de *Ooo!* and de *Oow!* an de *Ouch!* come only in a weak tired whisper.

Brer Fox and Brer Bear, dey listen an grin. Den dey shake hands an dey slap each other on de back.

"Brer Rabbit ain't goin' ter be sassy no more!" say de Brer Fox.

"Brer Rabbit ain't goin' ter be bossy no more!" say de Brer Bear.

"Brer Rabbit ain't goin' ter do *nothin'* no more!" say de Brer Fox an de Brer Bear.

"Dis is de end! *Brer Rabbit is dead!*"

But right den, Brer Fox an Brer Bear hear a scufflin' mongst de leaves, way at de other end of de brier-patch. And lo an behold, who do dey see scramblin' out from de bushes, frisky ez a cricket, but Brer Rabbit hisself! Brer Rabbit, whistlin' an singin' an combin' de last bit of tar outer his mustarshes wid a piece of de brier-bush!

"Howdy, Brer Fox an Brer Bear!" he hol-ler. "I told you an told you not to fling me in dat brier-patch. Dat's de place in all dis world I love de very best. Dat brier-patch is de place wher I wuz born!"

Wid dat, he prance away, *lippity-clippity*, laffin' an laffin' till he can't laff no more.

ELMER ELEPHANT

DEEP IN THE FOREST lived a little boy elephant. His name was Elmer, and he was as bright and plump and healthy an elephant child as anyone could ask. He would have been a happy one, too, but for one thing. The other animal children in the forest, the lion and tiger, the giraffe and the rhinoceros and hippopotamus children, laughed at his nose. It was a fine, long, curly elephant nose, but just because it was different from theirs, they laughed at it.

Of all the animal children in the forest, Elmer liked Tillie Tiger best. Tillie was a pretty little girl tiger, she was friendly and sweet, and, best of all to Elmer, she did not make fun of his nose.

So when Tillie Tiger's birthday came, and Elmer was invited to her birthday party, he picked her a beautiful bouquet of jungle flowers for a birthday present, and he went skipping down the forest path to Tillie's home, whistling happily.

All the children were standing around a table set up on the lawn, when Elmer arrived. In the center of the table stood a big, beautiful birthday cake with lighted candles.

Tillie looked up from the cake as Elmer came in.

"Hello, Elmer," she called. "You're just in time. I'm going to blow out my birthday candles." Then she saw the flowers in his hand. "Oh, Elmer, flowers for me?" she cried, taking the bouquet. "How sweet of you."

Then she turned back to the table, where the candles were still burning brightly. Tillie took a deep, deep breath. Whoosh! She blew at the candles. The flames bowed and fluttered, but they did not go out.

Again she took a deep, deep breath. And whoosh! She blew again. The flames quivered and danced, but still they did not go out.

Tillie's face was quite red now, and her paws were tightly clenched as she took another breath, deeper, deeper, deeper. Then she blew out as hard as she could! But the flames only flickered and winked as if they were laughing at her.

"Oh, dear," said Tillie.

"Let me help," said the hippopotamus child. He took a very deep breath, then opened his mouth and blew! Whoosh! Candles, frosting and all went flying across the table and right into Elmer Elephant's face.

"Ho ho ho! Ha ha ha!" laughed all the animal children at the party.. "Happy birthday, Elmer. You take the cake!"

Elmer just stood there, with frosting dripping down his trunk and cheeks and his big, drooping ears. As the children laughed and joked about him, he could feel his face getting hotter and hotter, right down to the tip of his curly trunk.

But Tillie Tiger was not laughing at him. She came over and wiped the frosting all off, every last sticky bit of it. Then she gave Elmer a kiss, right on the tip of his trunk.

That made Elmer happy, but it just made the other children tease him worse than ever. The moment Tillie went up into her house to get another cake, they all clustered around, making fun of him.

The monkey child flapped his hands beside his head to imitate Elmer's big ears. The lion child waddled along in Elmer's swinging walk. The hippopotamus child dangled a long stem from the end of his nose like Elmer's swaying trunk. And all of the other animals chanted, "Funny-face Elmer, Big-nose Elmer. Hiya, Elmer?"

Poor Elmer. He tried to take it as a joke, but soon the hippopotamus child pulled his trunk while the monkey ran between his legs to trip him, and Elmer went rolling down the hill and out the gate. He did not stop until he landed Plonk! against a coconut palm tree.

When he pulled himself together, Elmer walked off through the forest, feeling very sorry for himself. He tried to roll his trunk up in a ball. He tried to tuck it under his blouse. He even tied a knot in it. But nothing helped. It was always still there. Tears trickled down his cheeks as he realized at last there was nothing he could do.

"My, my!" said a voice far above Elmer's bowed head. "Whatever is going on here? It looks mighty bad."

Elmer wiped his eyes with the back of his paw and looked up—way up to the very tip-top of the trees, where old Mr. Giraffe's smiling face came poking through the leaves.

"G-good morning, Mr. Giraffe," said Elmer politely, but his voice shook as he said it.

"Having nose trouble, Elmer?" asked Mr. Giraffe with a wise, kind look.

"How did you know?" asked Elmer.

"Just figured, Elmer, just figured," chuckled Mr. Giraffe. "You see, I used to have the same trouble myself over my neck. But folks stopped laughing when they saw me eating the fresh, green, top leaves they couldn't reach. Same thing with noses. Look at those pelicans over there if you want to see funny beaks. But do you think they complain? No, sir! They're too busy eating all the good fish they can scoop up in those beaks to worry about being laughed at. Same thing with your trunk. You'll find plenty of use for it. . . . Say, what goes on over there?"

The pelicans had risen into the air and were flying away, cawing loudly. And way up above the treetops plumes of smoke started to streak through the air.

"Looks like a fire," said Mr. Giraffe. "Jump on, Elmer, let's have a look."

So up the hill they raced, with Elmer bouncing on top of Mr. Giraffe's long neck.

"It's Tillie's house!" cried Elmer, as they came in sight of the fire. "And she's up there on top of that high pole in the middle of the flames. We'll have to save her!"

"Don't worry, son," said Mr. Giraffe. "We'll save Tillie Tiger.

When they raced in through the gate, Mr. Giraffe and Elmer found the animal children running around in all directions. They did not know what to do. When they held out a blanket for Tillie to jump into, a burning chip dropped down and burned up the blanket. When the monkey child tried to climb the pole, flames slapped at his hands and face and he had to drop back. So by the time the giraffe came charging up, they all just stood and watched, to see what he would do.

Mr. Giraffe and Elmer had their plans all made. They did not waste a moment.

"Come on, boys," called the giraffe. "Get your squirter busy, Elmer."

Up flew the pelicans, one after another, with their beaks full of water. Elmer sucked up the water into his long trunk and sprayed it out on the flames. Splash! Splat! the water

sizzled against the fire. Soon the flames were pushed back, and Elmer could see Tillie Tiger standing on her little charred front porch.

"I'll save you, Tillie," cried Elmer, and he curled his trunk firmly around Tillie's waist. "Okay, Mr. Giraffe," said Elmer.

Then slowly and gently Mr. Giraffe let down his long neck, and Elmer and Tillie stepped to the ground.

"Elmer, you're my hero!" cried Tillie Tiger, and she gave him a big kiss.

Now all the animal children, and a lot of grown-ups who had hurried over to see the fire, crowded around Elmer and Tillie. But this time they did not make fun of Elmer's trunk. Oh, no! Now they would all gladly have traded their little round ears and their little blunt noses and their twirly tails for a wonderful curly trunk like his.

"Look at how he can curl it right up to his mouth," said the hippopotamus child.

"Let's see you squirt some more water," said the young monkey.

"Gee, that really is something!" said the little lion admiringly.

"I think it is the nicest nose in the whole world," said Tillie Tiger.

Elmer Elephant grinned a broad happy grin. He did not say so, but he did not think his nose was bad himself, now. In fact, he thought it was a pretty nice nose. And so do I. Don't you?

Lady
and
the
Tramp

From the Motion Picture "Lady and the Tramp"
Based on the story by Ward Greene

It was on Christmas Eve that Lady came to live with her People, Jim Dear and Darling. They loved her at once, but as often happens they needed some training from her.

For example, they thought she would like a little bed and blankets of her own. It took some howls and whining on Lady's part to show them their mistake. But it was not long before they understood that her place was at the foot of Jim Dear's bed—or Darling's in her turn. People are really quite intelligent, as every dog knows. It just takes a little patience to make them understand.

By the time spring rolled around, Lady had everything under control. Every morning she wakened Jim Dear with a bark and a lick at his hand. She brought his slippers and stood by until ·he got up.

Then out she raced, through her own small swinging door, to meet the postman at the gate. After the postman came the paper boy; and then it was breakfast time. Lady sat beside Jim Dear and Darling to make certain that not a bite or a crumb go to waste.

After making certain that Darling did not need her help with the housework, Lady went out to circle the house to keep all danger away. She barked at sparrows and dragonflies in a brave and fearless way.

Then she was free to visit around. Lady had two close friends of her own, who lived in the houses on either side of hers. One was an old Scotsman, known to his friends as Jock. The other was a fine old Southern gentleman, Trusty by name. Trusty was a bloodhound, and in the old days he'd had one of the keenest noses south of the Mason-Dixon Line. Lady, Jock and Trusty spent many happy days playing together.

Perhaps the nicest part of the day came toward the evening. That was when Jim Dear came home from work. Lady would fly to meet him at his whistle, and scamper home at his side. It took only a moment to reach the little house, and then the family was together again, just the three of them—Jim Dear, Darling, and Lady.

And all this added up to making her the happiest dog in the world.

It was autumn of that year when a bit of urgent business brought a stranger to the neighborhood. The stranger was a cocky young mongrel known around the town sim-ply as "The Tramp." This day he was two jumps ahead of the dog catcher's net, rounding the corner near Lady's house. Just then along the street came a stately open carriage, followed by two proud carriage hounds. The Tramp fell in step with the two proud carriage hounds until the dog catcher gave up the chase and ambled away.

"Understand the pickings are pretty slim around here, eh?" said the Tramp. "A lid on every trash can, a fence around every tree," he had just said, when he saw, from the corner of one twinkling eye, the dog catcher wandering away. "Oh oh!" he barked, and dropped out of step—no marching to someone else's tune for this cocky mongrel!

"Well," the Tramp thought, with a merry cock of his head, "I may as well have a look around this neighborhood as long as I'm here and my time's my own."

And his feet led him down the shady street to the house where Lady lived.

Poor Lady was in a very sad state when the Tramp appeared. The first dark shadow had fallen over her life.

"Why, Miss Lady," Trusty asked her, "is something wrong?"

"Well, Jim Dear wouldn't play when I went to meet him—and then he called me That Dog!" Lady admitted sadly.

Jim Dear called you, "That Dog!" cried Jock. He and Trusty were shocked. But they tried to make light of it.

"I wouldn't worry my wee head about it," Jock told her as cheerily as he could. "Remember, they're only humans after all."

"Yes, I try," said Lady, with tears in her dark eyes. "But Darling and I have always enjoyed our afternoon romps together. But yesterday she wouldn't go out for a walk at all, and when I picked up a soft ball she dropped, and got ready for a game, she said, 'Drop that, Lady!' And she struck me—yes, she struck me."

To Lady's surprise, Jock and Trusty were laughing now.

"Don't take it too seriously," Jock explained. "Don't you see, Lassie, Darling's expecting a wee bairn?"

"Bairn?" said Lady.

"The old Scotsman means a baby, Miss Lady," Trusty said.

"What's a baby or a bairn, Jock?" Lady wanted to know. Just as Jock started to answer Lady's question, the Tramp came along.

"Well," said Jock, staring thoughtfully, "they resemble humans, only they're smaller. They walk on all fours—"

"And if I remember correctly," Trusty broke in, "they holler a lot."

"They're very expensive," Jock warned her. "You'd not be permitted to play with it."

"But they're mighty sweet," smiled Trusty.

"And very very soft," said Jock.

"Just a cute little bundle of trouble," a new voice broke in. It was the Tramp, who swaggered up to join the group. "They scratch, pinch, pull ears," he went on to say, "but any dog can take that. It's what they do to your happy home! Homewreckers, that's what they are! Just you wait, Miss, you'll see what happens when Junior gets here.

"You get the urge for a nice comfortable scratch, and—'Put that dog out,' they say. 'He'll get fleas on the baby.'"

"You start barking at a strange mutt, and —'Stop that racket,' they say. 'You'll wake up the baby.'"

"No more of those nice juicy cuts of beef. Left over baby food for you!

"Instead of your nice warm bed by the fire —a leaky dog house in the rain!"

"Oh dear!" sobbed Lady.

Jock rushed to her side. "Don't you listen, Lassie," he growled. "No human is that cruel."

"Of course not, Miss Lady," Trusty put in. "Don't believe it. Everyone knows, a dog's best friend is his human!"

"Ha ha," laughed the Tramp, as he turned to leave. "Just remember this, pigeon. A human's heart has only just so much room for love and affection, and when a baby moves in—the dog moves out!"

Poor Lady! She had a long time to worry—all through the long dreary winter months. At last, on a night of wind and rain, in a most confusing flurry, the baby came.

Now there was a stranger in Lady's old room. Lady was scarcely allowed inside the door. And when she did follow Darling in, all she could see was a small high bed, and a strange wrapped-up shape in Darling's arms. But there was a smile on Darling's lips, and a softness in Darling's eye. When she spoke she spoke softly, and often sang sweet songs. So Lady began to think the baby must indeed be something sweet—if only they could be friends and play! Perhaps it might have worked out that way soon, if only Jim Dear had not been called away!

"I'll only be gone a few days," Jim Dear explained to Lady, with an old-time pat on the head. "Aunt Sarah will be here to help you, and I'm counting on you to—"

Knock! Knock!

The door shook under a torrent of bangs. It was Aunt Sarah. Lady watched from between Jim Dear's legs as a stern-faced lady marched in, leaving a stack of luggage on the door step for Jim Dear to bring in.

"I'll put your bags away for you, Aunt Sarah," Jim Dear offered.

"No need for that, James. You just skedaddle or you'll miss your train."

"Oh—er, all right, Aunt Sarah," Jim Dear said. As he rushed toward the door, he managed a last pat for Lady. "It's going to be a little rough for a while," she understood from

his pat. "But it won't be long, and remember, Lady, I'm depending on you to watch over things while I'm away."

Then Jim Dear was gone, quite gone.

Lady knew her job. She raced upstairs, to the bed where Darling was having her afternoon rest. And Lady snuggled down on the coverlet, within patting distance of her hand.

Not for long though!

"What is that animal doing here?" Lady heard Aunt Sarah's voice.

"Oh, it's just Lady," Darling smiled.

"Get off that bed," snapped Aunt Sarah—and she pushed Lady. "You'll get fleas on the baby! Shoo! Shoo!"

Poor Lady! She was hustled straight out of the room, back down to the front hall. There, still waiting, stood Aunt Sarah's bags, so she gave them an experimental sniff.

There was something peculiar about one basket—an odor unfamiliar to Lady and one she did not understand. She sniffed again. She circled the basket. Zip! Out shot a silken paw and clawed her from behind!

Lady pounced on the basket. Suddenly out shot two large forms! Yes, two Siamese cats. They were very sly, they were very sleek, they were tricky as could be.

They walked across the mantelpiece, scratched the best table legs, they bounced on the pillows Lady never touched—but whenever Aunt Sarah came into the room, they made it seem that Lady had done everything bad, and they had been angel twins!

"Get away, little beast!" Aunt Sarah would say, kicking at Lady with a toe. "Poor darlings," she would coo, scooping up the Siamese cats in her arms. "Dogs don't belong in the house with you!"

Poor Lady! She was blamed for trying to catch the goldfish, when really she was just protecting them from the cats. And when the cats opened the canary cage and were chasing the poor frightened little thing—it was Lady who was blamed by Aunt Sarah, of

Lady could stand no more. She reared back on her strong little legs until her leash snapped through. And away our Lady ran.

She had never been alone in the city. The large crowds of people frightened her, and the clatter of hurrying wheels. Down a dim and quiet alley she ran, and she found a hiding place behind a big barrel. There she lay and shook with fright.

"Well, pigeon, what are you doing here?" she heard a brisk voice say.

It was the Tramp, and how handsome he looked to Lady, how big and strong! She snuggled her head on his manly chest and had herself a good cry.

"There there," he said in a gentler tone. "Get it out of your system and then tell me what this is all about."

So Lady told him the whole sad story.

"And I don't know what to do next," she told him with a sob.

course, and put out at night in the rain! Everything was just as the Tramp had said. Oh, what a sad, sad life!

The worst day of all was still to come. That was the day Aunt Sarah took Lady to the pet shop and bought her a muzzle!

"It isn't safe to have this beast around in the house with a baby unmuzzled," she said. Tears filled poor Lady's eyes. Then the muzzle was snapped on. "There now, you little brute!" said Aunt Sarah.

"First of all we've got to get rid of that catcher's mitt," said the Tramp, with a nod at her muzzle. "Let's see—a knife? No, that's for humans. A scissors? A saw? Teeth! That's what we need. Come on, we'll visit the zoo."

Lady had never heard of a zoo, but she trustingly followed along. And Lady did just as the Tramp told her to, until they were safely past the No Dogs sign, strolling down the sunny paths inside the zoo.

The paths were lined with high fences, and beyond the fences—well, never in her wildest dreams had Lady imagined that animals came in such a variety of sizes and shapes and colors. But though all of them were nice about it, there did not seem to be one who could help remove the muzzle—until they came to the Beaver House.

"Say," said the Tramp, "if ever a fellow was built to cut, it's Beaver. Let's call on him." So they did.

"That's a pretty cute gadget," Beaver said, pointing at Lady's muzzle. "Did you make it yourself?"

"Oh no," said Lady.

"We were hoping you could help us get it off," the Tramp explained.

"Get that muzzle off? Hm, let's have a look at it. No, I'm afraid not. The only way I can get it off is to chew through it, and that seems a shame . . ."

"That's exactly what we had in mind," grinned the Tramp.

"It is?" The Beaver was surprised. "Well, it's your thingamajig. Hold still now. This may hurt a bit."

Lady held as still as could be.

"There!" said Beaver. And with a smile he handed her the muzzle. She was free.

"It's off! It's off!" cried Lady, bouncing up and down the paths with joy. "Oh, thank you, thank you," she stopped to say, as the Tramp prepared to lead her off.

"Here!" said the Beaver. "You're forgetting something—your gadget."

"Keep it if you wish, Beaver," said the Tramp with a lordly air.

"I can?" marveled Beaver. "Well, say, thanks." And as they looked back he was trying it on with a happy smile.

"The question is, what do you want to do now, pigeon?" the Tramp asked, as they left the zoo behind.

"Oh, I'll have to go home now," Lady said.

"Home?" said the Tramp. "You go home now and you'll just be sliding your head into another muzzle. Stay away a few hours, let them worry. Give Aunt Sarah a chance to cool off. Have dinner with me at a little place I know, and then I'll show you the town."

Lady had never known anyone so masterful. She found herself following along. And she had to admit that dinner on the back step of a little restaurant was the best meal she'd had for weeks. Then they went to the circus—Lady's first; they had wonderful seats under the first row.

After the circus, Lady and Tramp took a stroll in the park, and since it was spring and the night was warm, and they were young, time passed all too quickly. The first rays of morning caught Lady by surprise.

"Oh dear," she said. "I must go home."

"Look," said Tramp, "they've given you a pretty rough time. You don't owe them a thing. Look at the big wide world down here. It's ours for the taking, pigeon."

"It-sounds wonderful," Lady admitted, "but it leaves out just one thing—a baby I promised to watch over and protect."

The Tramp gave a deep sigh.

"You win," he said. "I'll take you home."

But on the way they passed a chicken yard. Tramp could not resist.

"Ever chase chickens Lady? No? Then you've never lived." In a flash, he was scraping a hole under the fence.

"But we shouldn't," said Lady.

"That's why it's fun," the Tramp explained.

So she followed him in; and when the chickens squawked and the farmer came running, it was Lady who was caught. Oh, the Tramp tried to warn her, but she simply didn't know her way around. The next thing she knew, she was in the Dog Pound!

Lady had never met dogs like those she found in the Pound. At first they frightened her. But she soon found they had hearts of gold—and she found they knew the Tramp.

"Now there's a bloke what never gets caught!" said one.

"Yup, his only weakness is dames," said another. "Got a new one every week."

"He does?" said Lady. "Well, I certainly hope I wouldn't give a second thought to a person like that!" But really she felt very sad. She was sure now the Tramp had let her be caught so he could go on to another "dame."

Her reception when she got home did not make her feel any better. She was put out in the dog house on a stout chain!

When the Tramp came around to call, early the next day, Lady would not even speak to him. That was just what one stranger in the yard had hoped to see. That stranger was slinking silently along under the cover of the tall grass near the fence. From the end of the fence it was a short dash to the shelter of the woodpile. And there the stranger lurked, waiting for the darkness—that arch-enemy of all society, the rat!

The rat was no stranger in one way. He had often poked around this house, trying to find a way in. But always he had been frightened off by the thought of a dog on guard.

Now, seeing Lady safely chained far from the back door, and having watched her send the Tramp away, the rat thought his big chance had come at last!

So in the dim light of dusk, he left his hiding place and scurried toward the back door.

Lady was standing at her dog house doorway, looking sadly after the Tramp, and wondering if she had been too cruel, not to let him try to explain—when she saw it—that sly, evil figure slinking toward her house—toward Darling and the baby!

Lady had never seen a rat before, but some instinct told her that this creature was evil and vicious. She knew this stranger must not be allowed in the house!

When she saw it slinking through her own little swinging door, Lady went wild with rage! Barking wildly, she lunged against the chain. Far down the street, the Tramp heard her and stopped in his tracks.

Upstairs in the house, Aunt Sarah heard too, but she was not one to understand.

"Lady! Stop that racket!" she snapped, then slammed the window and turned away.

Darling heard the uproar. "What is it, Aunt Sarah?" she asked.

"Nothing, Elizabeth, but that spoiled brat carrying on because she's chained up."

"But she's never carried on like this before," Darling worried. "Could someone be trying to break into the house? Perhaps if we went down to see?"

"Nonsense," snapped Aunt Sarah. "Stop being ridiculous and go back to sleep, Elizabeth. And you—hush up, you little beast!"

At that very moment the evil rat was pulling himself step by step up the stairs.

But at that moment, too, the Tramp came back. He wondered why Lady was barking.

"What's wrong, pigeon?" he asked.

"A horrible creature—went in the house," Lady panted anxiously.

"Horrible creature? Sure you're not seeing things, pigeon?"

"Oh, please, please!" cried Lady. "Don't you understand? Tramp, please! The baby—we must protect the baby!"

With one last lunge she snapped the chain; staggering forward, she broke into a run, and raced fearlessly for the back door.

The Tramp was close behind her. "Take it easy," he told her in his firm soothing tones, "remember I'm right with you."

Through the kitchen they raced, side by side in the darkness; then into the hall and up the stairs. Lady led the way to the baby's room and the Tramp followed close behind. But just inside the door they both stopped short, for there sure enough was the rat!

The Tramp knew what to do, and he wasted no time. He disposed of the rat behind a chair in the corner, while Lady stood guard over the crib.

The Tramp was just returning, still panting from his battle with the rat, when Aunt Sarah, broom in hand, appeared. "Take that, you mangy cur!" she cried, lowering the broom on the Tramp.

He winced and ran before the weapon— and found himself locked in a dark closet!

Now Darling was there too, cuddling the baby, as she sang sweet songs.

"Lady," Darling said in surprise, "whatever got into you?"

"Humph!" said Aunt Sarah. "She's jealous of the baby and brought one of her vicious friends in to attack the child."

"Oh, I'm sure not," cried Darling. "I believe that she saw the stray and came in to protect the baby."

"Rubbish!" said Aunt Sarah. "But Lady is your responsibility. If you don't know your duty, I know mine. I will notify the authorities. They'll take care of this other brute once and for all. As for you—" she picked Lady up by the scruff of her neck—"I'm locking you in the kitchen for the night."

Bad news travels fast in the animal world. By morning everybody in the neighborhood knew—every pigeon, canary and squirrel— that the Tramp had been picked up and was to be taken off to be executed. Aunt Sarah's cats knew, and for once even they felt something like sympathy as they tiptoed past the kitchen where Lady sobbed alone.

Jock and Trusty heard it; they watched from behind the shrubbery as the Dog Pound Wagon stopped at the door, and the catcher came out, leading the Tramp to his doom.

"We misjudged him badly," Jock admitted.

"Yes," said Trusty. "He's a very brave lad. And Miss Lady's taking it very hard."

"There must be some way we can help," said Jock to Trusty. But they could not think what it would be.

Lady knew, though, there was just one chance. And it came when a taxi stopped at the door. Jim Dear was home at last!

Darling told Jim Dear the story of their terrible night as soon as he came in.

"But I still don't understand," said Jim. "Why should a strange dog—and Lady—?"

Lady, leaping at the kitchen door, tried to say that she could explain.

Jim Dear opened the door and knelt beside her while she jumped up to lick his face.

"Lady, what's all this about, old girl? You know the answer, I'm sure," he said.

For a reply, Lady jumped past Jim Dear and raced up the stairs to the baby's room.

"She's trying to tell us something," he said.

Jim Dear was at Lady's heels.

"You're right, dear," she said. And when Lady showed her the dead rat behind the chair, at last she knew what it was.

"Don't you see?" he cried. "That strange dog wasn't attacking the baby. He was helping Lady protect it instead."

"Oh, Jim Dear, and we've sent him to be—" Darling wailed, clasping her hands.

"I don't see the reason for all this fuss," Aunt Sarah sternly said.

"Aunt Sarah," said Jim, "I'm going to save that dog. And when I come home I trust that you will be ready to leave."

"Well, I never!" Aunt Sarah gasped.

Then off raced Jim Dear in the taxicab, on the trail of the Dog Pound cart. But Lady was ahead of him. With Trusty and Jock beside her, Lady was off, down through the street and through the town on the wagon's trail.

They made some wrong turns. There were some dead ends. But at last they sighted the cart ahead, with the Tramp watching them through the wire mesh.

Straight to the horse's feet the three dogs ran. Then barking and snapping and leaping about, Trusty, Jock, and Lady set the horse to rearing nervously until the whole cart swayed and tipped! They had won!

Now up rattled Jim Dear's taxicab.

"That dog," cried Jim Dear, pointing to the Tramp, rubbing noses with Lady through the bars. "It's all been a terrible mistake."

"You mean that mongrel is yours, Mister?" the driver asked.

"Yes," said Jim Dear. "He's mine."

So home Lady and the Tramp went, in a taxicab with Jim Dear. And that was the end of the story—almost.

Let us visit that little house once more, at merry Christmas time. See the Baby playing on the floor, surrounded by wiggling puppy dogs. Jim Dear and Darling are watching Baby, with love and pride in their eyes. And watching the puppies every bit as proudly— are Lady and the Tramp.

SCAMP

LADY was the mother. Tramp was the father. Their puppies were the finest ever. They were sure of that.

Three were as gentle and as pretty as their mother.

But the fourth little puppy—

"Where is that puppy? Where is that Scamp?" they cried.

At mealtime three little gentle pretty puppies would line up, waiting for their bowl.

But the fourth little puppy, that Scamp of a puppy, would rush in ahead of them all.

At playtime three little gentle pretty puppies would play with their own puppy toys.

But the fourth little puppy, that Scamp of a puppy, would nibble at anything.

At bedtime three gentle pretty puppies would snuggle down to sleep.

But the fourth little puppy, that Scamp of a puppy, chose that time to learn to howl, loud and long.

One day the four little puppies started off for a picnic with nice puppy biscuits for lunch.

Three little puppies went straight to the

park and hunted for a nice, green shady spot.

But the fourth little puppy, that Scamp of a puppy, went off on an adventure.

He found some new squirrel playmates.

Their game looked like fun.

But Sss-ss-sst! they didn't want Scamp to play.

So Scamp got out of there.

He found another playmate.

It was a busy gopher, digging as fast as it could dig.

"Looks like fun," said Scamp. "How did you learn to do it?"

"By digging," Mr. Gopher said. So Scamp dug, too.

He dug and dug and dug.

And what do you think he found?

A big, juicy bone.

It was a great big bone for a small dog.

Scamp pulled at it.

He tugged and hauled.

Finally he got the bone out of the ground.

He tugged that bone all the way to the park.

Just as Scamp got there, a big bad dog was saying, "Ha! I smell puppy biscuits."

So he sneaked up on those three little puppies and took their puppy-biscuit lunch.

Poor little puppies!

They were really very hungry. And they felt very sad.

Just then, who should appear but the fourth little puppy, that Scamp of a puppy.

He was tugging his great big bone!

"Hi, folks," he said. "Look what I found. How about joining me?"

So they ate the big, juicy bone for lunch. And they all had a fine time.

When picnic time was over those three pretty puppies all went happily home.

And the fourth little puppy, that Scamp of a puppy, walked proudly at the head of the line.

Donald the Explorer

It was snowing. Donald Duck was indoors reading. His book was about an explorer who had been to the South Pole.

There were three or four pictures of penguins in the book. Donald liked to look at these pictures.

"I'd like to see some penguins," said Donald to himself. "This book says they are very hard to catch.

"The explorer didn't bring any back with him. He had some, but they got away. When I go to the South Pole, I shall bring back a lot of penguins. They won't get away from me."

He turned the page and went on reading. The more he read, the more he wanted to go to the South Pole.

By and by, he looked out of the window. He was surprised to see Goofy coming slowly through the deep snow.

Goofy was walking on skis. He was dragging a sled. The sled was piled high with all kinds of bundles and packages.

Donald pulled on his sweater. He grabbed his muffler and cap. Then he ran out to meet Goofy.

"Hi, Goof," he said, "where are you going with all that stuff?"

"I'm going to the South Pole," said Goofy. "I hear it's a fine trip. I have blankets and food and other things on my sled."

"Will you let me go, too?" asked Donald.

"Yes," said Goofy, "if you'll help pull the sled."

"I will," said Donald. "Just wait till I get some things. I can put them on your sled."

He ran quickly into the house. In a short time he came back carrying a butterfly net, a large bird cage, and a package. He put these on Goofy's sled with the other things.

"What are you going to do with those things, Donald?" asked Goofy.

"I shall catch some young penguins with the net," said Donald, "and I'll bring them back in the cage."

"What's in the package?" asked Goofy.

"A black coat and a white shirt," said Donald. "I'm going to wear them. That ought to fool the penguins. They'll think I'm another penguin when they see me all black and white."

"They say penguins are pretty smart," said Goofy.

"Well, even if they are, I'm going to catch one," said Donald. "They aren't any smarter than I am."

They started out. Goofy pulled the sled and Donald pushed.

Perhaps you think it took them a long time to reach the South Pole. But they went very fast and got there very quickly.

They made a hole in the ice and caught some fish. They put these away to cook for supper.

"We'd better make a snow house," said Goofy.

"You start the house. I'm going to catch a penguin right away," said Donald.

Goofy helped Donald dress himself in the black coat and white shirt and he really did look a little like a penguin.

Then Donald tied a fish to a short pole by a string. This was bait for catching penguins. He also carried with him the butterfly net and the bird cage.

Donald walked along for some time. At last he saw something small and black in the snow. He set down the bird cage and walked toward the little black thing.

Sure enough, he had found a baby penguin.

The baby did not run away. It stood and stared at Donald.

Donald held out the stick he carried, so that the fish hung right in front of the little penguin's bill.

But the penguin suddenly grew frightened. It turned and began to hurry away. Donald followed. He tried to get the butterfly net over the baby penguin's head. But the little penguin was too quick. It hurried off crying, "Oo-lah! Oo-lah! Oo-lah!"

In no time at all penguins rushed in from all sides—big penguins, little penguins, and middle-sized penguins. It seemed to Donald that there must have been a penguin hiding behind every snowbank.

Two of the biggest penguins took hold of Donald, one on each side, as though they were policemen.

Donald tried to tell them that he did not mean to hurt the little penguin. But the penguins could not understand him, and he could not understand them. He was sure of only one thing. This was that the penguins were angry at him.

As the penguins stood holding Donald, the biggest penguin of all came up.

What do you suppose he was carrying? Donald's bird cage.

One of the penguins opened the door of the cage. The two policemen penguins pushed Donald in and shut the door.

Donald was badly frightened. "How can I ever get out?" he thought.

The penguins all walked around the cage

Donald took off his black coat. He hung it on one side of the cage. Then he quickly dropped to the floor, pushed the door open, and crawled out.

He hoped the penguins would see the black coat and think he was still in the cage. He had on the white shirt. This would keep them from seeing him as he crawled along in the snow.

The penguins didn't see Donald. Or else they saw him and didn't mind. They had thought it was a good joke to scare him. But now they were busy coasting. They had lost interest in him. Penguins are like that.

Donald crawled a long way in the snow before he dared stand up and walk. At last he saw Goofy and the snow house. Goofy was out looking for him.

"Hurry, Donald! The fish have cooked till they are all dried up," called Goofy.

"I've had a terrible time, Goofy!" said Donald.

"That's too bad," said Goofy. "Come inside and tell me about it. Did you see any penguins?"

"Yes, I did," said Donald, "and I never want to see another penguin—never, never, NEVER! I don't like the South Pole, anyhow. You ought not to have brought me here."

"Well, we don't have to stay," said the good-natured Goofy. "We'll go back in the morning."

So they went back home the next day. That was the end of the famous Goofy-Donald Polar Expedition.

and made fun of him. He was sure they were laughing at him, though everything they said sounded like "Oo-lah!"

After a while they stopped laughing and joking. They all gathered in a huddle and talked together. Donald felt that they were planning what to do with him. He grew more and more worried.

Suddenly he thought of Goofy. Perhaps Goofy could scare away the penguins. He began to shout and pound on the cage. He hoped Goofy would hear him.

But Goofy did not come and Donald at last stopped shouting. It was no use. He was sure of that.

The penguins came out of their huddle and went to a snow hill a little way off. There they began coasting. They sat on flat pieces of ice and slid down hill on these. They seemed to be having a great deal of fun.

Donald knew he could open the cage door if he had a chance. He hoped that the penguins would stop watching him.

When they seemed very busy coasting, he unfastened the door. He unfastened it, but left it closed. He would push it open when he had a chance.

One penguin on his ice sled ran into another penguin on his. There was quite a mix-up. The penguins did not seem to be watching the cage.

Mrs. Cackle's Corn

ONE DAY, it was Clara Cluck's turn to tell a story, and this is the story she told:

My old friend, Katie Cackle is a good hen, if ever there was one. She works hard, brings up her children well, and is kind.

I never saw Katie cross but once. I will tell you about that time. You will not blame her.

That year, her children were very little when it was time for her to plant her corn. They needed a great deal of care.

So she went to Daniel Duck and Patsy Pig and asked them to help her. She had often helped them.

What do you think they said?

They told Katie that they did not feel well enough to work.

Patsy Pig said, "I am sorry, Mrs. Cackle. I should like to help you, but I have a very bad pain."

Katie said, "You were eating apples when I came along. You did not seem to have a pain."

"I have one now," said Patsy.

"Can you help me, Daniel?" said Katie to Daniel Duck.

"No," said Daniel, "I am sorry, but I can't help you. I have a pain."

"I saw you eating seeds just now," said Katie, "you did not seem to have a pain."

"I have one now—a bad one," said Daniel.

"I am sorry for you both," said Katie; and she walked away.

Katie asked some of her other friends to help her, but they were all too busy.

She went home very sad.

She told her children that she could not find anyone to help her plant the corn.

"We will help you, Mother," said the children.

"I am afraid you are too little," said Katie.

"But there are ten of us," said the children. "If we each do a little, that will be a good deal."

"You are good children," said Katie. "Perhaps you *can* help."

So the next day Katie Cackle and her children planted the corn.

You should have seen how hard they all worked.

They scratched and dug and planted.

By night the seed corn was all in the ground. Katie and her children were very tired, but they were happy.

When it was time to hoe the corn, Katie Cackle again went to Patsy Pig.

She said, "Patsy, there are a good many weeds in my corn. Will you help me hoe it?"

Patsy said, "I am sorry, but I can't help you. I don't feel very well today."

Then she went to Daniel Duck. He said, "I should like to help you, Mrs. Cackle, but I don't feel at all well today."

So Katie and her children worked hard and kept the weeds out of the corn themselves.

When the corn was ripe, Katie said it was the best corn she had ever seen.

She and the children did not ask any help. They took the corn into the barn themselves.

Always before this when Katie Cackle's corn was in the barn, she had cooked a big dinner and asked all her friends to come.

But this year she was tired when the corn was all in. So she decided to have a fine dinner just for the children and herself.

Of course the children helped. They swept and dusted. They stirred the cakes. They set the table with the best dishes. They put on their own bibs. When they all sat at the table looking very clean and polite, their mother was proud of them.

What a dinner that was! Corn soup and roast corn, corn cake and corn pudding—so many good things! It smelled good, too, and who do you think passed by and smelled it? Yes, Patsy Pig and Daniel Duck!

"Mrs. Cackle must have cooked a good dinner today," said Patsy. "How nice it smells!"

"We may as well eat with her, said Daniel.

So they rang Mrs. Cackle's bell.

"How do you do, Mrs. Cackle?" said Patsy. "We thought we would stop and have dinner with you."

"Are you sure you are well enough?" said Katie Cackle.

"Oh, yes indeed," said they.

"My table is full," said Katie, "but wait. I have something that will be just right for you."

They waited, and Katie came back and gave them something.

What do you think it was?

She gave them a bowl and spoon and a bottle of *castor oil.*

Mickey Mouse and Pluto Pup

MICKEY MOUSE came down the stairs whistling. He planned on a fine day's fishing with his loyal Pluto Pup.

He fixed a big dog breakfast in Pluto Pup's own bowl. Then he whistled for Pluto at the back door. But Pluto did not come.

"That's strange," said Mickey. "Pluto is always ready to eat."

He set Pluto's dish down on the back step and Mickey went out looking for his dog.

He looked in Pluto's dog house, but Pluto was not there.

He looked under the front porch, where Pluto liked to lie.

Mickey looked in the back seat of his car, out in the garage. He even looked in the big trash barrel, out in the yard. But Pluto Pup was not to be found.

Mickey noticed that the back gate was open.

"Aha!" thought Mickey. "That's the answer. Pluto has gone to see Minnie, I'll bet."

So Mickey Mouse jumped into his car and drove to Minnie's house.

"I came for Pluto," Mickey said, when Minnie came to the door. "Is he here?"

"Why, no," answered Minnie. "Do you suppose he's lost? I'll come and help you look for Pluto Pup."

So Mickey and Minnie jumped into the car and drove to Donald Duck's house, where Donald was out raking leaves.

"We've come for Pluto," they told Donald Duck. "Is he here with you?"

"Why, no," said Donald. "Is he lost? I'll help you look for him."

So Donald Duck jumped into the car.

"Hey, Unca Donald!"

"Hey, Unca Mickey!"

"Where are you going?"

There came Donald's nephews, one, two, three, Hughie, Louie, and Dewey, all running towards the car.

"We're going to look for Pluto," Donald said to his nephews.

"Can't we come along?"

"Okay," said Mickey. So in they piled. And they all rode over to Clarabelle Cow's.

Clarabelle Cow was out picking tomatoes.

She straightened up and waved to Mickey, Minnie, Donald, and the nephews.

"Hello," she called. "How are you all?"

"Fine," called the nephews. "But we can't find Pluto Pup."

"Oh, dear," said Clarabelle. "I'll help you look for him."

So into the car she came. Soon they met Goofy on the street.

"Gawsh," said Goofy. "Where are you folks all headed for today?"

"Looking for Pluto," Mickey called. "Have you seen Pluto Pup?"

"Nope," said Goofy to Mickey. "But I'll help you look for him."

"Come along," said Mickey. And Goofy jumped into the car.

"Pluto might have gone to Horace Horsecollar's house," said Minnie.

"We'll soon see," Mickey said.

Horace had not seen Pluto Pup, but he was glad to come along to look.

All around the town they drove. Mickey drove very slowly, and they whistled and they called. But Pluto never answered them.

"Wait!" cried the nephews, all at once. "Stop here a minute, Unca Mickey, please."

Mickey stopped. They all listened. Sure enough, from a big tent came all sorts of woofs and barks.

"The Dog Show!" cried Mickey. "Why didn't we think of that?"

He parked the car and they all hurried in. The Dog Show was almost over. Blue rib-

bons had been given to the best of the span-iels, the best of the terriers, to the best of the poodles and work dogs and hounds. Now there was just one blue ribbon left. It was for the Most Popular Dog in the Show.

As the dogs started marching past the judges' platform, who should come marching along with the rest but Mickey Mouse's dog, Pluto Pup!

"Pluto!" cried Mickey.

"There he is!" cried Mickey's friends.

And Pluto Pup was wild with joy. He jumped and cavorted. He rolled his eyes and flapped his ears. Everyone at the Dog Show began to laugh and clap.

Soon Pluto had a blue ribbon all his own for being the Most Popular Dog in the Show.

Then everyone piled back into Mickey's car—with Pluto Pup in the midst of them. And they all went back to Mickey's house, to cel-ebrate the triumph. They ate lots of ice cream and cake.

Pigs is Pigs

Based on the Story by Ellis Parker Butler

In the Westcote Railway Station
In the year nineteen-o-five,
The agent there was Flannery,
The best there was alive.

Flannery ran his station
Exactly by the rule.
He tried to learn each one by heart,
Just like a kid in school.

Whenever a customer chanced to call
Flannery let him wait
Until he could look up the rule
That would be appropriate.

One morning came McMorehouse,
A thrifty, crusty Scot,
To pick up a shipment of guinea pigs—
He wanted them on the dot!

"Good morning to you," says Section Two,
"And don't forget to smile."
"Morning it was," McMorehouse said.
"I've been standing here a while."

"I'm supposed to say, 'I'm sorry, sir,'"
Flannery read from Rule Three.
"Dry your tears," said McMorehouse.
"Have you got some pets for me?"

"Indeed I have—two guinea pigs—
See pigs, page forty-three—
According to the book of rules,
Your pets are pigs, you see."

"Pigs forty-eight cents, pets forty-four!"
McMorehouse read the rule.
"Guinea pigs is pets at forty-four!"
He cried. "You stubborn fool!"

"Pigs is pigs at forty-eight!"
Flannery insisted.
But paying freight at the higher rate
McMorehouse still resisted.

"Whenever an agent gets in a debate,"
Flannery read, "Concerning the rate,
The agent must wire for a ruling up high,
And hold onto the package awaiting reply."

"Hold them then," McMorehouse said,
"And when you find you're wrong,
Deliver them to my address,
Healthy, hale, and strong."

Then Flannery sat down and sent
A telegram away,
Not dreaming he'd regret this move
Until his dying day.

"Big Town, on the Drive,
Flannery to Morgan,
May sixth, nineteen-o-five.

"Holding two animals in a crate;
Big dispute regarding rate.
Is a guinea pig a pig or pet?
Give ruling on the rate to set."

The supervisor's office was
The pride of the company.
It received old Flannery's telegram
With trained efficiency.

They examined the wire and immediately
    dated it,
Stamped the receipts, then communicated it
To the department that quadruplicated it.
Copies were sent out to all of the staff.

Each copy received was filed and related
To copies of copies, then checked and
    notated,
Nine copies of each were then validated
And contents were noted in ink on a graph.

Meanwhile Flannery tended the pigs.
"I'll call one Pat and the other Mike!"
But he changed it to Marie
When Mike became a mother!

Soon Flannery sent off a message:
"Regarding last wire of mine,
Instead of just two guinea pigs,
I now am holding nine!"

The legal department was next delegated
To study the problem now so complicated,
When all of the data was accumulated
To make a report and to tell what they knew.

The president wanted a full explanation
As well as an overall clarification
Of Flannery's wire that wanted to know
If a pig was a pig and to please tell him so.

The Board of Directors convened and debated
The question of pigs and were they related
To pigs or to rabbits as once indicated
By evidence found by the fact-finding staff.

A boy in the office first advocated it,
Then a professor formally stated it,
The office force tripled and quadruplicated it,
And this is the answer that Flannery got:

"The guinea pig makes a very nice pet,
But in family, shape, and size
It is certainly not a common pig,
So the forty-four cent rate applies."

With monotonous regularity,
Those pigs had produced more pigs,
While Flannery tried to stem the tide
By playing them Irish jigs.

Now each grandchild of the first two pigs
Had grandsons by the dozens,
And every time the clock would strike,
There were fifty brand-new cousins.

When Flannery got the telegram,
Straight down the road he tore
To take the news to McMorehouse, but—
McMorehouse didn't live there any more!

They unloaded the pigs at the office station,
And filled up the warehouse first;
Then they stored away pigs in the office,
Till the building almost burst.

Flannery heard, and he wired:
"It's not so bad," he said.
"What if all those guinea pigs
Had been elephants instead?"

So Flannery wired the office,
"Tell me quick, what do I do?
There is no rule to cover this case
So now it's up to you."

It was a clever young clerk at last
Who made the recommendation
That the pigs should simply be crated up
And sent to the main-office station.

Flannery loaded the pigs in crates
In boxes, bags, and sacks.
He filled six hundred box cars up,
If you want to know the facts.

Just as he finished, chuckling,
He glanced out the station door—
There stood a long circus train
With elephants galore!

When Flannery recovered, he swore:
"No more will I be a fool!
Whenever it comes to livestock,
Dang every single rule."

"If the animals come in singles,
Or if they come in sets,
If they've got four feet and they're alive,
They'll be classified as pets!"

Peter Pan

*From the Walt Disney Motion Picture "Peter Pan," based
upon "Peter Pan" by Sir James Matthew Barrie**

IN A quiet street in London lived the Darling family. There were Father and Mother Darling, and Wendy, Michael, and John. There was also the children's nursemaid, Nana—a St. Bernard dog.

For Nana and the children the best hour of the day was bedtime, for then they were together in the nursery. There Wendy told wonderful stories about Peter Pan of Never

Land. This Never Land was a magical spot with Indians and Mermaids and Fairies— and wicked pirates, too.

John and Michael liked best of all to play pirate. They had some fine, slashing duels between Peter Pan and his arch-enemy, the pirate, Captain Hook.

Father Darling did not like this kind of play. He blamed it on Wendy's stories of

Peter Pan of Never Land, and he did not approve of those stories, either.

"It is time for Wendy to grow up," Father Darling decided. "This is your last night in the nursery, Wendy girl."

All the children were much upset at that. Without Wendy in the nursery there would be no more stories of Peter Pan! Then to make matters worse, Father Darling became annoyed with Nana and decided the children were too old to be treated like puppies. So he tied Nana in the garden for the night.

When Mother and Father Darling had gone out for the evening, leaving the children snug in their beds with Nana on guard below, who should come to the nursery but Peter Pan! It seemed he had been flying in from Never Land to listen to the bedtime stories, all unseen. Only Nana had caught sight of him once and nipped off his shadow as he escaped. So back he came, looking for his lost shadow and hoping for a story about himself. With him was a fairy, Tinker Bell. When Peter heard that Wendy was to be moved from the nursery, he hit upon a plan.

"I'll take you to Never Land with me, to tell stories to my Lost Boys!" he decided as Wendy sewed his shadow back on.

Wendy thought that was a lovely idea—if Michael and John could go, too. So Peter Pan taught them all to fly—with happy thoughts and faith and trust, and a sprinkling of Tinker Bell's pixie dust. Then out the nursery window they sailed, heading for Never Land, while Nana barked frantically below.

Back in Never Land, on the pirate ship, Captain Hook as usual was grumbling about Peter Pan. You see, once in a fair fight long ago, Peter Pan had cut off one of the pirate captain's hands, so that he had to wear a hook instead. Then Pan threw the hand to a crocodile, who had enjoyed the taste of Hook so much that he had been lurking around ever since, hoping to nibble at the rest of him. Fortunately for the pirate, the crocodile

had also swallowed a clock. He went "tick tock" when he came near, which gave a warning to Captain Hook.

Now, as Captain Hook grumbled about his young enemy, there was a call from the crow's nest.

"Peter Pan ahoy!"

"What? Where?" shouted Captain Hook, twirling his spyglass around the sky. "Swoggle me eyes, it is Peter Pan!" Hook gloated. "Pipe up the crew. Man the guns. At last. We'll get Peter Pan this time!"

"Oh, Peter, it's just as I've dreamed it would be—Mermaid Lagoon and all," Wendy was saying when the first of the pirates' cannonballs ripped through the cloud close beside their feet and went sizzling on past.

"Look out!" cried Pan. "Tinker Bell, take Wendy and the boys to the island. I'll stay here and draw Hook's fire."

Away flew Tinker Bell, as fast as she could go. In her naughty little heart she hoped the children would fall behind and be lost. Especially was she jealous of the Wendy girl, who seemed to have won Peter Pan's heart.

Straight through the Never Land jungle flew Tink, down into a clearing beside an old dead tree called Hangman's Tree. She landed

on a toadstool, bounced to a shiny leaf, and pop! a secret door opened for her in the knot of the hollow tree.

Zip! Down a slippery tunnel Tink slid. She landed at the bottom in an underground room—the secret house of Peter Pan.

Ting-a-ling! she tinkled, flitting about from one corner of the room to the next. She was trying to awaken the sleeping Lost Boys, who lay like so many curled-up balls of fur.

At last, rather grumpily, they woke up and stretched in their little fur suits. And they listened to Tinker Bell.

"What? Pan wants us to shoot down a terrible Wendy bird? Lead us to it!" they shouted, and out they hurried.

When Wendy and Michael and John appeared, flying wearily, the Lost Boys tried to pelt them with stones and sticks—especially the "Wendy bird." Down tumbled Wendy, all her happy thoughts destroyed—for without them no one can fly.

"Hurray! Hurray! We got the Wendy bird!" the Lost Boys shouted.

But then Peter Pan arrived. How angry he was when he discovered that the boys had tried to shoot down Wendy, even though he had caught her before she could be hurt.

"I brought her to be a mother to us all and to tell us stories," Peter said.

"Come on, Wendy," said Peter, "I'll show you the Mermaids. Boys, take Michael and John to hunt some Indians."

So Peter Pan and Wendy flew away, and the boys marched off through the forest, planning to capture some Indians. There were wild animals all around, but the boys never thought to be afraid, and not a creature harmed them.

"First we'll surround the Indians," John decided. "Then we'll take them by surprise."

John's plan worked splendidly, but it was the Indians who used it. Disguised as moving trees, they quietly surrounded the boys and took them by surprise!

Soon, bound with ropes, the row of boys marched away, led by the Indians to their village on the cliff.

"Don't worry, the Indians are our friends," the Lost Boys said, but the chief looked stern.

Meanwhile, on the other side of the island, Wendy and Peter Pan were watching the Mermaids swim and play in their peaceful Mermaid Lagoon. As they were chatting together, Peter suddenly said, "Hush!"

A boat from the pirate ship was going by. In it were wicked Captain Hook and Smee, the pirate cook. And at the stern, all bound with ropes, sat Princess Tiger Lily, daughter of the Indian chief.

"We'll make her talk," sneered Captain Hook. "She'll tell us where Peter Pan lives, or we'll leave her tied to slippery Skull Rock, where the tide will wash over her."

But the proud and loyal Princess Tiger Lily would not say a single word.

Peter and Wendy flew to Skull Rock. Peter, by imitating Hook's voice, tried to trick Smee into setting Tiger Lily free. That almost worked, but Hook discovered the trick, and came after Peter with his sword. Then what a thrilling duel they had, all over that rocky cave where Princess Tiger Lily sat, with the tide up to her chin!

Peter won the duel and rescued Tiger Lily just in the nick of time. Then away he flew to the Indian village, to see the Princess home.

When Peter and Wendy brought Tiger Lily home, the chief set the captives all free. Then what a wonderful feast they had! All the boys did Indian dances, and learned wild Indian chants, and Peter Pan was made a chief! Only Wendy had no fun at all, for she had to help the squaws carry firewood.

"I've had enough of Never Land," she thought grumpily. "I'm ready to go home right now!"

While the Indian celebration was at its height, Smee, the pirate, crept up through the underbrush and captured Tinker Bell.

Trapped in his cap, she struggled and kicked, but Smee took her back to the pirate ship and presented her to Captain Hook.

"Ah, Miss Bell," said Hook sympathetically, "I've heard how badly Peter Pan has treated you since that scheming girl Wendy came. How nice it would be if we could kidnap her

and take her off to sea to scrub the decks and cook for the pirate crew!"

Tink tinkled happily at the thought.

"But, alas," sighed Hook, "we don't know where Pan's house is, so we cannot get rid of Wendy for you."

Tink thought this over. "You won't hurt Peter?" she asked, in solemn tinkling tones.

"Of course not!" promised Hook.

Then she marched to Captain Hook's map of Never Land. Tinker Bell traced a path to Peter's hidden house.

"Thank you, my dear," said wicked Captain Hook, and he locked her up in a lantern cage, while he went off to capture Peter Pan!

That night when Wendy tucked the children into their beds in the underground house, she talked to them about home and mother. Soon they were all so homesick that they wanted to leave at once. Wendy invited all the Lost Boys to come and live with the Darling family. Only Peter refused to go. He simply looked the other way as Wendy and the boys told him good-by and climbed the tunnel to Hangman's Tree.

Up in the woods near Hangman's Tree waited Hook and his pirate band. As each boy came out, a hand was clapped over his mouth and he was quickly tied up with ropes. Last of all came Wendy. Zip, zip, she was bound up too, and the crew marched off with their load of children, back to the pirate ship.

"Blast it!" muttered Captain Hook. "We still don't have Peter Pan!"

So Captain Hook and Smee left a wicked bomb, wrapped as a gift from Wendy, for poor Peter to find. Very soon, they hoped, Peter would open it and blow himself straight out of Never Land.

Imagine how terrible Tinker Bell felt when she saw all the children prisoners, and knew it was her fault!

The boys were given the terrible choice between turning pirates and walking the plank. To the boys the life of a pirate sounded fine, sad to say, and they were all ready to join up. But Wendy was shocked at that.

"I will never become a pirate," said Wendy.

"Very well," said Hook. "Then you shall be the first to walk the plank, my dear."

Everyone felt so terrible, though Wendy was ever so brave. Captain Hook and Smee did not notice Tinker Bell escaping, as she flew off to warn Peter Pan.

What a dreadful moment when Wendy said good-by to everyone on the ship and bravely walked out the long narrow plank that led to the churning sea!

And then she disappeared. Everyone listened, breathless, waiting for a splash, but not a sign of one came! What could the silence mean?

Then they heard a familiar, happy crow. It was Pan in the rigging, high above. Warned by Tinker Bell, he had come just in time to scoop up Wendy in mid-air and fly with her to safety.

"This time you have gone too far, Captain Hook," Peter cried.

He swooped down from the rigging, all set for a duel. And what a duel it was!

While they fought, Tinker Bell slashed the ropes that bound the boys and they forced the pirates into jumping overboard and rowing away in their boat. Then Peter Pan knocked Captain Hook's sword overboard, and Hook jumped, too. When the children last saw the wicked Captain Hook, he was swimming for the boat, with the crocodile tick-tocking hungrily behind him.

Peter Pan took command of the pirate ship. "Heave those halyards. Up with the jib. We're sailing for London," he cried.

"Oh, Michael! John!" cried Wendy. "We're going home!"

And sure enough, with happy thoughts and faith and trust, and a liberal sprinkling of pixie dust, away flew that pirate ship through the skies till the gangplank was run out to the Darlings' nursery window sill.

But now that they had arrived, the Lost Boys did not want to stay.

So Wendy, John, and Michael waved good-by as Peter Pan's ship sailed off through the sky, taking the Lost Boys home to Never Land, where they still live today.

Cinderella

From the Walt Disney Motion Picture "Cinderella"

ONCE UPON A TIME in a far-off land, there lived a kindly gentleman. He had a fine home and a lovely little daughter, and he gave her all that money could buy—a horse of her own, a funny puppy dog, and many beautiful dresses to wear.

But the little girl had no mother. She did wish for a mother and for other children to play with. So her father married a woman with two daughters. Now, with a new mother and sisters, he thought, his little daughter had everything to make her happy.

But alas! the kindly gentleman soon died. His fine home fell into disrepair. And his second wife was harsh and cold. She cared only for her own two ugly daughters. To her lovely stepdaughter she was cruel as cruel could be.

Everyone called the stepdaughter "Cinderella" now. For she had to work hard, she was dressed in rags, and she sat by the cinders to keep herself warm. Her horse grew old, locked up in the barn. And her dog was not allowed in the house.

But do you suppose Cinderella was sad? Not a bit! Cinderella made friends with the birds who flew to her window sill each day. Cinderella made friends with the barnyard chickens and geese. And her best friends of all were—guess who—the mice!

The musty old house was full of mice. Their homes were in the garret, where Cinderella lived. She made little clothes for them, and gave them all names. And they thought Cinderella was the sweetest and most beautiful girl in the world.

Every morning her friends the mice and birds woke Cinderella from her dreams. Then it was breakfast time for the household— with Cinderella doing all the work, of course. Out on the back steps she set a bowl of milk for the stepmother's disagreeable cat, who watched for his chance to catch the mice. The faithful dog had a tasty bone. There was grain for the chickens and ducks and geese. And Cinderella gave some grain to the mice —when they were out of reach of the cat, of course. Then back into the house she went.

Up the stairway she carried breakfast trays for her stepmother and her two lazy step-sisters. And down she came with a basket of mending, some clothes to wash, and a long list of jobs to do for the day.

"Now let me see," her stepmother would say. "You can clean the large carpet in the main hall. And wash all the windows, upstairs and down. Scrub the terrace. Sweep the stairs—and then you may rest."

"Oh," said Cinderella. "Yes. I will finish all those jobs." And off to work she went.

Now across the town from Cinderella's home was the palace of the King. And in the King's study one day sat the King himself, giving orders to the Great Grand Duke.

"The Prince must marry!" said the King to the Great Grand Duke. "It is high time!"

"But, Your Majesty, what can we do?" asked the duke. "First he must fall in love."

"We can arrange that," said the King. "We shall give a great ball, this very night, and invite every girl in the land!"

There was great excitement all through the land. And in Cinderella's home, the stepsisters were delighted, when the invitations to the King's ball arrived.

"How delightful!" they said to each other. "We are going to a ball at the palace!"

"And I—" said Cinderella, "I am invited to the ball, too!"

"Oh, you!" laughed the stepsisters.

"Yes, you!" mocked the stepmother. "Of course you may go, if you finish your work," she said. "And if you have something suitable to wear. I said IF Cinderella." And she smiled a very horrid smile.

Cinderella worked as hard as she could, all through the long day. But when it was time to leave for the ball, Cinderella had not had a moment to fix herself up, or to give a thought to a dress to wear to the ball.

"Why, Cinderella, you are not ready. How can you go to the ball?" asked her stepmother, when the coach was at the door.

"No. I am not going," said Cinderella sadly.

"Not going! Oh, what a shame!" the stepmother said with her mocking smile. "But there will be other balls."

Poor Cinderella! She went to her room and sank sadly down, with her head in her hands.

But a twittering sound soon made her turn around. Her little friends had not forgotten her. They had been scampering and flying about, as busy as could be, fixing a party dress for her to wear.

"Oh, what a lovely dress!" she cried. "I can't thank you enough," she told all the birds and the mice. She looked out the window. The coach was still there. So she started to dress for the ball.

"Wait!" cried Cinderella to the coachman. "I am coming too!"

She ran down the long stairway just as the stepmother was giving her daughters some last commands. They turned and stared.

"My beads!" cried one stepsister.

"And my ribbon!" cried the other, snatching off Cinderella's sash.

"And those bows! You thief! Those are mine!" shrieked the stepmother.

So they pulled and they ripped and they tore at the dress, until Cinderella was in rags once more. And they flounced off to the ball.

Poor Cinderella! She ran to the garden behind the house. And there Cinderella sank down on a low stone bench and wept as if her heart would break.

But soon she felt someone beside her. She looked up, and through her tears she saw a sweet-faced woman. "Oh," said Cinderella. "Good evening. Who are you?"

"I am your fairy godmother," said the little woman. And from the thin air she pulled a magic wand. "Now dry your tears. You can't go to the ball looking like that!

"Let's see now, the first thing you will need is—a pumpkin!" said the fairy godmother.

Cinderella did not understand, but she brought the pumpkin.

"And now for the magic words!" The fairy godmother began, "Salaga doola, menchika boola — bibbidi, bobbidi — bibbidi, bobbidi, boo!"

Slowly, up reared the pumpkin on its pumpkin vine, and it turned into a very handsome magic coach.

"What we need next is some fine big— mice!" said the fairy godmother.

Cinderella brought her friends the mice. And at the touch of the wand they turned into prancing horses.

Then Cinderella's old horse became a very fine coachman.

And Bruno the dog turned into a footman at the touch of the magic wand and a "Bibbidi, bobbidi, boo!"

"There," said the fairy godmother, "now hop in, child. You've no time to waste. The magic only lasts till midnight!"

"But my dress fairy godmother," said Cinderella as she looked at her rags.

"Good heavens, child!" laughed the fairy godmother. "Of course you can't go in that!"

The wand waved again, and there stood Cinderella in the most beautiful gown in the world, with tiny slippers of glass.

The Prince's ball had started. The palace was blazing with lights. The ballroom gleamed with silks and jewels. And the Prince smiled and bowed, but still looked bored, as all the young ladies of the kingdom in turn curtsied before him.

Up above on a balcony stood the King and the Duke, looking on. "Whatever is the matter with the Prince?" cried the King. "He doesn't seem to care for one of those beautiful maidens."

"I feared as much," the Great Grand Duke said with a sigh. "The Prince is not one to fall in love at first sight."

But just then he did! For at that moment Cinderella appeared at the doorway of the ballroom. The Prince caught sight of her through the crowd. And like one in a dream he walked to her side and offered her his arm.

Quickly the King beckoned to the musicians, and they struck up a dreamy waltz. The Prince and Cinderella swirled off in the dance. And the King, chuckling over the success of his plan to find a bride for the Prince, went happily off to bed.

All evening the Prince never left Cinderella's side. They danced every dance. They ate supper together. And Cinderella had such a wonderful time that she quite forgot the fairy godmother's warning until the clock in the palace tower began to strike midnight. Bong! Bong! the clock struck.

"Oh, dear!" cried Cinderella. She knew the magic was about to end!

Without a word she ran from the ballroom, down the long palace hall, and out the door. One of her little glass slippers flew off, but she could not stop.

She leaped into her coach, and away they raced for home. But as they rounded the first corner the clock finished its strokes. The spell was broken. And there in the street stood an old horse, a dog, and a ragged girl, staring at a small round pumpkin. About them some mice ran chattering.

"Glass slipper!" the mice cried.

And Cinderella looked down. Sure enough, there was a glass slipper on the pavement.

"Oh, thank you, godmother!" she said.

Next morning there was great excitement in the palace. The King was furious when he found that the Great Grand Duke had let the beautiful girl slip away.

"All we could find was this one glass slipper," the Duke admitted. "And now the Prince says he must marry the girl whom this slipper fits. And he will not marry anyone else."

"He did?" cried the King. "He said he would marry her? Well then, find her!"

All day and all night the Grand Duke with his servant traveled about the kingdom, trying to find a foot on which the glass slipper would fit. In the morning, his coach drove up before Cinderella's house.

The news of the search had spread. The stepmother was busy rousing her daughters and preparing them to greet the Duke. She was determined that one of them should wear the slipper and be the Prince's bride.

"The Prince's bride!" whispered Cinderella. "I must dress, too. The Duke must not find me like this."

She went off to her room, humming a waltzing tune. Then the stepmother suspected the truth—that Cinderella was the girl the Prince was seeking. So the stepmother followed Cinderella—to lock her in her room.

The mice chattered a warning, but Cinderella did not hear them—she was off in a world of dreams.

Then she heard the key click. The door of her room was locked.

"Please let me out—oh, please!" she cried. But the wicked stepmother only laughed and laughed and went away.

"We will save you!" said the loyal mice. "We will somehow get that key!"

The household was in a flurry. The Great Grand Duke had arrived. His servant held the glass slipper in his hand.

"It is mine!" both stepsisters cried.

And each tried to force her foot into the tiny glass slipper. But the stepsisters failed.

Meanwhile, the mice had made themselves into a long, live chain. The mouse at the end dropped down into the stepmother's dress pocket. He popped up again with the key to Cinderella's room! At once the mice hurried off with the key.

Now the Grand Duke was at the door, about to leave. Suddenly, down the stairs Cinderella came flying.

"Oh, wait, wait, please!" she called. "May I try the slipper on?"

"Of course you may try," said the Great

Grand Duke. And he called back the servant with the slipper. But the wicked stepmother tripped the boy. Away sailed the slipper, and crash! it splintered into a thousand pieces. "Oh my, oh my!" said the Duke. "What can I ever tell the King?"

"Never mind," said Cinderella. "I have the other here." And she pulled from her pocket the other glass slipper!

So off to the palace went Cinderella in the King's own coach, with the happy Grand Duke by her side. The Prince was delighted to see her again. And so was his father, the King. For this sweet and beautiful girl won the hearts of all who met her.

In no time at all she was Princess of the land. And she and her husband, the charming Prince, rode to their palace in a golden coach to live

Happily Ever After!

Mickey Mouse
GOES CHRISTMAS SHOPPING

MORTIE MOUSE dried the breakfast dishes. Ferdie Mouse swept the floor.

They both made their beds and picked up their clothes.

Because today was the day Uncle Mickey and Aunt Minnie had promised to take them Christmas shopping, if they were very good.

They all rode down town in Uncle Mickey's car. What a wonderful day it was! There were snow flakes spinning in the air. There were frosty breezes blowing around the buildings.

Every street corner was a-tinkle with the sound of Santa's helpers' bells.

Every shop window was a-twinkle with colored lights and toys.

Best of all was the big Department Store. Mortie Mouse and Ferdie Mouse took Mickey and Minnie firmly by the hand, and they led those grown-ups through the crowd, straight into the busy store.

What a hustle! What a bustle! What a clatter! What a crowd! But Mortie and Ferdie knew where they were going.

Whenever Mickey Mouse or Minnie Mouse tried to hang back to look at sweaters or mittens or socks, Mortie and Ferdie tugged at their hands and pulled them straight ahead. For they had seen a big sign saying TOYS!

Z-z-zoop! Up they went in an elevator, straight to the Toy Floor.

What a wonderful place it was!

There was a room full of dolls—but they raced by that. There were tables of games,

and balls and bats and skis. But Mortie and Ferdie had no time for those.

"What we want for Christmas are things that go!" they shouted, racing on to the toy cars and trucks and trains, and some extra-special toy airplanes.

"Stay with Uncle Mickey while I go to shop," Minnie whispered to Mortie.

Mickey wanted to buy a present for Minnie, too. "Stay with Aunt Minnie," he told Ferdie. "We'll meet at the car at closing time."

So there were Ferdie and Mortie in the great big Toy Shop on their own!

And what a wonderful time they had! They tried out every single toy that moved!

They bought tickets for the space ship, which advertised *Quick Trip to the Moon, 10c.* And during the thrilling ride through space, Mortie and Ferdie fell asleep.

At the end of the ride, the other children piled out. The pilot climbed out of his space suit and stretched.

"Glad this day is over!" he said to the Santa Claus' helper who worked at that store, getting messages from children all day.

Then the space pilot went home, and all the clerks in the entire Toy Shop went home.

Just then Mortie woke up. He looked around. It was dark and strange. "Where are we, Ferdie?" he asked.

"In the space ship," said Ferdie, waking up too. "Maybe we're on the moon." So they opened the door and peeked cautiously out.

There was the toy department. But how strange it looked now! For everything was shadowy and still. There was plenty of space to drive the toy cars and trains. But the boys did not seem to care.

Just then they saw a beam of light.

"Let's see what that is," they whispered, both at once. So hand in hand they tiptoed toward the light, squeak, squeak, squeak in the dark.

When they reached the open door and peeked through, imagine their surprise. For there sat Santa's helper at a desk.

"Well, well," he said, when he saw them there. "What brings you youngsters here this time of day?"

So Mortie Mouse and Ferdie Mouse told him their tale.

"I see," said Santa's helper, with a wise and kindly nod. And he stood up and took them each by one hand.

Then down through that big, still depart-ment store they marched with a fine, big clomping sound. Through the big front door they saw Mickey and Minnie Mouse.

"Wherever have you been?" cried Minnie.

"Here they are," said Santa's helper, "as good as new." Then he turned to the boys with a serious look. "Next time you're out shopping you'll stay close to your grown-ups, won't you?"

"Yes, sir," said Mortie and Ferdie Mouse. And they meant it from their hearts.

Then Santa's helper smiled and held open the big door, while they all ran out to the car.

"See you Christmas Eve!" he called as he waved good-by. "Merry Christmas and Good Night to you all!"

PLUTO PUP GOES TO SEA

"WHY CAN'T you be a hero like that ship's dog?" Mickey Mouse asked Pluto Pup one day.

They were standing beside an ocean liner, looking up at the deck.

On the deck lay a huge dog, staring proudly out to sea.

"There was a story in the paper about all the lives he's saved," said Mickey. "Why can't you be a dog like that?"

If all you had to do to be a hero was to lie on a deck staring out to sea, Pluto was willing to try it. The next gangplank they came to, up Pluto went.

Mickey did not miss him for a few minutes. Then he whistled and called and looked all around, behind crates and barrels and in coils of rope. But not a trace of Pluto could he find.

High above, on the deck of a sleek white

yacht, Pluto was sitting all alone, looking proud and haughty, gazing out to sea.

No one on the yacht knew Pluto was on board until they had left the harbor for the open sea. There the waves rose and fell, and the yacht pitched and tossed, and Pluto was unhappy as a dog can be.

Down below, the sailors shuddered at the dismal moans that came from the deck above. Checking, they soon found the stowaway and led him to a corner of the dark hold, where they fixed him a bed of old rags.

"Too bad he isn't a smarter mutt," said the second mate to the first. "We could use a smart watchdog for the captain's jewels."

"Sh!" The first mate put a finger to his lips. "No one must know about those jewels!"

It was too late, though they did not know it. The tough-looking sailor who had found Pluto, coming back to report, had heard.

"Aha! Them jewels will line my pockets soon, and I'll jump ship at the very first port, or my name's not Pegleg Pete!"

Next day Pluto's nose led him to the galley, where the ship's cat lived with the cook.

Pluto heard that catty sizzle, he saw her back arch, and he took off, racing for the deck.

The cat came behind him, traveling so fast that as the ship lurched she slid across

231

the deck, under the rail, down into the sea!

Pluto started over for a better look—and skidded, with a yelp, right after her!

When the sailors rescued them, they thought Pluto had jumped in to save the cat. They called him a hero. They fussed over him, and the mates moved his bed to the captain's cabin.

"He's just the dog we need to guard the captain's jewels, in spite of his looks," they said.

Pluto did not like being shut in the cabin, though. He set up such a howl that night that the captain shouted for the mates. "Take that mutt away. I'd rather be guarded from him than by him!" he cried.

So Pluto went back to his first spot on deck, looking proudly out to sea. He kept a sharp

eye for anyone about to fall overboard, because he liked the life of a hero.

That was the night Pegleg Pete had picked to steal the captain's jewels. The ship lay close to shore. His friends would meet him with a boat.

So Pete slipped down to the cabin where the captain lay asleep, and he hit him with a blackjack and stole the jewels!

With the jewels safely stowed in a small leather pouch, Pegleg Pete signaled to his friends on shore.

When a small light answered, he kicked off his shoe, laid his blackjack beside it, and over the rail he dove into the dark waters below.

Splash! He landed and started to swim, but Pluto had heard that splash, too.

One of his friends must be overboard! Time to be a hero again!

"Arf arf arf!" Pluto yelped, and he jumped in too.

"Man overboard!" the lookout yelled. The sailors came running, turned the searchlight on, and soon they picked up Pluto and Pegleg Pete, bobbing in the waters below.

Pete was still sputtering about his cursed luck, and "that blasted mutt," but he soon changed his tune. "I saw the dear mutt slide in," he claimed, "and I couldn't bear to think of nothing happening to him, so I jumped in to save him, of course."

"Is that so?" said the first mate. "Then what were you doing with the blackjack here beside your shoe?"

"Come to think of it, where's the captain?" the second mate cried. And he ran to the cabin to see.

Pegleg Pete knew then that it was all up with him. "Let me go!" he cried, and he ran for the rail.

But Pluto did not want another bath in that cold water that night! He made a frantic jump for Pegleg's trousers and hung on to them!

Soon the second mate was back, with the captain on his arm and a blackjack lump on the captain's head.

"Put Pete in the brig," the captain said. "And we'll get you a medal, sir," he went on. He was speaking to Pluto Pup!

So when the yacht came home at last, with Pluto sitting proudly up on deck, he wore the biggest, shiniest medal to be had. "Our Hero!" it said in gold.

Mickey was wandering down by the docks, as he did every lonely day, looking for his lost pup, when the yacht came into port.

"Arf!" cried Pluto, when he spied Mickey.

"Pluto!" cried Mickey. "Where have you been? and that medal? What does it mean?"

The sailors told Mickey the whole proud tale.

"I guess you won't want to come back home," Mickey said at the end.

For his answer, Pluto gnawed his medal off and laid it at Mickey's feet. He still thought the finest thing of all was to be Mickey Mouse's dog!

Davy Crockett

KING OF THE WILD FRONTIER

Long ago, America was a land of woods and forests. And deep in the green woods, high on a mountain top, a baby was born. His Ma and his Pa called him Davy . . . Davy Crockett. And it happened in the state of Tennessee.

Little Davy was raised in the woods. He learned to know every tree. He learned to know the critters, too. From the little possum to the big bear, Davy knew them all.

As Davy grew up, he learned how to shoot. He was a real rip-snorter with a rifle.

Once a bear came at Davy from one side. A panther came at him from the other side. Davy fired his rifle at a rock between them. The bullet hit the rock, splitting into two pieces. One piece hit the bear, the other hit the panther. That way, Davy got him two critters with one shot.

No mistake about it—Davy was one of the greatest hunters that ever was.

He liked to tell the story of the time he saw a raccoon up a tree. Before he raised his rifle, Davy grinned at the coon.

"Don't shoot, Davy! I'll come down!" said the coon.

It wasn't long before Davy tried his grin on a bear. He looked the bear right in the eye. The bear looked Davy right in the eye. Davy grinned and grinned, trying to grin that bear to death. Then, snarling and growling, the bear rushed at Davy.

"Well, b'ar," said Davy, "guess we'll have to fight."

And they did. Davy and the bear rolled through the bushes, shaking the ground like an earthquake.

Davy won the fight, of course. But he had to give up grinning at bears. He saved his grin for the little critters, like the coons and the possums.

Besides hunting, Davy liked fun and frolics. He was always ready to dance. He'd stomp and step with the other folks, singing:

> Old Dan Tucker was a good old man,
> Washed his face in a frying pan,
> Combed his hair with a wagon wheel,
> And died with a toothache in his heel.

But when the Indians started a war, Davy stopped his hunting and dancing. With his friend, George Russel, he joined General Andy Jackson's army.

They fought the Indians in the forest and the swamp. Davy was a brave fighter, and a good fighter. And yet, he did not like war.

As soon as he could, Davy helped make peace with the Indians. After that, he and the Indians were friends.

Folks liked Davy's way of doing things. They thought Davy ought to be a Congressman and help run the country. The critters seemed to think so, too. Even the crickets all chirped:

"Crockett for Congress! Crockett for Congress!"

At least, they sounded like that to Davy.

Sure enough, Davy was elected to Congress. He went to the nation's capitol in Washington City. There he made a speech.

He said, "I'm Davy Crockett, fresh from the backwoods. I'm half horse, half alligator, and a little tetched with snappin' turtle. I got the fastest horse, the prettiest sister, the surest rifle, and the ugliest dog in Tennessee."

Folks all over the country were talking about Davy. They wanted to see him. They wanted to hear his funny stories. Davy took a trip, stopping in the cities to make speeches.

In Philadelphia, the folks gave him a fine new rifle. Davy liked it so much he called it old Betsy.

Davy could hardly wait to get back to the woods and try out old Betsy. But more and more folks were making their homes in the forest. It was getting too crowded for Davy.

He and George Russel went west, where there was more room. They traveled part of the way by boat.

At last Davy and George reached the west. They saw the wide, wide prairies. They saw the tall, tall grass. They saw herds and herds of wild buffalo.

"This is a fine country," said Davy. "It's worth fighting for. Guess we'll head for the fort called the Alamo, where the Texans are fighting for liberty."

Whatever Davy said, he did. He helped fight a great battle at the Alamo.

Ever since, folks have told stories about

Davy. They tell about Davy riding a streak of lightning.

And they tell of Davy catching a comet by the tail, before it could crash into the earth. Davy threw the comet back into the sky, where it couldn't do any harm.

Another story folks tell is of the time of

the Big Freeze. It was so cold the sun and earth were frozen, and couldn't move.

Davy saw that he would have to do something. He climbed up Daybreak Hill. He thawed out the sun and the earth with hot bear oil. Then he gave the earth's cogwheel a kick, and got things moving.

As the sun rose, Davy walked down the hill, with a piece of sunrise in his pocket.

And some folks say that Davy is still roaming the woods. And right with Davy is his friend, George Russel, singing:

Born on a mountain top in Tennessee,
Greenest state in the Land of the Free,
Raised in the woods so's he knew every tree,
Kilt him a b'ar when he was only three.
Davy — Davy Crockett,
King of the Wild Frontier!

dARBY O'GILL

Now IRELAND, as you may know, is a green
and lovely land. There's many a thousand of
Irishmen there, in every valley and town.

But there are others in Ireland, too, who
make their homes snug underground. You
may not see a one of them from New Year's
Eve to year's end. But they are there, make no
mistake. They're the Little People, the leprechauns.

A canny lot of wee folk are they, dressed in
their suits of green. And many's the crock of
gold they have miserly hidden away. But will

they share it with human folk? They'll give you
a trick instead!

Take the case of Darby O'Gill, which happened not long ago:

Darby was chasing his horse one night. The
skittish mare led him across the sloping
meadow and off toward the mountain beyond.

Now Darby knew as well as the next what
dangers that mountain held. For it had the
name of Knocknasheega, the hill of the fairy
folk.

And sure enough, elfin music seemed to

rise up from the place. Darby heard it plain enough. It came from an open well. And a strange sort of light seemed to rise from there too.

Well, Darby was a man with his share of wonder. He bent down to peek down the hole.

As he did so, the fairy music grew wilder. Darby heard his horse give one strange, wild neigh. Then he felt her hooves upon his shoulders. And he tumbled down that well!

When he came to himself, he was flat on his back, lying on the floor of a cave.

Suddenly, spang, a wee man landed on Darby's middle!

Darby waved his stick.

"You wicked little creatures!" he cried.

"Watch your stick!" cried one of the leprechauns. And Darby's own trusty blackthorn flew out of his hands and beat its master's head!

"Come on," said the other leprechaun. "We'll take you to our king."

Darby had nothing better to do, so he followed the little men. Many were the wonderful sights he saw, in those caves deep underground. He saw leprechauns shoveling crocks full of gold. He saw others cobbling small fairy shoes.

"Well, Darby O'Gill!" cried the Little People's king, laying aside his pipes. "I'm pleased and delighted to see you!"

"Thank you sir," Darby said.

"Sit down," said the king, and waved his hand at a chest by the foot of his throne.

"Drop the lid, man," he said, as Darby just stared. "It's only an old chest of jewels."

Darby closed the lid and sat down.

Then Brian the king showed him the treasures here and there, scattered about the room.

"I declare to my soul!" cried Darby O'Gill.

"When I tell this at home, they'll never believe me."

"Oh, you'll not do that, Darby," said the king with a smile. "Once you're here, there's no going back, you know."

"But I've got to go back!" cried Darby.

"Ah, no," said the little king. "You can say goodbye to the tears and the troubles of the world outside. There's nothing but fun and dancing here. Be a good lad now and give us a tune."

"Well," said Darby, with a glint in his eye,

"I'm no great hand with the pipes or harp. But give me my old fiddle, and I can play you a tune worth going a mile o'ground to hear."

"Grand, grand," said Brian the King.

"But I'll have to go home," said Darby O'Gill. "To get the fiddle, you see."

"None of your tricks," said King Brian sternly. "I said you were here to stay."

He gave a snap of his fingers, and a fine old fiddle and its bow dropped into Darby's hands.

"Go ahead," said King Brian. "Give us a good one."

Darby tucked the fiddle under his chin and tried a chord or two. They sounded so magnificent that a bold plan came to him.

"I'll play you the Fox Chase," said Darby O'Gill. For he knew that the Little People loved both the dance and the hunt. They could not resist them at all.

Well, he played the gathering of the huntsmen and the hounds, and the start of the hunt.

"Off we go!" cried Darby, tapping his foot. And the little men started to dance.

He played them the long, lone sound of the horn and the fine, fast music of the chase. You could hear the hounds baying and the riders galloping.

Soon the Little People were racing off to mount their white hunters. With the king at their head, they circled the cave, while Darby fiddled the baying of a hound.

"Tally ho!" cried the king, with a crack of his whip. And the mountainside opened before him.

Then the moonlight flooded in, dazzling Darby's eyes. But he kept on fiddling as never before. And out streamed the king, with his hunters behind him, toward the night sky

241

filled with the glory of all the stars above.

When Darby was alone in the cave, he laid down the fiddle and started after them. But of a sudden he thought of the chest of jewels beside the throne.

Back he went and he lifted the lid and began to stuff his pockets with jewels.

A strange grating sound made him turn his head. The mountainside was closing again! Darby reached for one last handful of jewels. But he saw there was not a moment to lose! So he raced for the opening, narrowed now to a crack in the mountainside.

Out he dove headlong. And as he sprawled in the night-chilled grass, with a crash the mountain behind him closed. He shuddered at his narrow escape!

Then his hand went to his jewel-crammed pocket. Not a thing was there. Deeper he dug. Still only cloth. And then, at the bottom, he found a hole. As he had fled from the cave, all the jewels had trickled out!

So that was how it came about that Darby O'Gill came back to his home from a night with the Little People, with not a glint of a treasure to show.

There were even those who doubted his word. But you and I understand.

THE OLD MILL

It was early spring when the mother and father robin found the old mill.

"This is the place for our nest," said the father robin, as they flew into the dim, cool, peaceful place.

"Let us start right away," said the mother robin. "I like it here."

"Everyone likes it here," said a little mouse who scampered over to visit.

He waved a tiny paw, and in the shadows the robins could see drowsy bats hanging from the rafters high above, and an owl dozing on a lofty beam. And in the corners spiders were spinning.

"Oh, we shall have neighbors," said the mother robin. "How nice!"

So they chose a hollow in the old mill wheel's stone base, and there they built their nest. Soon after the nest was finished, the mother robin laid five speckled eggs in it.

"We have five speckled eggs in our nest," sang the mother robin to the sleepy bats and the drowsy owl and the spinning spiders and the scampering mice in the old mill.

"We have five speckled eggs in our nest," sang the father robin to the cows in the meadow and the ducks swimming on the pond and the frogs hiding under the lily pads outside the old mill. Then he hunted until he found the plumpest, most delicious worms to take home to the mother robin.

So the spring days drifted softly past the old mill. Every morning the cows came out to pasture nearby, and at twilight they plodded homeward through the thick meadow grass, with the ducks waddling along close behind them.

Then the frogs popped up, one by one, among the lily pads. And the deep chug-a-rum of the frog chorus drifted into the old mill, where the mother robin was waiting on her nest.

243

turn, and inside the old mill, wheels rumbled and rusty chains clanked.

"Oh, dear," chirped the mother bird, as the great mill wheel came clanking toward the nest. "A storm! A storm! What shall we do?" She said to the father robin.

"We shall have to leave the nest if the wheel comes closer," said the father bird, ruffling his feathers in alarm.

"Leave our nest, our precious eggs?" chirped the mother bird. "Oh, never! We would never do that!"

So the father and mother robin huddled to-

"We shall not have much longer to wait," said the mother robin one evening as the twilight deepened to soft, black night.

"Soon our eggs will hatch," said the father bird to the friendly little mouse.

And the kind old round-faced moon smiled down on them all, safe and sound in the sturdy old mill.

But as the robins sat close together in the darkness, chirping softly to one another, a sly old wind came skimming over the meadow grasses. The wind rustled the reeds at the duck pond's edge. It rattled the tall cattails. The wind blew a cloud across the face of the kind old moon.

The frog choristers disappeared under the lily pads. The crickets were silent in the quivering reeds. But now the saucy wind began to howl and scream, and it shivered the windmill sails high above.

With an uneasy creak the sails began to

gether there in the creaking darkness. Meanwhile the ropes of the old mill groaned and strained. And shutters banged themselves to pieces at the old mill's windows. Now rain came pouring down and lightning flashed. And far across the meadow deep thunder growled and roared.

Each time the mill wheel creaked around, it seemed as if it would be the last moment for the little nest, but the father and mother robin stayed on through it all, keeping their eggs warm and dry.

Now the beating rain forced its way into the mill itself, and sent the mice scamper-

and the drowsy owl, the spinning spiders and scampering mice.

"We have five hungry babies in our nest," chirped the father robin to the cows and the ducks and the crickets outside the mill, as he scratched and pulled and hunted for big, plump, delicious worms.

"And how is the world outside, now that the storm is over?" asked the mother robin when the father robin returned.

"It is all washed fresh and clean by the storm," said the father robin, as he dropped a fat chunk of worm into each wide-open beak. "And the mill, the dear old mill, looks more beautiful than ever," he chirped.

"The good old mill," said the mother robin with a happy sigh. "How lucky we are to have our nest here. Let us never, never leave the dear old mill."

ing to find new holes. The wind tore angrily at the old mill. Finally the storm in its fury flung a lightning bolt straight at the mill's flailing arms. The whole building rocked and shuddered. The robins on their nest quivered in alarm. Then with a groan the mill slouched down on its foundation. Its broken sails creaked to a stop. The old wheel stood still. And the robins' nest was safe.

The storm swept on across the meadow, and in the calm it left behind, the battered old mill slept.

Soon it was morning. The cows came plodding back to their meadow. The ducks waddled back to the pond. And inside the mill, at the mother and father robins' nest, there was great excitement.

"We have five hungry babies in our nest," called the mother robin to the sleepy bats

Johnny Appleseed

From the Walt Disney Motion Picture "Melody Time"

THERE WAS one thing Johnny Appleseed liked to do better than anything else. That was to find a sunny spot and dig a little hole and plant an apple seed. For he knew the seed would grow into a sturdy apple tree.

Johnny dug his little holes and planted apple seeds, and he dug and he planted some more, until the whole countryside around his home was dotted with fine young apple trees.

"I don't know what I'll do when there's no place left for planting apple trees," said Johnny to his animal friends on the farm.

One day as he was walking down the road, looking for a spot to plant just one more apple tree, Johnny heard the sound of singing, coming closer and closer.

"Git on a wagon rolling West,
Out to the great unknown!
Git on a wagon rolling West,
Or you'll be left alone."

Then, as Johnny watched, down the road came a very long line of covered wagons drawn by great oxen. Beside each wagon walked a tall, strong man dressed in deerskin. Each man had a rifle swinging at his side. These were the pioneers.

The pioneers were taking their families off into the great empty lands of the West, to build new homes.

"Come along, boy!" the pioneers shouted to Johnny, when they saw him standing there at the roadside. "Come West, young fellow. Come along with us."

"But I can't be a pioneer!" said Johnny. "I'm not tall and strong. I couldn't chop down trees to build a log cabin. I couldn't clear fields to plant corn. I guess there's nothing much that I can do out West."

The pioneers were not listening. They were marching ahead, still singing as they went. Soon their wagons vanished from sight around the turn of the road.

Only the words of their song floated back to Johnny on the breeze:

"—*you'll be left alone.*"

"I wish I could go West, too," said Johnny to himself.

"You can Johnny!" said a voice beside him. It was Johnny's Guardian Angel speaking. "Not all the pioneers have to cut down trees.

You can be a pioneer who plants them. Wherever there are homes, Son, the folks will need apple trees.

"Why Johnny Appleseed! You just think of the things that apples make. There's apple pies and apple fritters, apple cores to feed the critters, tasty apple cider in a glass. There's apples baked and boiled and frizzled, taffy apples hot and sizzled, and there's always good old apple sass!

"You're needed in the West, young Johnny Appleseed! You have a job to do!"

"But I have no covered wagon," said Johnny. "I have no knife and gun."

"Shucks," said the Guardian Angel to Johnny, "all that you will need out West is a little pot to cook in, and a stock of apple seed —and the Good Book to read!"

"That's wonderful!" said Johnny. "I have a

pot to cook in, and my Book and apple seed. I can start right away. I'm off for the West, Mr. Angel, this very day!"

Of course, before he left for the West, Johnny stopped to see his friends, the animals on the farm.

"I hate to say good-by," he told them, "cause you've been such good friends to me. I sure will miss you when I'm out there all alone."

The animals looked sorrowful. They knew they would miss Johnny, too.

"Well, so long," he said at last. Then away down the road to the West he went, young Johnny Appleseed.

The West was mostly forest in those days. And that forest was big and deep and dark—a mighty fearsome place, you might think, for one young man to be all alone, without a knife and without a gun.

But Johnny Appleseed never thought of being afraid. He just marched along the narrow forest trail, singing a merry song. And as he marched, he looked to the right and to the left, watching for bright sunny spots to plant his apple seeds.

No, Johnny was not afraid in the forest, but he was lonely. He had to admit that. It had been some days since he had seen a covered wagon train or a single pioneer. And he missed his animal friends, back on the farm.

Of course, Johnny was not really all alone in the forest. He just thought he was. On every side, from behind every tree, sharp little, bright little forest eyes kept watch as he marched along.

And as they watched, the little forest folk wondered. For the animals did not like Men. The only Men they knew were the tall, strong pioneers. They cut down trees to build cabins. They cleared away thickets to make fields. They shot wild animals for food and fur. Naturally, the forest folk did not like that.

So they hid and watched as Johnny Appleseed came down the path, all alone.

"He doesn't look like the others," whispered a chipmunk.

"He is not very tall. He does not look very strong," said a squirrel.

"He has no knife, and he has no gun," said the smallest bunny.

"Still, he is a Man," the gentle deer reminded them, "so we must be very careful."

And they were. They watched, ever so

quietly and ever so cautiously, as Johnny Appleseed walked along.

At last he came to a sunny little open spot among the forest trees, and there Johnny Appleseed stopped short.

"This looks like a right nice spot," said he, "for me to plant an apple tree."

So Johnny set down his little cooking pot and his Bible and his packet of apple seeds. And he picked up a long straight stick which he found there on the ground.

"This is a fine straight stick for digging my little holes," said he.

But the animals watching, from behind the trees, thought it was a gun.

"Danger!" they whispered. "The Man has a gun! Run, run, run!"

At the signal, all the animals started to run as fast as they could. Off in all directions they scattered through the forest.

But just as the smallest bunny started to run, he caught one foot in a twisted vine. He

250

squirmed and twisted as hard as he could, but he could not jerk himself loose.

"Oh, dear! How sad!" whispered the other animals, as soon as they knew. And from their hiding places farther back in the woods, they watched to see what would happen to the smallest bunny.

"Is someone there?" called Johnny Appleseed. For he had heard the forest folk racing away to their new hiding places.

"It would be nice to find a friend," said Johnny to himself.

He called again.

But there was no answer.

Pushing the bushes aside with his long, straight stick, Johnny Appleseed stepped into the forest.

And there, while the watching animals held their breath in fright, Johnny Appleseed found the smallest bunny with his foot caught in the twisted vine.

"Well," said Johnny Appleseed softly. "What has happened to you, little fellow?"

And very gently Johnny Appleseed untwisted the vine from around the foot of the smallest bunny, and set him free. Just as soon as the smallest bunny was free, he started to run into the forest.

"I wish you wouldn't run away," called Johnny Appleseed after the smallest bunny. "It is lonely in the forest for me, and I would like to be your friend."

The smallest bunny did not answer. Instead, he turned and hopped back to where Johnny was still sitting. Then, he put his soft nose into Johnny Appleseed's hand, and twiddled his whiskers in a friendly way.

The other animals were amazed.

"Why, this Man is not bad," they said. "He is nice and friendly."

So one by one the animals crept out from their hiding places farther back in the woods and gathered around Johnny Appleseed. Before long Johnny was surrounded by his new forest friends.

"Well," he chuckled happily, "this is as nice as being home on the farm."

And from that day on, Johnny Appleseed was never lonely again. He wandered on through the lands of the West. Whenever he came to a sunny little open spot among the forest trees, he planted his apple seeds.

And as Johnny Appleseed planted his trees, he sang his merry song:

"—*apple pies and apple fritters,*
Apple cores to feed the critters,
Tasty apple cider in a glass.
Apples baked and boiled and frizzled,
Taffy apples hot and sizzled,
And there's always good old apple sass."

As the years passed, there were more and more farms through the wide land, and farmhouses and people.

And in almost every farmyard, throughout the West, there were spreading apple trees which had been planted by Johnny Appleseed.

He was a welcome guest in all these farm homes. And Johnny liked to come and visit for a barn-raising or a house-raising or a quilting or corn-husking bee, for then friends would gather from far and near.

But between times Johnny kept on the move. There was still much woodland there in the West. Days often passed when Johnny did not see a covered wagon or a log cabin or a sign of a pioneer.

But he was never lonely in those wild Western woods. For as he came singing along, out from behind the bushes and trees came squirrels and deer and bunnies and all the other forest folk.

"This is the Man," they would whisper. "He carries no knife and he carries no gun. He is a true friend to us all."

And the smallest bunny would hop up close to Johnny Appleseed and twiddle his whiskers in the friendliest way.

No, Johnny was never lonely now. For every animal in the whole wide forest was a friend to Johnny Appleseed.

The Grand Canyon

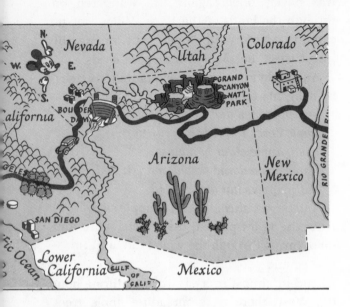

We OUGHT to see something of the Indians while we're here," said Mickey. "They're the first Americans really. The Pueblo Indians have a rain dance in August. We're just in time for it."

They were in New Mexico and had crossed the Rio Grande River. The road ran across the desert. Queerly shaped rocks and mountains rose from the barren ground. The colors of the rocks were purples, pinks, and reds. It was a strange and beautiful land.

"This is different from anything we've seen before," said Mickey in amazement. "Look at that flat-topped hill over there. It must be a mesa."

They stopped for lunch near an Indian trading post. Minnie was delighted with all the things the Indians made. She bought a lovely silver necklace and a bracelet set with turquoise as blue as the desert sky. Donald bought a Navajo belt of silver, and Mickey bought a Navajo rug.

The next morning they left the main route and drove across the desert to the pueblo, and there they saw the famous rain dance of the Indians.

They decided that that was one of the best sights on the trip, but Mickey said, "Tomorrow you'll see something even better."

"What?" asked Minnie and Donald.

"The Grand Canyon, in Arizona," said Mickey, and the others cheered with delight.

When Mickey and Minnie and Donald peered over the edge of the Grand Canyon, they could scarcely believe their eyes.

"It's not real," gasped Minnie. "Somebody painted it!"

Down, down, down, they looked into the great gash in the earth. During the ages, the Colorado River had carved this canyon through the layers of colored rocks. It had left strangely shaped islands and towers.

"It's the strangest, most beautiful place I ever saw," sighed Mickey. "The book says it's a mile deep."

They stayed at the Canyon for several days, for there were many things to see and do. They watched the sunrise and the sunset light up the colors in the mysterious depths below. They took trips with the forest rangers, who told them how the Canyon had been made. They sat around the campfire in the evening

and sang songs with the other tourists there.

Then one day Donald asked, "What about going down into the Canyon, Mickey?"

"Well—" said Mickey. He had watched the parties start down the Canyon on mule-back, for there was a narrow trail down the steep rock wall. In the evening he had seen the parties coming back looking very tired and lame. Mickey was not sure that he wanted to go down into the Canyon.

Minnie was perfectly sure that she did not want to go, but Donald begged Mickey to go, and finally Mickey said that he would.

The next morning Donald and Mickey started out on burros.

"What have you got on your back?" asked Minnie, as she saw them off.

"That's my affair," said Donald.

"It looks like a lunch box," suggested Mickey. But it was not a lunch box; it was Donald's parachute.

"You can't tell what might happen," he muttered.

Down the narrow trail they started with the rest of the party and a guide. The path was very steep and narrow. On one side rose the rock wall. On the other the cliff dropped straight down for over a mile. No sooner had Donald started than he felt he had made a bad mistake to come. He peered over the edge

of the precipice, and he wished that he were back with Minnie and Pluto.

Every now and then the trail made a sharp hairpin curve. Donald felt as though he were hanging in space while his burro humped himself around the turn. After a while, the burro grew hungry. There were a few blades of grass growing in the cracks in the rock at the side of the path. Donald's burro stopped and stretched his long neck down to reach the grass. There he stood and nibbled away.

"Hi there, come back!" shouted Donald. With the burro's head down, it was very hard not to start sliding down his neck. Donald gave a tug at the burro's head, but the animal only stretched his neck further over the edge.

"Help!" shouted Donald.

"Just give your burro a kick and make it go on," called the guide. "You're blocking the way."

But when Donald tried to give his burro a kick, he lost his hold. He began slipping down the length of the beast's smooth neck.

It was a terrible moment for Donald. He quacked nervously, and grabbed at the animal's ears. The burro gave a little shake. Donald lost his hold. Over the burro's head he coasted. Then he plunged off into the air.

"Donald! Donald!" cried Mickey, but there was nothing he could do to help.

Luckily, at that moment Donald remem-

Then they saw him. His parachute had caught on a rock and he was hanging just a few feet above the rushing water.

"Hold on, Donald!" Mickey shouted. "We're coming!"

But Donald couldn't help holding on. He was caught fast. The men steered the boat so that it went right under Donald. Mickey had his knife ready, and he clutched Donald with one hand. With the other hand, he slashed at the ropes. For a few seconds it was a question who would win, Mickey or the swift current. But Mickey won. The ropes were cut. Donald fell safely into the bottom of the boat.

bered to pull the cord on his parachute. Slowly the big umbrella opened above him, and he drifted slowly toward the ground.

Mickey sighed with relief, but the guide said, "He'll probably land in the river."

"We'd better hurry down as fast as we can," Mickey exclaimed, "and try to save him."

They raced down the winding path. Donald had long since disappeared from view.

"Maybe he's already in the river," Mickey thought, urging his burro on. "He'll be carried down the river through the rapids.

There was a ranch house at the bottom of the Canyon, and Mickey hired a boat. He telephoned back to Minnie.

"Get a plane to take you over to Boulder Dam," he said. "We'll be coming down the Colorado River. I've hired a boat and crew to chase Donald. Don't worry about us."

"I won't," said Minnie.

The boat was soon ready, and Mickey started out on the dangerous trip. Down the rapids they plunged. The boatmen crouched with long poles, ready to push the boat away from the cruel teeth of rocks that seemed waiting to tear it to pieces. Down the dark depths of the canyon they went, searching for Donald.

"I hate to lose my parachute," said Donald sadly.

"I'll get you another," Mickey promised him.

All that day they sped down the Colorado River. They passed wrecks of boats that had tried to go through, but had failed. Mickey's crew was strong and clever. The men brought the boat to safety. At last the current grew less and less swift. Then the boat floated out on the wide and beautiful Lake Mead in Nevada.

"Boulder Dam makes this lake," said one of the men as he lay back, resting.

They reached Boulder Dam ahead of Minnie, so Mickey and Donald took time to explore it. A great wall of steel and cement blocked the canyon. Inside the dam there were elevators.

"What do you think of that?" cried Mickey in amazement.

They went down to see the big power houses at the foot of the dam.

"You have no idea how much electricity this country gets from water power each year," Mickey told Donald. "My book says that we get millions of kilowatt-hours a year."

"Kilo-whats?" demanded Donald.

"That's how they measure electricity," said Mickey.

They went up in the elevator. There was Minnie waiting for them on the roadway that runs across the top of the dam. She had a big car and a truck with her.

"Here you are at last," she called. "What do you think has happened?"

"Something good, I hope," Mickey said.

"I telephoned to the Studio in Hollywood and told them all about what had happened," she said. "They want to make a movie of Donald and the Grand Canyon. I've got the burro here in a truck."

"I don't ever want to see that burro again!" cried Donald hotly. "And I'm not going down into the Grand Canyon again!"

"But you were so brave and wonderful," exclaimed Minnie, "and they'll take your picture at the Studio with the Canyon as a background."

"Well-ll—" said Donald, who was beginning to like the idea.

"I'll drive the car and you drive the truck with the burro in it, Mickey," said Minnie. "We'll soon be home."

They hastened across the lower end of Nevada and were soon on the home stretch to California.

Beaver and his Brothers

BEAVER and his brothers were looking for a place to build a house. They came to a little stream in the woods.

"The water in this stream is not deep," said Beaver to his brothers. "The water must be deep where we build our house."

"What shall we do?" asked Beaver's brothers.

Old Wise Beaver was sitting nearby. He heard the beavers talking about their house. "Build a dam across the stream," said Old Wise Beaver.

"Why must we build a dam?" asked the Beavers.

Old Wise Beaver looked up and said, "A dam will make the water deep. It will make the water deep for your house."

"How can we build a dam here?" asked Beaver's brothers.

"Cut down trees to build your dam," said Old Wise Beaver.

Beaver and his brothers began to build their house. Old Wise Beaver sat nearby and watched the beavers work.

"Snap, snap," went their big teeth as they cut down trees. The trees fell near the water.

"Cut off the branches," said Old Wise Beaver, "and make a dam with the branches. You must gather sticks for your dam too."

"Snap, snap," went their big teeth as they

cut off the branches for their dam. The beavers found sticks in the woods. They found sticks on the ground and in the stream. They were going to build their house with branches and sticks and mud.

Suddenly a big wind came up. The wind blew the bushes and the trees. It blew across the water in the stream. The wind blew and blew. But Beaver and his brothers kept working on their house.

Then the rain came. The rain fell on the hills beside the little stream. It fell on the water in the stream. The rain fell all day and all night. The water ran down from the hills into the little stream.

The little stream grew and grew into a big stream. The big stream grew into a flood. The flood rose higher and higher. And the water came faster and faster.

Beaver was on the bank getting sticks for the house. He saw the flood coming.

"The flood will wash the dam away! Then it will wash our house away," he said to himself.

Beaver raced along the top of the dam. He saw water coming through a little hole in the dam. Beaver put his paw in the hole. His paw held back the water.

Beaver saw water coming through another hole in the dam. It came through a hole here. It came through a hole there. Beaver just couldn't put his paws in all the holes.

"Oh, what can I do to save the dam?" he cried. He looked around and saw some little

sticks. He gathered the sticks and put them in the holes. But the little holes grew bigger. They grew into one big hole. Beaver could not fill the big hole with his paw. The hole was too big.

"Oh, what can I do to save the dam?" he cried. Beaver thought and thought. His tail was big. It was bigger than all his paws put together. Beaver put his tail into the one big hole.

Beaver's tail filled the big hole and went through on the other side. Turtle was on the other side of the dam. Turtle saw Beaver's tail coming through the dam. He snapped at the tail.

"Oh, oh, oh!" said Beaver.

Turtle held fast to his tail.

"Let go! Let go!" said Beaver. But Turtle held fast to his tail.

"All right," said Beaver. "If you won't let go of my tail, you can fill the big hole yourself."

Beaver pulled Turtle into the big hole in the dam.

"Now will you let go?" said Beaver.

"No," said Turtle.

When Turtle opened his mouth to say "No," he let go of Beaver's tail. Then Beaver climbed up on the dam. But Turtle was still in the hole. He was bigger than Beaver's tail. Turtle kept the water from coming through the big hole.

The flood came faster and faster and faster against the dam.

"Hold fast, Turtle," called Beaver.

Beaver saw the flood wash away part of the dam.

"Hold fast, Turtle," called Beaver. "Hold fast. You must save the dam and our home."

"Help," called Turtle. "Get help. I cannot hold the dam alone."

"Help!" called Beaver to his brothers. "Come and help save the dam."

The beavers ran to a big tree on the bank of the stream.

"Snap, snap," went their big teeth. They worked quickly. Then the big tree began to fall. The beavers splashed into the stream. The big tree fell across the stream.

Beaver was in the water and the top of the big tree fell near his head. Beaver climbed out of the water through the top of the big tree. When he climbed out, Beaver had a bird's nest on his head!

But Beaver was very happy. The big tree kept the water from washing the dam away.

"We have saved the dam," said Beaver to Turtle.

"We have saved the dam," said Beaver to his brothers.

Peter and the Wolf

A Fairy Tale
Adapted from Sergei Prokofieff's Musical Theme

Far up in the north of Russia, in a cozy cottage at the edge of a great forest, Peter lived with his grandfather.

Peter loved the forest. In summer he roamed its shady paths, visiting his friends the wild animals and birds. He loved the

forest in winter, too, when a thick blanket of white snow covered the ground and the frozen lake and clung to the top-most branches of the trees. But in winter Peter could not go into the forest.

"Hungry wolves roam about in the winter,"

As Peter and Sasha stood there, quaking, the shadow moved toward them, and out from behind a tree stepped—another old friend of the summer, Sonia, the duck.

"Hello, Sonia," grinned Peter. "We're out to hunt the wolf."

"Oh," said Sonia, "may I come along?"

Of course, Peter and Sasha were glad to

his grandfather told him when he caught Peter trying to steal out. "You must wait until you are old enough to hunt them."

But Peter was certain he was old enough for anything—and too smart for any wolf— right now! So he waited his chance, and when his grandfather dozed, off went Peter, armed with a coil of rope and his own little wooden gun. Down the path he went, ever so quietly, through the gate, across the snowy bridge and into the white, mysterious winter forest.

At first Peter felt rather cold and lonely, with whiteness and silence on every side.

Then "Hello, Peter!" twittered a little voice like a flute, and down flew his old friend Sasha, the bird. "What are you doing alone in the forest in the winter?" asked Sasha.

"I'm out to hunt the wolf," said Peter stoutly. "Want to come along?"

Sasha did want to, so on they went together.

Suddenly, on the snowbank ahead, they saw a great threatening shadow. Could it be the wolf?

have Sonia with them, so she fell into line as they started on again.

But now as they marched along a slinking figure followed them, hidden among the reeds. It was Ivan, the sly cat, who kept hungry eyes on Sonia and Sasha.

As they reached a clearing, pounce! out jumped the cat and sprang at the bird. Only Peter's quick leap saved Sasha from Ivan's jaws.

Peter was shocked.

"Why, Ivan!" he said. "You're a bully!"

Ivan dropped his head guiltily.

"Come on, Sasha," said Peter. "Ivan is sorry. He won't do it again."

With a doubtful glance at Ivan, Sasha hopped back into line.

So once again the brave hunters marched on.

Suddenly, crunch! a lump of snow broke noisily behind them. The line of little hunters spun about.

There was the wolf!

Peter made the leap of his life to a low tree branch. Sasha fluttered up beside Peter on the low tree branch. Ivan scrambled up, too. But Sonia could not fly!

From their hiding places Peter and Sasha

and Ivan anxiously watched Sonia scuttle across the snow with the wolf's breath hot upon her. Sonia disappeared from sight behind a fallen log, and they waited, breathless with suspense.

Then the wolf reappeared, alone. And there were duck feathers clinging to his jaws.

Poor Sonia! Poor Sonia! But there was little time for sadness, for the wolf was snarling below Peter, Ivan, and Sasha.

A plan came to Peter! He whispered it to Sasha and Ivan, who twittered and purred their agreement.

First, Sasha flew down from his perch, and flew back and forth in the face of the wolf until the beast was frantic.

Then, down Peter's rope crawled Ivan the cat. Inch by inch Ivan moved closer to where the wolf was battling Sasha.

Ivan crept up behind the angry wolf, with

the loop of rope ready for action. Down went the rope over the wolf's tail! Zing! Ivan pulled the loop tight and Peter, on the bough above, pulled in the slack.

Soon the wolf felt the rope's pull. He reared around, snarling with fresh rage. But Ivan was back on the branch beside Peter, and they were both tugging. They were tugging with every bit of their strength.

There they were, Peter and Ivan, up on their tree branch, and there was the wolf snarling and snapping as he swung by his tail in mid-air.

Now it was Sasha's turn to fly into action again. For off in the forest sounded a hunter's horn. With a tweet of encouragement to his friends, Sasha flew off toward the sound. In and out among the branches he flew until below him he spied three stout hunters marching along.

What could the little bird do to make them follow him? He tried to imitate a wolf howl.

He sputtered and he chirped. Still the hunters did not understand.

"Something must be wrong," said one.

"This little fellow is trying to tell us something," agreed the second.

"Let us take a look," said the third.

So they followed Sasha back to the tree. But what was this? The wolf was snugly bound with the rope, and Peter and Ivan were sitting on him, swinging to and fro.

And who was that coming out from behind the log? It was Sonia, safe and sound, though still a little wobbly on her feet.

And what a gay parade as they entered the village—Sasha and Ivan and Sonia, and the three hunters carrying the wolf. And at the head of them all, Peter marched proudly. Now even his grandfather had to be impressed. For Peter the hunter and his friends had captured the wolf!

THE BRAVE LITTLE TAILOR

ONCE UPON A TIME there was a little kingdom which was a happy place to live in. It would have kept on being happy but for one thing—a big, enormous giant moved in and went stamping about the countryside, trampling houses and crops under his great boots.

The king himself had offered a reward for the capture of the giant, dead or alive. Everyone wanted him to be captured, but somehow no one knew how to do it. So the giant went on until the whole kingdom was in a terrible state.

Now in the royal city was a little tailor shop. There Mickey Mouse, the tailor, sat and worked all day. The giant did not bother him. What bothered him was flies! Flies swarmed on the ceiling; flies crawled over the table where Mickey sat and sewed; flies zoomed around his nose as he tried to work.

At last, in a great burst of annoyance,

Mickey picked up two swatters and slammed them together as a whole swarm of flies went buzzing by. Down fell the victims to the floor, and Mickey smiled.

"O boy! Seven at one blow!"

Running to the window, he thrust his head out just as one villager passing by said to another, "Did you ever kill a giant?"

"I killed seven at one blow!" cried Mickey, thinking of his swatted flies.

"Seven at one blow!" echoed the villagers, picturing a kingdomful of giants laid out at Mickey's feet.

Mickey nodded happily, and the villagers rushed away to spread the news. Soon the whole town was buzzing with talk of Mickey's great deed.

At last word came to the King himself and his daughter, Princess Minnie.

"The little tailor, Your Majesty, killed

265

seven giants with one blow!" panted a guard.

"Seven!" shouted the King. "Bring the tailor here!"

So Mickey Mouse to his great surprise, found himself being hustled to the palace of the King.

"Did you kill seven at one blow?" thundered the King, as Mickey was brought before the throne.

"Yes, Your Honor. I killed seven." said Mickey, gaining courage from Princess Minnie's smile. "And how!"

"Well," said the King. "How?"

Mickey took a deep breath, glanced up at Princess Minnie, and started in.

"I was all alone," he explained. "I heard 'em coming. I looked up and I was surrounded. They were here, there, everywhere —a whole bunch of 'em. They came at me from the left, right, left, right—"

The king was hanging on Mickey's every word. "Yes, yes," he encouraged. "Go on!"

"They were coming closer. The fight was on. I swung and missed—I missed and swung. I swung again and again and again. They were right on top of me." Mickey was all excited himself now.

"And then?" said the King.

Mickey drew his long tailor's scissors through the air like a sword.

"Then," he finished proudly, "I let 'em have it!"

"Wow!" said the King. "Brave tailor, I appoint you Royal High Killer of the Giant!"

Mickey's smile faded. He almost collapsed.

"Giant!" he squeaked. "But-but-but-Your Majesty—I-I-I—"

"And your reward," the King continued, "shall be one million pazoozas!"

"Th-thank you, sir," Mickey stammered, "but I-I-I couldn't—"

"Two million pazoozas!" said the King.

"But—I-I-I-I don't know—," Mickey tried to explain.

Now Princess Minnie tugged at her father's sleeve and whispered in his ear.

"Three million pazoozas," smiled the King, "and the hand of the Princess Minnie!"

"The Princess!" gasped Mickey. "Gee! I'll cut that giant down to my size!"

And away he marched, out of the long throne room, down the palace halls, through the royal city to the great gate in the walls. The streets were filled with cheering people as the hero strode along; banners and handkerchiefs fluttered at windows, and from high in the palace tower, Princess Minnie waved and threw him a kiss.

Mickey Mouse marched along triumphantly to the gates of the city. But as he stood alone on the road outside, and the drawbridge clanked up behind him, he suddenly felt very lonely indeed.

"Gosh," sighed the brave little tailor to himself as he sank down upon a stone. "I don't know how to catch a giant."

As he sat there, with his head in his hands, Mickey felt the rock beneath him tremble, and a great shadow fell across the ground.

"The giant!" Mickey gasped, and he began to run as fast as his legs would carry him.

He ran fast, but the giant's footsteps clomped closer and closer. Soon Mickey came to the shore of a little lake. For a moment he was stopped. But then he spied a rowboat moored near by. Leaping into it, he rowed away at top speed. But his fastest rowing could not save him. The giant splashed into the water behind Mickey, and a great wave from his boot flung the little rowboat up onto the far shore.

Mickey jumped out and raced away, but the huge black shadow of the giant spread across the landscape and the thudding footsteps were very close now. As the giant overtook him, Mickey dove into a cartload of pumpkins and burrowed in among them. He peeked out of his hiding place once, only to see the giant seating himself on a cottage roof beside him. The cottage crumpled softly beneath the tremendous weight, and the

giant grunted a comfortable grunt. Then he spied the load of pumpkins and a hungry smile spread across his face. He reached out and scooped up a great handful of pumpkins —and in the handful was Mickey Mouse!

Mickey scarcely had time to figure out what was happening. He felt himself being lifted through the air. He saw a great dark hole opening before him. It was the giant's mouth, he realized with horror! As the giant flung the pumpkins down his gullet, Mickey managed to catch hold of his great upper lip. From there he swung himself up to the giant's nose. The poor giant twitched uncomfortably, for his nose began to tickle, but as he reached up to rub it, Mickey scrambled to his eyebrow. The giant wrinkled his forehead in a worried frown, and this unexpected motion shook Mickey loose from his hold. Down he plummeted, down through thin air!

"This is the end!" Mickey thought grimly. But with a soft thud he landed unhurt on the giant's palm.

"What a spot!" Mickey groaned.

The giant raised his other palm, ready to squash Mickey flat, but the brave little tailor darted up the giant's big sleeve. As the giant reached in after him, Mickey began sewing, faster than he had ever sewed in his life. Soon the giant's hand was sewed into his sleeve, and as he struggled to free it, Mickey raced up his side, sewing his arms down flat, until the big fellow was completely helpless.

Then Mickey scampered on up until he reached the giant's head, and, still keeping a firm grip on his string, he jumped! Down swung Mickey, whirling round and round the giant's frame until he was completely bound up in the string. Mickey had just jumped to the ground and started to run for all he was worth when the giant, who could not move a muscle, began to topple.

Cr-runch! BANG! The giant crashed down full length to the ground, and the earth quivered and shook for miles around. The giant himself was knocked out completely.

Mickey drew a deep, deep breath, dusted off his hands, and started back to the city and the palace of the King.

What a welcome he received there when the people realized that the giant was in their power! What a celebration there was for the whole countryside! With the giant furnishing wind power, a great, glorious carnival was set up.

Mickey, with millions of pazoozas' reward in the bank, was the hero of the day. But for Mickey, the best reward of all was having the Princess Minnie's hand in his.

So the brave little tailor became prince of the realm, and married his princess and lived happily ever after.

101 Dalmatians

Based on the book "The Hundred and One Dalmatians"
by Dodie Smith, published by The Viking Press

Dognapping! FIFTEEN PUPPIES STOLEN!" said the newspaper headlines.

It was a sad day in the small London house of Roger and Anita Radcliff. Only yesterday they had been the proud owners of seventeen beautiful Dalmatians. Now only two—Pongo and Perdita—remained.

And Pongo and Perdita were heartbroken.

There had been articles in the newspapers . . . friends had helped in the search . . . and even Scotland Yard had been called in to find the missing puppies.

"I'm afraid we've done everything possible," said Roger sorrowfully. "I don't know how we can ever find the puppies."

Pongo looked sadly at his human owners and walked slowly back to the kitchen.

"Perdy," he said to the puppies' weeping mother, "our humans are getting nowhere in the search. It looks as if it's up to us."

"What will we do?" asked Perdita tearfully.

"I have a plan," said Pongo. *"The Twilight Bark.* It's the fastest way to send news. And if our puppies are anywhere in the city, the

London dogs will know. We'll send word *tonight*."

It was almost dark that evening when the Radcliffs took Pongo and Perdita to the park.

Pongo barked the alert . . . three loud barks and a long howl.

"Pongo!" admonished Roger. "Quiet, boy. You'll wake up the whole neighborhood." Pongo was silent, for he was awaiting the answer that soon came. A Great Dane over in Hampstead replied.

Pongo barked the news of the stolen puppies and asked for help. Soon, all over London, setters and bulldogs and mongrels and dogs of all shapes and sizes were relaying the message.

Far out in the country, the distant barking reached the shaggy ear of Colonel, a retired army dog. With him was his friend, a cat called Sergeant Tibs.

The Colonel lifted his ear and listened, while he tried to decode the faint message. "Hmmm," he pondered. "Spotted puddings . . . no . . . fifteen spotted puddles stolen. No . . . wait . . . *fifteen spotted puppies* have been stolen!"

"Fifteen puppies!" exclaimed Sergeant Tibs. "That's funny: I heard puppies barking down at the old deserted mansion the other night."

"Balderdash, Tibs," growled the old sheep dog. "Nobody's lived there for years!"

"Someone is there now," replied the cat. "Look! There's smoke coming from the chimney."

"By Jove," said the Colonel. "So there is. Hop aboard, Tibs, and we'll investigate." The cat climbed onto the shaggy dog's ample back, and the Colonel floundered his way through the snowdrifts to the old ruin.

"Climb in through that broken window," instructed the Colonel, "and see what is going on. Maybe the puppies we're looking for *are* inside."

Sergeant Tibs, who had heard frightening tales about the old crumbling house, was more than a little frightened. But bravely he eased himself in through the window, and started his search.

Suddenly he saw a streak of light through a hole in a broken door. Tibs could hear loud voices. Ever so carefully and silently he slipped through the hole and into the room.

The startled cat could hardly believe his eyes...or ears. In the room were three villainous looking characters, two men and a woman. *And* (Tibs counted them carefully) there were *ninety-nine Dalmatian puppies!* Fifteen of them wore collars and licenses. They *must* be the missing puppies!

The evil-looking woman was Cruella De Vil, whose ancestors had once lived in the huge old house. She was screaming at the two men, Horace and Jasper Badun. "I tell you the job's got to be done tonight," she shrieked. "I have no time to argue."

"But the pups ain't big enough," answered one of the Baduns, as Cruella departed in fury. "You couldn't get a dozen fur coats out of the whole kaboodle."

"Oh, my!" thought Sergeant Tibs. "Those pups are going to be made into *coats...dog-skin* coats! I've got to warn the Colonel." He crept out noiselessly to where the shaggy dog awaited him.

The Colonel lost no time in sending the message that the stolen puppies had been found. An old hound picked up the news and relayed it to a small dog floating down the River Thames on a barge. The barge dog yelped into the night, and a collie in a nearby cowbarn sent along the news with yips and barks and howls.

In the little house in London, Pongo and Perdita waited.

"Oh, Pongo," wailed Perdy. "I'm afraid it's no use. There's been no answer for..."

"Wait!" cried Pongo. "Listen! It's the Great Dane over at Hampstead." The two dogs listened breathlessly. "Our puppies have been *found!*" cried Pongo. "The Dane's going to meet us at Primrose Hill and give us directions."

Quickly, the two dogs nosed their way through a partly open window, leaped to the ground and were off running, running into the night.

In the old, crumbling mansion in Suffolk, Tibs had returned to help the puppies. It was no easy task. While the two Baduns, Horace and Jasper, watched television, Sergeant Tibs had cautiously urged the puppies to escape, one by one, through the hole in the room's door. But the last fat puppy, struggling through the hole, had yelped. And now they had been discovered. Tibs and the Dalmatian puppies were cornered under the staircase.

Jasper and Horace, one armed with a heavy poker and the other with a broken chair leg, advanced menacingly.

Pongo and Perdita had been following directions through the barking chain all night. Now they hesitated at a crossroad. Perdita was discouraged. "Pongo," she wept, "I'm afraid we're lost!"

"I don't think so," answered Pongo. "It can't be far." And once again he barked the alert.

The answer came from near at hand. It was from the gruff throat of Colonel, the old sheep dog.

"Quick! Follow me," he said, as he turned to lead the way. "I'm afraid there's trouble." But the old fellow, slipping and sliding on the icy road, soon fell behind. Pongo and Perdita raced on . . . for from the old house they could

hear the sound of dozens of whimpering puppies.

The Baduns were jubilant.

"We've got 'em now," gloated Jasper. Then he gave a startled yelp. There was a crash of glass, and two furious Dalmatian dogs jumped into the room through a window.

"Hey! What's this?" shouted Horace. "Looks like a couple of spotted hyenas!"

Sergeant Tibs turned to the puppies. "Come on, kids," he said. "Now is our chance to escape." In a jiffy the puppies swarmed through the broken door and were away, floundering through the snowdrifts after the cat.

The Baduns did their best to defend themselves against Pongo and Perdita, but in the confusion many of their blows landed on each other. The fight ended abruptly. Jasper and Horace collided with each other, and stumbled into a wall. It was old and crumbling, and the impact of their weight made it crack widely from floor to ceiling. There was a rain of plaster, boards and debris, and the two men were buried up to their necks.

"Come on, Perdy. Let's go," said Pongo, and the two ran after Sergeant Tibs and the puppies.

Jasper shouted furiously after them: "I'll get even with you! I'll skin every one of you spotted hyenas if it's the last thing I do!"

The Pongos followed the trail of the puppies to the Colonel's living quarters, a warm barn. They were promptly surrounded by their joyous, squirming puppies, all of them talking at once.

"Are all fifteen of you here?" asked Pongo anxiously. Pongo and Perdita started to count. Then they noticed for the first time that the barn was filled with dozens and dozens of Dalmatian puppies.

"Ninety-nine of you!" gasped Pongo.

"Most of us were bought at pet shops," explained one of the puppies. "That mean wom-

an wants to make dogskin coats out of us."

"Then we can't leave you here. We'll have to take you all back to London with us," said Pongo.

"It's time to retreat," said the Colonel, who was on guard at the door. "I see a truck following our tracks through the snow. Better be off. We'll delay your pursuers as much as possible."

"Goodbye, Colonel. Goodbye, Sergeant . . . and thank you," said Pongo and Perdita.

"It was nothing," growled the Colonel. "All in the line of duty, you know."

Quickly the dogs swarmed through the back door and were soon lost to sight in the thick underbrush.

Mile after mile the Baduns followed the

dogs' trail...and now Cruella De Vil, in her big, powerful car had joined them. For a while Pongo eluded them by having all the puppies walk single file down a frozen creek, which showed no tracks.

Still, they were almost caught once, when the Baduns' truck stopped on a bridge, under which the trembling puppies were hidden. At last the truck drove on, and the dogs contin-

ued toward the sound of distant barking. Someone was trying to reach them with a message.

It turned out to be a big, black Labrador. "Pongo," he panted, as he came bounding up, "I've got a ride home for all of you, if we can get there in time. Follow me." He led them through the back streets of the little town of Dinsford, into a deserted blacksmith shop.

"Do you see that van out the window?" asked the Labrador. "As soon as the engine is repaired, it's going to London."

"Pongo, look!" said Perdita. "There's Cruella!"

"And here come the Baduns," groaned Pongo. The rickety truck and Cruella De Vil's huge roadster drew to a stop in the street.

As Pongo pondered on the problem, two of the puppies tumbled out of the fireplace.

"Dad," yipped one of them, "Lucky pushed me in the fireplace. I'll push *him* in, too." And Pongo turned to see two coal black puppies tumbling in the soot from the forge.

"Perdita," said Pongo, "I've got an idea.

"We'll *all* roll in the soot. We'll *all* be black Labradors... and if we travel in small groups, I think we can reach the van undetected."

277

Perdita hated to soil her beautiful coat, but the pups joyously rolled in the soot, and soon Pongo and a dignified Perdita joined them.

Outside, Cruella and her henchmen were searching the village.

"Hurry," urged the Labrador. "The van's almost ready to leave. I'll take the first bunch of puppies to the van and then I'll stay there to help the rest of them aboard. Follow me in little groups."

The army of black puppies began their trek past Cruella De Vil and into the van. Cruella studied them with narrow eyes. She had never seen so many black Labradors in her life.

Then Cruella's eyes widened. As the last puppy left the smithy, a lump of melting snow from the eaves fell on his back. The soot dripped away, to show Cruella the white coat and black markings of a Dalmatian puppy.

"It can't be!" she screamed. "It's impossible! Horace! Jasper! Come here, quickly!"

The van was already on the move, with Pongo running desperately after it, the last puppy in his mouth. With a last burst of speed he grasped a precarious hold on the tailgate, and Perdita pulled the two to safety.

"There they go!" shrieked Cruella. "The puppies are in that van! After them!"

She tried to turn her big car around in the narrow village street. But the Baduns had driven up at her summons, and were blocking the way.

"That'll delay them for a while," said Pongo with satisfaction.

The van sped along toward London. The driver was going as fast as he could, for he was anxious to get home for Christmas Eve. Pongo was exultant. "Perdita," he said happily, "we made it."

But his happiness was short-lived. The bright headlights of a fast, pursuing car suddenly flashed into their eyes.

"Pongo! It's her! It's Cruella!" cried Perdita.

Cruella urged her big car to the side of the speeding van and tried to force it off the road.

The driver fought to keep out of the ditch. "Crazy woman driver!" he shouted. "What on earth are you trying to do?" He maneuvered as best he could, but Cruella continued to push him to the side, and the van teetered precariously over the deep ditch.

Inside the lurching van, Pongo and Perdita desperately tried to keep their feet. The van was full of furniture, and the frightened pups were hidden in various drawers and cabinets. Their safety was debatable, however, for Cruella viciously and recklessly kept up her efforts to push them off the road.

Then Fate intervened in the form of Jasper, the tall Badun. He and Horace were following closely behind Cruella at the highest speed their rickety truck had ever accomplished.

"Watch, Horace, me lad," shouted Jasper gleefully, "watch *me* shove them into the ditch." With an extra burst of speed he drew up alongside the two careening vehicles. But he'd forgotten that the road was narrow and slippery...and at a curve Cruella's car and the Baduns' truck crashed off the road amid a shower of broken metal.

The van swerved out of the way and then sped on. Behind, Horace and Jasper picked themselves out of the broken wreckage, and ignoring Cruella, began a dreary trudge to London.

Cruella watched them leave, and looked at what was left of her once magnificent car. "Oh," she sobbed furiously. "I give up!"

It was Christmas Eve, but nobody in the little house at Regents Park felt happy. Roger had written a song that was a great success, and the Radcliffs were no longer poor. But all they could think of was their beloved Dalmatian dogs.

Then, suddenly, a host of happy, barking black dogs swarmed through the front door. The Radcliffs were almost knocked off their feet by the sea of black puppies. Then Roger saw something familiar in the shape of a big dog's head, and dusted it off.

"Pongo! It's Pongo!" he cried, and grabbing the big dog's forepaws, did a joyous dance around the room. At last, with the help of a pair of feather dusters, the familiar white coats and black spots of their Dalmatians came to view. Pongo, Perdita and their fifteen puppies were all dusted and accounted for.

"But look, Anita," exclaimed Roger, "there are *more* puppies...*everywhere!* There must be a hundred of them. Let's see...there are six...and twelve makes eighteen...and..."

Roger finally finished counting. "That's eighty-four puppies! Add Pongo and Perdita and their pups, and we have *one hundred and one Dalmatians!* Where did they all come from?"

"What will we *do* with all of them?" gasped Anita.

"We'll *keep* them," Roger answered.

"What?" said Anita. "In this little house?"

In answer, Roger picked his way through the puppies to the piano. He made room for himself on the bench, which was covered with more puppies, and started to play.

"We'll buy a big place in the country," said Roger, as the first notes tinkled forth. "We'll have a plantation...er...a *Dalmatian* plantation."

SLEEPING BEAUTY

ONCE UPON A TIME, in a distant, lovely place, there were two tiny kingdoms side by side. One was ruled by a king named Hubert, a fine and noble man whose greatest pride was in his baby son.

The other was ruled by King Stefan, a good and generous man whose greatest sorrow was that he and his lovely queen had no child. So when, after years of longing, a princess was born to them, you may well believe that she at once became her parents' greatest joy. They chose for her name Aurora, which means "the dawn" because she brought sunshine to their hearts.

The day of the baby princess's christening they set apart as a holiday, so that everyone in the kingdom might share their joy. Every human being in the country was invited, by a royal proclamation cried aloud.

And three golden invitations were sent out by a royal proclamation to the three Good Fairies of the land, though even the king scarcely dared hope they would come; for it is only on very special occasions indeed that the fairy folk appear to human kind.

Everyone else, though, was delighted to come, King Hubert among them of course. He rejoiced with his friend in his great joy—

and showed him some pictures of small Prince Philip, which he happened to have along. And the two proud and happy fathers agreed that some day in the distant future their two children would be wed.

All of Stefan's subjects were on hand—every shop in the town and countryside was closed so that everyone could attend the reception on the palace grounds following the christening of Princess Aurora.

It was indeed a happy day for King Stefan and his Queen, as all their subjects, from the highest to the lowly, paid homage to the Little Princess. But just when it seemed there was nothing that could make the day happier, the best dream of all came true—with a fanfare of trumpets, a herald announced the arrival of the three Good Fairies, Mistresses Flora, Fauna, and Merryweather.

The King himself came forward to greet the three Good Fairies.

"Welcome, good Mistresses," he said with a bow. "Your presence here is a great honor."

"We are happy to be invited," said Mistress Flora, with a little flutter of delight.

"And for this happy occasion each one of us has a gift to give the Princess," added Mistress Fauna.

"Oh, Stefan!" the Queen whispered happily. "Did you hear that?"

"Mistress Fauna," said Flora, "will present the first gift."

Mistress Fauna came forward with tiny dancing steps, beaming to right and to left.

"Sunbeams!" Mistress Fauna called, stretching out her arms, and the room was flooded with golden light. Then Mistress Fauna presented her gift:

"May her life be filled with laughter,
May her heart be free from woe.
Let happiness, like dancing sunbeams
Follow wherever she may go."

"Happiness is the first gift," the murmur went around.

Mistress Merryweather came second:
"You shall have hair of finest gold,
Eyes of sapphire blue.
There will never be one
'Neath the moon or sun,
Half as beautiful as you."

"Beauty is the second gift," the crowd murmured happily, and around them unseen voices seemed to sing:
"She shall be beautiful now and ever after.
She shall have happiness filling her life
with laughter."

But the happy voices were cut short by a burst of evil laughter. Suddenly a blast of chill wind swept in through an open window. A shaft of lightning shot down from the cloud-darkened sky. A shudder swept through the frightened crowd as Mistress Maleficent, the Fairy of Darkness, appeared!

"Dear me!" she cackled with evil delight. "I'm afraid I startled you. You didn't expect me now, did you? And yet I see everyone else is here, from the highest to the low."

She swept down the long steps, to where the Good Fairies stood. "And how do you do, my dears?" she cooed. The three of them looked away. Maleficent, the Fairy of Darkness, then approached the King and Queen.

"Now tell me, why wasn't I invited to this charming ceremony?" Maleficent hissed.

"You know quite well," the King replied, depending on his dignity to hide his quaking heart. "Where you go, the shadow of sorrow follows. I command you to leave."

"Ha! First you insult me, then you command!" Maleficent cried in a rage. "Do you think I am one of your peasant rabble? Why, at one stroke I could . . ."

"Please, your Excellency," begged the Queen, "I ask you for the sake of our child, please leave us in peace."

"Hmm, the child, yes. Your Majesty's gentle plea touches my heart," sneered Maleficent. "I shall go, but first let me see the Princess."

Maleficent stepped toward the cradle, but

the three Good Fairies stood before her, barring her evil way.

"Very well," said Maleficent. "I shall be content to give her my blessing. Now listen, all of you—she shall have beauty and happiness, I don't deny—but there will come a time when tears will follow laughter."

At these words the King and Queen and their guests stiffened with fear.

"Before the sun sets on her sixteenth birthday the Princess will prick her finger with the spindle of a spinning wheel—and die!" cried Mistress Maleficent.

The King sprang from his seat, unsheathing his sword. "Seize her! Seize the Fairy of Darkness!" he cried to the guards.

"Stand back, you fools!" screamed Maleficent—and in a great burst of flame and smoke she vanished quite away.

The Queen knelt weeping beside Princess Aurora's cradle. "Oh, my child, my little one," she sobbed.

Mistress Flora stepped to her side. "Take heart, your Majesty," she said. "All is not lost. Remember, we still have one gift to bestow. Perhaps I can undo this wicked prophecy." For long moments she stood, frowning thoughtfully, before she extended her magic wand over the Princess's bed.

"If there comes a day of evil,
This my promise from above—
She'll not die, but sleep till wakened
By the kiss of her true love."

The company had listened breathlessly to this last of the magic gifts. But now the King stepped forward slowly, his kindly face still creased with pain.

"But Mistress Flora," he protested. "You did not destroy Mistress Maleficent's prophecy. You only softened it."

Mistress Flora sadly shook her head.

"I did my best, Sire," she said. "The powers of evil are great—and my magic is simple."

"That cursed hag can't do this to my

daughter," the King vowed solemnly. "I'll stop her if I have to burn every spinning wheel in the kingdom to do it!"

The King was as good as his word. Before long the spinning wheels were gathered and the countryside was bright with the light from a huge burning heap of them.

From a distant crag Mistress Maleficent watched the blaze. "So," she cackled to the pet hawk perched on her bony shoulder, "to destroy a magic prophecy, King Stefan builds a bonfire. He thinks he can blot out my sorcery with a trifling cloud of smoke. He will learn soon enough the stupid error of his ways, eh, Diabolo?"

The hawk joined her laughter with an eerie scream, as his eyeballs reflected the blaze.

The three Good Fairies also knew that the fire was to no avail. But they had powers of their own. Best of all, the Good Fairies had the power of love.

"We must love her enough," Mistress Flora explained, "to give up our magic, you see."

"But I don't see," Merryweather insisted. "Why should we give up our magic?"

"It's part of the disguise," said Flora.

"Maleficent will be looking for us, not for three simple peasant women. As for me, I've always wanted to be a mortal. It's such a pleasant life, plowing the fields, chopping wood, scrubbing floors—"

Fauna and Merryweather looked unconvinced, but before they had time for more conversation, the King and Queen drew near.

"Well, good Mistresses, what of the evil prophecy now?" smiled the King, waving a royal arm at the last embers of the fire.

The Good Fairies hesitated. At last Mistress Flora spoke.

"It's no use, your Majesties," she said.

"Maleficent can conjure up a whole kingdomful of spinning wheels with a flick of her finger," Fauna added.

The King's face fell.

"But there must be a way!" he insisted.

"Perhaps there is," said Flora. "Our way."

"What do you mean—your way?" asked the eager Queen.

"You must give us the Princess," Flora explained, "to keep until her sixteenth birthday is past. We shall hide her away—oh, we have a plan—" She glanced at Fauna and Merry-

283

weather and they nodded eagerly. "Not even the King and Queen shall know where she is —nor where we are, of course."

It was a bitter thing to ask. But the unhappy King and Queen had faith in their Good Fairy friends. They agreed at last, and they said good-by to their lovely little daughter for many long years.

The lonely years passed, as years will do. In the echoing palace the King and Queen imagined what their Princess would be doing, how she would look, every day of their lives.

But deep in the forest, in a tiny cottage, the little Princess was not sad at all. Her three Good Fairy godmothers had named their little charge Briar Rose, and with her gifts of joy and beauty they had brought her up to be a lovely young girl.

Briar Rose had no thought of being a Prin-cess, but she knew she had all any girl could ask—a loving family, a pleasant home, a host of lively animals for friends. Oh, yes, she was certain she had everything—but deep in her heart, as her sixteenth birthday drew near, a yearning sprouted and grew and bloomed. It was the yearning for Love.

She saw love all about her in the woods—in the nesting birds, in the animals watching tenderly over their little families. But how, wondered lovely little Briar Rose, would Love ever find her, deep in the woods? As she wondered, she sighed a little sigh.

She need not have worried; as is often the case, what she longed for was very close at hand.

In a clearing in the forest not far away, a handsome young man stopped to rest. He was none other than Prince Philip, son and heir of King Hubert of the kingdom nearby.

It was a warm day, and Prince Philip had wandered far from his company. He slipped off his cloak as he rested beneath a tree to let the soft breeze cool his brow.

In the branches above Prince Philip frolicked some birds who had heard Briar Rose's sad sigh. Perhaps this young man was what their friend needed to bring back her smiles, they thought.

So down swooped the birds, plucked up the cloak, and flew off with it to the Princess Aurora—or Briar Rose.

The cloak, as the birds swooped and dipped with it, seemed to dance along on the breeze. When Briar Rose saw it, her feet began dancing too, and soon she was twirling happily, with the empty cloak for a dancing partner.

Meanwhile Prince Philip had been following his cloak as the birds made off with it. They led him to the dancing little maiden in the woods. At first sight, he fell in love with Briar Rose.

Silently, Prince Philip stepped closer to her, until he could slip into his own cloak as it came twirling by.

What a surprise for Briar Rose! Here were all her dreams come true! Now the love which had taken root in the prince's heart took root in her own too.

"How has it happened that we have never met?" Prince Philip demanded, when the dance was done.

"I live very quietly here in the woods," Briar Rose explained, "with my three dear aunts. We go nowhere and we meet no one; it is not so surprising that we have not met, as that you should happen along today, just as I was dreaming of—something nice."

"It was my good fortune that brought me this way," Prince Philip told her. Thinking that she was a simple peasant girl, he knew he must not spoil her joy by telling her that he would one day be a king. "Let us meet here again tomorrow," he begged. And Briar Rose agreed to meet him in the woods.

Tomorrow, though Briar Rose little dreamed it, was to be her sixteenth birthday and the end of the spell which had hung over her whole life. If she little dreamed it, it was still uppermost in the minds of the three Good Fairies.

"Only to think," they kept saying with deep sighs, "that this is the last night dear Briar Rose will be at home with us here."

"We must do something special," said Fauna, fussing busily about. "We must decorate the cottage for this happy event."

"Oh, I agree," twittered Merryweather.

But Flora, the sensible one, was not sure.

"It would be safer to wait until tomorrow," she warned. "Wait until the danger is over before you celebrate."

"Oh, Flora, you spoil everything," Fauna wailed. "Then Briar Rose will be leaving us, and she will have no time to celebrate here."

"We must do some little thing tonight," Merryweather agreed. And the two of them bustled busily about, with paper streamers and bows and flowers and such.

"Ouch!" cried Merryweather, pricking her thumb. "Oh, dear, this is all so awkward, without any magic at all."

"All right," said Flora, giving in. "If you're going to do it, do it right." She pulled out her hidden magic wand, and touched the cottage lightly here and there. How magically lovely it looked!

The three Good Fairies could hardly wait for Briar Rose to come home from the woods. They were so pleased with all their plans for the happy day to come.

When at last she came, and the little women saw her face light up with joy, they felt repaid for all their magic work.

"Oh, how perfectly lovely the world is today!" cried Briar Rose.

And the three Good Fairies, having no idea that Love had come into their dear one's life, thought she was speaking of their beautiful decorations, which truth to tell, Briar Rose had not even seen.

"We planned it as a surprise for you," said Flora. "For your birthday, dear."

"You planned it? But how could you?" said Briar Rose, thinking of her meeting with the handsome young man, of course.

"Oh, we have certain magic powers, my dear," Merryweather explained.

"You mean—he wasn't real?" cried poor little Briar Rose.

Bit by bit it all came out—the Good Fairies' loving care of her to save her from the Evil Fairy's curse. Briar Rose listened with wonder in her heart to the story of her babyhood as Princess Aurora, and of the palace home to which she would return tomorrow, on her sixteenth birthday.

"Tomorrow!" she cried. "Oh no, I can't go. I can't go back to the palace tomorrow."

The dear Fairies thought she was grieving for them, and they were deeply touched. And when Briar Rose realized all they had given up for her—living in hiding for almost six-

"Ridiculous, my boy!" King Hubert cried. "You've been betrothed for sixteen years to King Stefan's daughter, Princess Aurora—the loveliest girl in the world."

"Why have I never seen this Princess Aurora?" asked Philip.

"She's been hidden away to avoid an evil spell, but she'll be home tomorrow, on her sixteenth birthday. And you and I will be on hand to arrange the wedding there and then."

"Not I," Philip insisted. "My heart and hand are promised to the loveliest girl in the world. No Princess shall win me away from the little maiden in the woods. Sorry, Father. This is one time I cannot obey."

Alas, a bitter quarrel grew up, and at the end Prince Philip gave up all his right to the throne, and stamped out of the castle, into the woods, to find his way to the meeting place and wait for Briar Rose.

Briar Rose did not come.

Instead, the next afternoon, dressed in royal robes, she stood on a balcony of her father's castle, watching the joyous people below celebrate her homecoming.

Everyone was so happy that no one saw the grim shadow of a hawk against the sky. It was Maleficent's hawk, and off he wheeled to take his evil mistress the news.

At the height of the celebration, Princess Aurora could stand it no longer. She felt that she must, must slip away to the meeting place in the woods.

In a dark castle hallway she met a little old woman—Maleficent in disguise.

"What's the trouble, dearie?" The little old woman was friendly, and led the sad Princess to her tower room. There Aurora told the story of her own true love, waiting at the woodland meeting place.

Outside the castle, sunset colors glowed. The power of Mistress Maleficent's spell was nearly gone. With sunset it would end. She had no time to lose.

"I can help you, my sweet," she whispered

teen years, giving up their magic powers for all that time, she knew she could never disappoint them. She must hide her secret love away in her heart and go back to the palace as a dutiful daughter.

"And there's a handsome Prince waiting for you too, my dear," Fauna reminded her.

But what was that to Briar Rose, whose true love would be waiting in the woods?

Prince Philip, though she never would have dreamed it, was having quite as difficult a time. He went straight home from the woodland glen and told his father of his new-found love. Good King Hubert had always been such a kind and understanding father that Philip was sure he would rejoice with him now. But no!

winningly. "Make a wish—any wish that is dearest to your heart—and touch the spindle of my magic spinning wheel. Then all your problems will be solved."

Princess Aurora took a deep breath; she made her wish—of her true love, of course—closed her eyes and touched the spindle.

With a crash and a puff of smoke, the evil prophecy came to pass. Princess Aurora lay deep in a magic sleep.

Meanwhile the three Good Fairies had missed their charge. They had started through the castle, searching for her. Through the state dining rooms, and the royal bedroom suites, at last up a dim little winding stairs that led to the tiny tower room, went the three Good Fairies.

There they found their Princess, fast in the fatal sleep. "We have failed," they cried. "We have failed."

"There is just one thing we can do to help," the sensible Flora said. "We can put the whole castle around her to sleep, so that when the kiss of true love awakens her—as we hope may happen somehow—everything can go on as if it were today."

So that is what they did. They put the whole castle under a sleeping spell—King

Stefan and King Hubert on their terrace, the Queen in her room, the cooks in the kitchens and courtiers in the court. All the guests slept, and the birds dozed off on the roof.

Everyone slept but Prince Philip, for he was far from the palace, deep in the woods, waiting at the meeting place. For hours he waited, with a growing sense of gloom, until at last a hooded figure approached.

"I can lead you to your lady," said a voice.

Philip did not know it was Maleficent, the Fairy of Darkness, of course. So he leaped to his feet and followed her. But she led him, not to the castle of the Sleeping Beauty, but to her own dark haunt. There, when he was imprisoned, she told him the tale of the Sleeping Beauty, Aurora or The Dawn, who was his own true love.

Poor Philip! He schemed and he struggled to escape, but the power of Mistress Maleficent was strong.

And while he lay in prison, seasons rolled around, and a forest of thorns grew up about the castle, to hold back knights and princes and such, who came to try to rescue the Princess for their own.

At last came a day when Maleficent dozed —and Philip escaped! It was a bare escape;

the dogs were at his heels as he reached the shelter of the great woods. But he broke free at last and made his way to the cottage of the three Good Fairies.

Poor dears, they were sad as sad could be, for they had almost given up their search for Princess Aurora's true love. But their kind hearts still warmed to the weary young man. They took him in and cared for him, and when he was rested he told them his tale.

How delighted they were! They helped him creep up to the hedge of thorns.

The thorn hedge parted before him; he strode straight to the castle walls. But Maleficent's hawk saw the hedge give way, and flew screaming off with the news.

In a trice the Prince found himself face to face with a dreadful enemy which changed its form whenever he was about to strike. At last it appeared as a fire-snorting dragon. Now the power of love strengthened the Prince's arm; he lunged with his sword at the creature's neck, and the Evil Spirit lay dead at his feet!

Into the castle the victor ran. And following directions the Good Fairies had given him, Prince Philip swiftly found his way up to the tiny tower room.

There lay Princess Aurora, deep in her magic sleep. The Prince knelt beside her, and at his kiss she opened her lovely eyes.

Around them, they heard the castle stirring into life. The cooks and courtiers awoke, the Queen and King Stefan awoke.

King Hubert awoke and was trying, as he had been years before, when they all fell magically asleep, to explain his trouble with his son Prince Philip. When to his amazement the Prince appeared, with a happy, blushing Princess on his arm.

What happiness bloomed in the old castle then, as wedding plans hastened along. And after the wedding, you may be sure, they lived happily ever more.

The Three Little Pigs

Once upon a time there were three little pigs who went out into the big world to build their homes and seek their fortunes.

The first little pig did not like to work at all. He quickly built himself a house of straw. Then he danced down the road, to see how his brothers were getting along.

The second little pig was building himself a house, too. He did not like to work any better than his brother. So the second little pig decided to build a quick and easy house of sticks.

Soon it was finished, too. It was not a very strong little house, but at least the work was done. Now the second little pig was free to do what he liked.

What he liked to do was to play his fiddle and dance. So while the first little pig tooted his flute, the second little pig sawed away on his fiddle, dancing as he played.

And as he danced he sang:

"I built my house of sticks,
I built my house of twigs.
 With a hey diddle-diddle
 I play on my fiddle,
 And dance all kinds of jigs."

Then off danced the two little pigs down the road together to see how their brother was getting along.

The third little pig was a sober little pig. He was building his house of bricks. He did not mind hard work, and he wanted a stout little, strong little house, for he knew that in the woods nearby there lived a big bad wolf who liked nothing better than to catch little pigs and eat them up!

So slap, slosh, slap! Away he worked, laying bricks and smoothing mortar.

"Ha ha ha!" laughed the first little pig, when he saw his brother hard at work.

"Ho ho ho!" laughed the second little pig.

"Come down and play with us!" he called to the third little pig.

But the busy little pig did not pause. Slap, slosh, slap! Away he worked, laying bricks and smoothing mortar between them, as he called down to his brothers:

"I build my house of stones.
I build my house of bricks.
 I have no chance
 To sing and dance,
 For work and play don't mix."

"Ho ho ho! Ha ha ha!" laughed the two lazy little pigs, dancing along to the tune of the fiddle and the flute.

"You can laugh and dance and sing," their busy brother called after them, "but I'll be safe and you'll be sorry when the wolf comes to the door!"

"Ha ha ha! Ho ho ho!" laughed the two little pigs again, and they disappeared into the woods singing a merry tune:

"Who's afraid of the big bad wolf,
   The big bad wolf, the big bad wolf?
   Who's afraid of the big bad wolf?
   Tra la la la la-a-a-a!"

Just as the first pig reached his door, out of the woods popped the big bad wolf! The little pig squealed with fright.

"Little pig, little pig, let me come in!" cried the big bad wolf.

"Not by the hair of my chinny-chin-chin!" said the little pig.

"Then I'll huff and I'll puff and I'll blow your house in!" roared the wolf.

And he did. He blew the little straw house all to pieces!

Away raced the little pig to his brother's house of sticks. No sooner was he in the door, when knock, knock, knock! There was the big bad wolf! But of course, the little pigs would not let him come in.

"I'll fool them," said the wolf. He left the little pig's house. And he hid behind a tree.

Soon the door opened and the two little pigs peeked out. There was no wolf in sight.

"Ha ha ha! Ho ho ho!" laughed the two little pigs. "We fooled him."

Then they danced around the room, singing gaily:

"Who's afraid of the big bad wolf,
   The big bad wolf, the big bad wolf?
   Who's afraid of the big bad wolf?
   Tra la la la la-a-a-a!"

Soon there came another knock at the door. It was the big bad wolf again, but he had covered himself with a sheepskin, and was curled up in a big basket, looking like a little lamb.

"Who's there?" called the second little pig.

"I'm a poor little sheep, with no place to sleep. Please open the door and let me in," said the big bad wolf in a sweet little voice.

The little pig peeked through a crack of the

door, and he could see the wolf's big black paws and sharp fangs.

"Not by the hair of my chinny-chin-chin!"

"You can't fool us with that sheepskin!" said the second little pig.

"Then I'll huff, and I'll puff, and I'll blow your house in!" cried the angry old wolf.

So he huffed
    and he PUFFED
        and he puffed
           and he HUFFED,
and he blew the little twig house all to pieces!

Away raced the two little pigs, straight to the third little pig's house of bricks.

"Don't worry," said the third little pig to his two frightened little brothers. "You are safe here." Soon they were all singing gaily.

This made the wolf perfectly furious!

"Now by the hair of my chinny-chin-chin!" he roared, "I'll huff, and I'll puff, and I'll blow your house in!"

So the big bad wolf huffed and he PUFFED, and he puffed and he HUFFED, but he could not blow down that little house of bricks! How could he get in? At last he thought of the chimney!

So up he climbed, quietly. Then with a snarl, down he jumped—right into a kettle of boiling water!

With a yelp of pain he sprang straight up the chimney again, and raced away into the woods. The three little pigs never saw him again, and spent their time in the strong little brick house singing and dancing merrily.

The Country Cousin

THERE WAS ONCE a little country mouse who lived in a cornfield. Abner—that was the country mouse's name—had a neat little pantry well stocked with seeds and grain, bits of cheese, and whole beans and peas. He was warm and snug and well fed, and content with his life.

But he had a cousin who was an elegant city mouse. Now this fine fellow would not let Abner rest until he agreed to come to town for a visit.

"I'll show you what life can really be," said Monte, the city cousin.

So Abner closed up his little house and started off one day for the city. With an extra pair of clean socks and a toothbrush slung over his shoulder in a red bandanna handkerchief, and his trusty umbrella tucked under his arm, Abner felt ready for anything the city might offer.

In town, he had no trouble finding the place Monte had described. It was just as Monte had said, a fine big town house with stone walls which stretched up and up and up, farther than Abner could see. He was looking about him wide eyed when the door opened and Monte appeared.

"Come on in," said Monte sharply. "We can't stand around in the streets here in the city. It's much too dangerous."

Abner obediently followed his cousin into the house and through a series of dim pas-

sageways. When they stepped out into a fine big room, Abner's eyes grew wide again. For there, right beside him, set out on a neat little wooden platform, was a large and tasty looking chunk of cheese.

"Hey!" said Abner happily. "This is swell!"

Monte, who was leading the way, spun around at Abner's words.

"Stop!" he cried. "Leave that alone!" And he slapped down Abner's hand just as it touched the cheese.

Zam! the trap slammed shut, whistling past Abner's fingers.

"Never touch cheese you find lying around!" said Monte very sternly.

Abner nodded meekly, and followed his guide on shaking legs.

"There!" said Monte proudly as they came into the next room and hopped onto a big table. "Feast your eyes on that!" added Monte.

He swept an arm out over the great white expanse of a dining room table laden with

Suddenly Monte shouted, "Look out!" But it was too late.

Abner had lurched against the rim of a plate. And as he clutched at it, the plate started rolling crazily across the table top, carrying poor Abner with it. It scooped up Monte, too, as it whirled and twisted along. Then over the edge of the table it went, plunging down toward the floor far below, landing on the floor with a crash!

In a flash Abner snapped open his trusty umbrella, which he always carried. He grabbed Monte's coat tail in his other hand, and together they floated to the floor, unharmed, after the plate crashed down.

But now a new danger awaited them! With eyes gleaming hungrily, the cat approached on padded paws!

"This way!" shouted Monte, and he dived for his mouse hole and safety. But Abner, in his haste and fright, ran in the opposite direction. As Monte peeked out of his mouse hole, he saw Abner heading out the door, inches ahead of the cat's bared teeth and snatching claws. And that was the last Monte saw of Abner.

Down into the street raced Abner, with the cat close behind.

food. There were fruits, cheeses, and mounds of jello. There were cakes and breads and great puddings, and so many other good things to eat.

"Ooh!" said Abner, in pure delight. But he did not dare touch a thing, for fear of traps.

"Go ahead," Monte told him. And to show the way, he snapped off a corner of cheese and munched daintily at it.

Abner waited no longer. He sampled the cheese, too. It was delicious cheese! Abner broke off a larger piece and tucked it away as fast as he possibly could.

"This is great, Monte," he admitted. "This is the life, all right!"

He dipped into a bowl of cream and smacked his lips in delight. He marveled at a great mold of jello. Next he came to another jar of what looked like darker cream, and he scooped up a big mouthful. But it was mustard, hot mustard! and tears rolled down Abner's cheeks as it sizzled his insides. He gulped down a glass of water at one swallow, but that only gave him the hiccups.

Poor Abner stumbled across the table top. His eyes were red and watering from the hot mustard. And Abner's whole body was shaken with great coughs.

Zip! a huge tire whistled past in front of his nose. Wh-whip! another sped close behind him.

Whoo-OO-oo! shrieked a siren.

Clang-g-g! snarled a noisy bell.

Rattle-rattle! went a heavy truck above his head.

Poor Abner raced along with his heart in his mouth. He was swerving this way and that way, as danger rushed at him from all sides! Poor Abner! He was running as fast as he could. And as he ran, he clutched his trusty umbrella in his right hand.

Not until he found himself in the open countryside once more did he dare stop to catch his breath and mop his dripping face. Then he began walking slowly down the country road toward his cornfield.

"If that's the city," he vowed, "no more of it for me! I'll stay in my cornfield where I can have a long life and a happy one!"

PINOCCHIO

From the Motion Picture "Pinocchio." Based on the Story by Collodi

ONE NIGHT, long, long ago, the Evening Star shone down across the dark sky. Its beams formed a shimmering pathway to a tiny village, and painted its humble roofs with stardust.

But the silent little town was deep in sleep. The only witness to the beauty of the night was a weary wayfarer who chanced to be passing through.

His clothes were gray with dust. His well-worn shoes pinched his feet; his back ached from the weight of the carpetbag slung over his shabby shoulder. To be sure, it was only a small carpetbag; but this wayfarer had a very small shoulder. As a matter of fact, he was an exceedingly small wayfarer. His name was Cricket, Jiminy Cricket.

He marveled at the radiant star; it seemed almost close enough to touch, and pretty as a picture. But at this moment Jiminy Cricket was not interested in pretty pictures. He was looking for a place to rest.

Suddenly he noticed a light in a window, and smoke curling from a chimney.

"Where there's smoke, there's a fire," he reasoned. "Where there's a fire, there's a hearth. And where there's a hearth, there *should* be a cricket!"

And with that, he hopped up to the window sill and peered in. The room had a friendly look. So Jiminy crawled under the door, scurried over to the hearth, backed up against the glowing fireplace, and warmed his little britches.

It was no ordinary village home into which the small wayfarer had stumbled. It was a workshop: the workshop of Geppetto the woodcarver. Old Geppetto was working late that night. He was making a puppet.

Geppetto lived alone except for his black kitten, Figaro, and a pet goldfish he called Cleo. But he had many friends; everyone knew and loved the kindly, white-haired old man. He had spent his whole life creating happiness for others.

It was the children who loved Geppetto best. He doctored their dolls, put clean sawdust into limp rag bodies and painted fresh smiles on faded china faces. He fashioned new arms and legs for battered tin soldiers—and there was magic in his hands when he carved a toy.

Now, the weary old fellow put his tools away and surveyed his newest handiwork. The puppet he had made had the figure of a small boy. He was the right size for a small boy. He had the cute, round face of a small boy—except for one feature. The nose! Geppetto had given him a very long and pointed nose, such a nose as no real boy ever possessed. A funny nose.

The old woodcarver stroked his chin and chuckled. "Woodenhead," he said, "you are finished, and you deserve a name. What shall I call you? I know—*Pinocchio!* Do you like it?" He worked the puppet's strings so that it nodded "Yes."

"That settles it!" cried Geppetto happily. "Pinocchio you are! And now," he yawned, "time for bed. Good-night, Figaro! Goodnight, Cleo! Good-night, Pinocchio!"

Jiminy Cricket was glad to hear these words, for he felt very sleepy. Geppetto put on a long white nightshirt and climbed creakily into bed, but he still sat admiring the puppet with its wooden smile.

"Look at him, Figaro!" he exclaimed. "He seems almost real. Wouldn't it be nice if he were alive?"

But the only answer from the kitten was a snore.

Long after Geppetto had gone to sleep, Jiminy Cricket lay awake thinking. It made him sad to realize the old man's wish could never come true.

Suddenly he heard something. Music—mysterious music! He sat up and looked around the room. Then he saw a strange light—a brilliant glow, which grew more dazzling every minute. It was a star—the Evening Star, floating down the sky and entering Geppetto's window!

Then in the center of its blinding glow appeared a beautiful lady dressed in robes of flowing blue.

"As I live and breathe!" Jiminy whispered in astonishment. "A fairy!"

The Blue Fairy bent over the old woodcarver and spoke to him ever so softly, so as not to disturb his slumber.

"Good Geppetto," she said, "you have given so much happiness to others, you deserve to have your wish come true!"

Then she turned to the wooden puppet. Holding out her glittering wand, she spoke these words:

> "Little puppet made of pine,
> Wake! The gift of life is thine!"

And when the wand touched him, Pinocchio came to life! First he blinked his eyes, then he raised his wooden arm and wiggled his jointed fingers.

"I can move!" he cried. "I can *talk!*"

"Yes, Pinocchio," the Blue Fairy smiled. "Geppetto needs a little son. So tonight I give you life."

"Then I'm a real boy!" cried Pinocchio joyfully.

"No," said the Fairy sadly. "There is no magic that can make us real. I have given you life—the rest is up to you."

"Tell me what I must do," begged Pinocchio. "I want to be a real boy!"

"Prove yourself brave, truthful, and unselfish," said the Blue Fairy. "Be a good son to Geppetto—make him proud of you! Then, some day, you will wake up and find yourself a real boy!"

"Whew! That won't be easy," thought Jiminy Cricket.

But the Blue Fairy also realized what a hard task she was giving Pinocchio. "The world is full of temptations," she continued. "You must learn to choose between right and wrong—"

"Right? Wrong?" questioned Pinocchio. "How will I know?"

Jiminy wrung his hands in desperation. But

the wise Fairy was not yet finished. "Your conscience will tell you the difference between right and wrong," she explained.

"Conscience?" Pinocchio repeated. "What are they?"

That was too much for Jiminy Cricket. He hopped down where he could be seen.

"A conscience," he shouted, "is that still small voice people won't listen to! That's the trouble with the world today!"

"Are *you* my conscience?" asked Pinocchio eagerly.

Jiminy was embarrassed, but the Blue Fairy came to his rescue. "Would you like to be Pinocchio's conscience?" she smiled. "You seem a man of the world. What is your name?"

Jiminy was flattered. "Jiminy Cricket," he answered.

"Kneel, Mister Cricket," commanded the Blue Fairy.

Jiminy knelt and trembled as her wand touched him.

"I dub you Pinocchio's conscience," she proclaimed, "Lord High Keeper of the Knowledge of Right and Wrong! Arise — *Sir* Jiminy Cricket!"

And when the dusty little cricket rose his shabby old clothes were gone and he was clad in elegant raiment from head to foot.

"Don't I get a badge or something?" he asked.

"We'll see," the Blue Fairy smiled.

"Make it a gold one?" urged Jiminy.

"Perhaps, if you do your job well," she said. "I leave Pinocchio in your hands. Give him the benefit of your advice and experience. Help him to be a real boy!"

It was a serious moment for the little cricket. He promised to help Pinocchio as much as he could, and to stick by him through thick and thin. The Blue Fairy thanked him.

"And now, Pinocchio," she said, "be a good boy—and always let your conscience be your guide! Don't be discouraged because you are different from the other boys! Remember— *any child who is not good, might just as well be made of wood!*" The Blue Fairy backed slowly away. There was one last soft chord of music and she was gone.

Pinocchio and Jiminy stared silently at the spot where the Fairy had stood, half hoping she might return. The little cricket finally broke the spell.

"Say, she's all right, son!" he exclaimed. "Remember what she told you—always let your conscience be your guide!"

"Yes sir, I will!" answered Pinocchio.

"And when you need me, whistle," said Jiminy, "like this!"

"Like this?" Pinocchio tried, but no sound came.

So Jiminy sang him a little lecture-lesson, which went something like this:

"When you get in trouble
And you don't know right from wrong,
Give a little whistle,
Give a little whistle.
When you meet temptation
And the urge is very strong,
Give a little whistle,
Give a little whistle."

Then he began dancing down the strings of a violin on the bench, balancing himself with his small umbrella.

"Take the straight and narrow path
And if you start to slide,
Give a little whistle,
Give a little whistle—"

Just then the violin string broke. Jiminy fell over backward, but picked himself up and finished, "and always let your conscience be your guide!"

Pinocchio watched entranced as the little cricket went on dancing. Finally he too jumped up and tried to make his wooden feet go through the same steps. But he danced too close to the edge of the work-bench, lost his balance and fell clatteringly to the floor.

The noise woke Geppetto. "Who's there?" he called.

Pinocchio, on the floor, answered, "It's *me!*"

Geppetto's teeth chattered with fright. "Figaro, there's somebody in here!" he whispered. "A burglar, maybe! Come, we'll catch him!"

Then to his surprise, he noticed his puppet, which he had left on the workbench, lying on the floor.

"Why, Pinocchio!" he exclaimed. "How did

you get down there?" He picked the puppet up and set him back on the bench. Imagine his surprise when Pinocchio answered!

"I fell down!" he said.

Geppetto stared. "What! You're talking?" he cried. "No! You're only a marionette. You can't talk!"

"Yes, I can," insisted the puppet. "I can move, too!"

The old man backed away. "No, no," he argued. "I must be dreaming! I will pour water on myself! I will stick me with pins!"

Geppetto made sure he was awake. "Now we will see who is dreaming," he challenged. "Go on—say something!"

Pinocchio laughed merrily. "Do it again!" he begged. "You're awful funny! I like you!"

"You *do* talk," said the old man, in a hushed voice. "Pinocchio! It's a miracle! Figaro! Cleo! Look—he's alive!"

Geppetto didn't know whether to laugh or cry, he was so happy. "This calls for a celebration!" he announced. He turned on a music box and began to dance. He went to his toy shelves and filled his arms with playthings. It was just like Christmas for Pinocchio. He couldn't decide which toy to play with first!

But the music box ran down and the celebration ended.

"Now it is time for bed," said the old woodcarver. "Come, Pinocchio. You shall sleep here in this dresser drawer." He tucked Pinocchio in and said, "Sleep fast, Pinocchio!"

That night Jiminy Cricket did an unusual thing—for him. He prayed. He prayed that Pinocchio might never disappoint that kind, happy old man or the lovely Blue Fairy, and that he himself might be a good conscience, so Pinocchio would soon earn the right to be a real boy.

All was still in the little shop. High in the sky the Evening Star twinkled softly, as though smiling approval of a good night's work.

Morning dawned bright and clear. As the school bells rang out over the village, their clamor sent pigeons flying from the old belfry like colored fans spread against the white clouds.

The school bells carried a special message of joy to old Geppetto. Today his own son was to join the other little ones on their way to school!

Pinocchio too was impatient. His face, shiny from scrubbing, beamed with excitement. Even Figaro and Cleo realized it was a gala day.

At last Pinocchio was pronounced ready. Geppetto opened the door. For the first time the puppet looked out at the wide, wide world. How beautiful it was!

"What are those?" he asked, pointing down the street.

"Those are the children, bless them!" Geppetto answered. "They are the boys and girls —your schoolmates, Pinocchio!"

"Real boys?" Pinocchio asked eagerly.

"Yes, my son. And if you study hard, you'll soon be as smart as they are. Wait a minute —your books!"

Little Figaro appeared at the door, tugging the strap which held Pinocchio's schoolbooks.

"Ah, thank you, Figaro. You too want to help! Pinocchio, here are your books. Remember, be a good boy. Choose your friends carefully; shun evil companions. Mind the teacher—"

"Good-by!" shouted Pinocchio, pulling carelessly away. But he thought better of it, ran back and threw his arms around Geppetto. "Good-by, Father," he said shyly; then off he marched, his books under his arm, chock-full of good resolutions.

Jiminy Cricket heard the school bell and jumped up in a great hurry. Suppose Pinocchio had gone off to school without him! If ever a small boy needs a conscience, it is on his first day at school. A fine time to oversleep, Jiminy thought. Then he stuffed his shirt hastily inside his trousers, grabbed his hat and rushed out.

"Hey, Pinoke!" he called. "Wait for me!"

Geppetto saw Pinocchio safely off to school, then went cheerily to his workbench.

"An extra mouth to feed, Figaro," he chuckled to the kitten. "Yet what a joy it is to have someone to work for!"

But alas, many a dreary day and night

"My dear young man! I'm so sorry," Foulfellow apologized, helping Pinocchio to his feet. "A most regrettable accident—Mr.—er—"

"Pinocchio," answered the puppet cheerfully.

"Ha ha, Pinocchio," began Foulfellow, "you were going a little too fast! A little too fast, and in the *wrong* direction. Now I have a plan for you. Come . . ."

"But I'm on my way to school," said Pinocchio.

"To school? Nonsense!" said Foulfellow. "I have a much better plan."

"You're too bright a boy to waste your time in school," said Foulfellow. "Isn't he, Gideon?" Gideon nodded.

"You deserve a trip to Pleasure Island, my boy," said sly old Foulfellow.

"Pleasure Island?" repeated Pinocchio.

"Pleasure Island!" cried Foulfellow. "Where every day is a holiday, with fireworks, brass bands, parades—a paradise for boys! Why, I can see you now—lolling under a doughnut

were to pass before the old woodcarver saw his boy again! For in spite of Geppetto's warning, Pinocchio fell into bad company. He met two scheming adventurers—a Fox and a Cat, the worst pair of scoundrels in the whole countryside.

Run down at the heel and patched at the seat, these villains managed somehow to look like elegant gentlemen out for a stroll. But as usual, they were up to no good.

Suddenly, "Look!" cried the sharp-eyed Fox, who went by the name of J. Worthington Foulfellow, alias Honest John. "Do you see what I see?" He pointed with his cane. The stupid Cat, who was called Gideon, stared at Pinocchio.

"A puppet that walks!" marveled Foulfellow. "A live puppet—a marionette without strings! A breathing woodenhead!"

And before Pinocchio knew what had happened, he was lying flat on his face. Something had tripped him up, and that something was a cane, thrust between his feet by the sly old fox.

304

tree, a lollipop in each hand, gazing off at the pink Ice Cream Mountains—think of it, Pinocchio!"

It was a tempting picture the sly fox painted. "Well, I *was* going to school," said Pinocchio. He hesitated. "But perhaps I could go to Pleasure Island first—for a little while . . ."

Jiminy Cricket came panting along just in time to see the three of them stroll off arm in arm.

"Oh, what a woodenhead he is!" thought Jiminy Cricket. But he followed loyally.

Soon they came to a great coach, piled to the brim with boys—eager, noisy, impudent boys! Laughing and shouting, Pinocchio climbed aboard.

"Good-by!" Pinocchio called to the Fox. "I'll never be able to thank you for this!"

"Think nothing of it, my boy," said the Fox. "Seeing you happy is our only reward. Our only reward—reward—*reward!*" he kept repeating, until the wicked-looking Coachman slipped him a large sack of gold. The Fox had sold Pinocchio for gold!

Jiminy Cricket saw the Coachman crack his long blacksnake whip, and the coach start to move. The coach was drawn by twelve sorrowful-looking little donkeys, who seemed to feel very badly. "Tsk! Tsk! Tsk!" they said, every time the Coachman's whip descended. But nobody could hear them because of the boys' shouting.

"Three cheers for anything," they yelled, throwing their caps into the air as the coach rolled away. "Hurray for Pleasure Island!"

Jiminy made a last desperate effort. He hopped onto the rear axle of the coach and rode along. Certain that Pinocchio was headed for disaster, the loyal little cricket went with him just the same.

The journey was an unhappy one for Jiminy. At the waterfront, the passengers boarded a ferryboat for Pleasure Island, and the little cricket suffered from seasickness during the entire voyage.

But physical discomfort was not what bothered him most. He was worried about Pinocchio, who promptly made friends with the worst boy in the crowd—a no-good named "Lampwick." Lampwick talked out of the corner of his mouth, and was very untidy. Yet Pinocchio cherished his friendship.

Jiminy tried to warn Pinocchio, but the

heedless puppet refused to listen. Finally the ferry docked and the boys swarmed down the gangplank onto Pleasure Island.

Bands played loudly; wonderful circuses performed along the streets, which were paved with cookies and lined with doughnut trees. Lollipops and cupcakes grew on bushes, and fountains spouted lemonade and soda pop. The Mayor of Pleasure Island made a speech of welcome and urged the boys to enjoy themselves.

Yes, Pleasure Island seemed to be all the Fox had claimed for it, and more. Only Jiminy Cricket was skeptical. He felt that there was more to all this than appeared on the surface. But weeks went by, and seldom did Jiminy get close enough to Pinocchio to warn him. He was always in the midst of the fun, and his friend Lampwick was the ringleader of the horde of carefree, mischievous boys.

They smashed windows and burned schoolbooks; in fact they did whatever they felt like doing, no matter how destructive. They ate until they nearly burst. And always the Coachman and Mayor encouraged them to "Have a good time—while you can!"

And all the while the poor little donkeys—who performed all the hard labor on the island—looked very sad and said "Tsk! Tsk! Tsk!"

One day Pinocchio and Lampwick were lazily floating in a canoe along the Lemonade River, which flowed between the Ice Cream Mountains. Chocolate cattails grew thickly along the banks, lollipop trees drooped overhead, and the canoe was piled high with sweets.

"This is too good to be true, Lampwick," Pinocchio sighed blissfully. "I could stay here forever."

"Aw, this is kid stuff," retorted Lampwick. "Let's go where we can have some real fun!"

"Where?" asked Pinocchio curiously.

"I'll show you," said Lampwick. So they pulled the canoe up on the bank, and Lamp-

wick then led the way to Tobacco Lane.

Here the fences were made of cigars, cigarettes and matches grew on bushes, and there were rows of cornstalks with corncob pipes on them. Lampwick lit a cigar and began smoking.

Pinocchio hesitated. Finally he picked a corncob pipe and began to puff timidly.

"Aw, you smoke like my granmudder," jeered Lampwick. "Take a big drag, Pinoke—like dis!"

Under Lampwick's instruction, Pinocchio soon found himself smoking like a chimney. Just then, along came Jiminy. How sad the little cricket felt when he saw this you will never know. While he had known for a long time that Pinocchio had fallen into evil ways, Jiminy did not realize he had sunk to such depths.

Well, he had tried everything—except force. Would that make the lad come to his senses? He'd decided to try. He shook his little fist angrily. "So it's come to this, has it?" he shouted. "SMOKING!"

Pinocchio gave him a careless glance. "Yeah," he answered out of the corner of his mouth, in imitation of Lampwick. "So what?"

"Just this!" Jiminy exploded. "You're making a disgusting spectacle of yourself. You're going home this minute!"

Lampwick, who had never seen Jiminy be-

fore, was curious. "Who's de insect, Pinoke?" he asked.

"Jiminy? Why, he's my conscience," explained Pinocchio.

Lampwick began to laugh. "You mean you take advice from a *beetle*?" he remarked insultingly. "Say, I can't waste time wid a sap like you. So long!" And he strolled away.

"Lampwick! Don't go!" cried Pinocchio. "Now see what you've done, Jiminy! Lampwick was my best friend!"

That was too much for the little cricket. "So *he's* your best friend," he said angrily. "Well, Pinocchio, that's the last straw. I'm through! I'm taking the next boat!"

Pinocchio hesitated but temptation was too strong. He couldn't give Lampwick up. He started off after him, full of apologies.

"Hey wait, Lampwick!" he called. "I'm coming with *you*!"

That was the end as far as Jiminy was concerned. "So he prefers to remain with that hoodlum, and allow him to insult *me*, his conscience?" he muttered. "Well, from now on he can paddle his own canoe. I'm going home!"

And he started toward the entrance gate, so upset that he did not notice how dark and forlorn Pleasure Island looked. There wasn't a boy in sight on the wide streets.

Jiminy's only thought was to get away quickly. He was just about to pound angrily on the gate when he heard voices on the other side. He tried to listen, and became conscious of a reddish glow which cast great, frightening shadows against the high stone walls. The shadows looked like prison guards, and they carried guns!

Jiminy jumped up and peered fearfully through the keyhole. In the cove, lit by flaming torches, he saw something that made his blood turn cold.

The ferryboat stood waiting, stripped of its decorations. The dock swarmed with howling, braying donkeys—fat ones and thin ones, many of whom still wore boys' hats and shoes. Huge, ape-like guards herded them into crates, assisted by the Coachman, who cracked his whip brutally over the poor donkeys' heads.

The little cricket shuddered. At last he understood the meaning of Pleasure Island. This, then, was what became of lazy, good-for-nothing boys! They made donkeys of themselves! This was Pinocchio's fate, unless—

Forgetting his anger, Jiminy leaped to the ground and started back toward Tobacco Lane. He must warn Pinocchio to leave at once.

"Pinocchio!" he yelled. "Pinocchio!" But his cries only echoed through the empty streets.

Not far away, Pinocchio was still looking for Lampwick. He wandered unhappily past pie trees and popcorn shrubs. The island suddenly seemed strange, deserted.

Then he heard a frightened voice say, "Here I am!"

"Lampwick!" Pinocchio answered joyfully. "Where are you?"

Just then a little donkey emerged from some bushes. "Ssh!" he whispered. "Stop yelling! They'll hear us!"

Pinocchio stared. The donkey spoke in Lampwick's voice!

"This is no time for jokes," Pinocchio said crossly. "What are you doing in that donkey suit?"

"This ain't no donkey suit, Pinoke," the frightened voice replied. "I *am* a donkey!"

Pinocchio laughed. "You a donkey?" For he still thought it was a joke. "Ha ha ha! *He-Haw! He-Haw! He-Haw!*"

Pinocchio turned pale, but he couldn't stop. He was braying like a donkey! He put his hand over his mouth.

The little donkey came closer to him. "That's the first sign of donkey fever," he whispered. "That's how I started."

"Then—you *are* Lampwick! What happened?"

"Donkey fever," replied Lampwick, "and you've got it too!"

Pinocchio's head began to buzz like a hive of bees. He reached up and felt something horrible. Two long, hairy ears were growing out of his head!

"You've got it all right!" whispered Lampwick. "Look behind you!"

Pinocchio looked and discovered that he had a long tail. He began to tremble, and was no longer able to stand up straight. Then he found himself on all fours, like a donkey!

"Help! Help!" he shrieked. "Jiminy! Jiminy Cricket!"

Jiminy ran toward them, but he saw that he was too late.

"Oh! Oh! Oh me, oh my!" he groaned. "Look at you! Come on! Let's get away from here before you're a complete donkey!"

This time nobody argued with the little cricket. As he fled toward the high stone wall, Pinocchio and the donkey that had once been Lampwick followed as fast as their legs would carry them. But as they rounded a corner, they came face to face with the Coachman and his armed guards. They turned and dashed toward the opposite wall.

"There they go! That's the two that's missing!" yelled the Coachman. "After them! Sound the alarm!"

Instantly the air was filled with the sound of sirens and the baying of bloodhounds. Searchlights began to play over the island, and bullets whizzed past the ears of the escaping prisoners. They expected any minute to be shot.

Pinocchio and Jiminy reached the wall and managed to climb to the top before the ape-like guards got within shooting distance. But Pinocchio looked down and saw a little

donkey choking and kicking as he was caught with a rope lasso. It was Lampwick.

"Go on, Pinoke!" he cried. "It's all over with me!"

A lump came in Pinocchio's throat. After all, Lampwick was his friend. But there was nothing he could do. He turned his back and said a silent prayer. Then he and Jiminy dove into the sea.

Bullets splashed all around them in the water, but by some miracle neither of them was hit. Finally a thick fog hid them from the glaring searchlights, and the sound of the guns died away. They had escaped!

It was a long, hard swim back to the mainland. When they reached shore, Pinocchio longed to see once more the cozy little cot-

tage and his dear, kind father. Pleasure Island, and all it stood for, now seemed like a bad dream. But they were by no means at the end of their journey, for home was still many weary miles away.

It was winter when at last one evening they limped into the village. They hurried through the drifting snow to Geppetto's shop. Pinocchio pounded on the door with eager fists.

"Father! Father!" he cried. "It's me! It's Pinocchio!"

But the only reply was the howling of the wintry wind.

"He must be asleep," said Pinocchio, and he knocked again. But again there was no answer.

Worried, Pinocchio hastened to the window and peered in. The house was empty! Everything was shrouded and dusty.

"He's gone, Jiminy," said Pinocchio sorrowfully. "My father's gone away!"

"Looks like he's gone for good, too," said Jiminy. "What'll we do?"

"I don't know." Pinocchio sat down on the doorstep shivering. A tear came from his eye, ran down his long nose and froze into a tiny, sparkling icicle. But Pinocchio didn't even bother to wipe it off. He felt terrible.

Just then a gust of wind blew around the corner, carrying a piece of paper. Jiminy hopped over to see what it was.

"Hey, Pinoke, it's a letter!" he exclaimed.

"Oh! Maybe it's from my father!" cried Pinocchio, and he quickly took the note from Jiminy and tried to read it. But alas, the marks on the paper meant nothing to him.

"You see, if you had gone to school you could read your father's letter," Jiminy reminded him. "Here—give it to me!"

The little cricket began to read the note aloud, and this is what it said:

"Dear Pinocchio:

"I heard you had gone to Pleasure Island, so I got a small boat and started off to search for you. Everyone said it

was a dangerous voyage, but Figaro, Cleo, and I thought we could reach you and save you from a terrible fate.

"We weathered the storms, and finally reached the Terrible Straits. But just as we came in sight of our goal, out of the sea rose Monstro, the Terror of the Deep—the giant whale who swallows ships whole. He opened his jaws. In we went—boat and all . . ."

Here Pinocchio's sobs interrupted Jiminy's reading of the letter as he realized Geppetto's plight.

"Oh, my poor, poor father!" the puppet moaned. "He's dead! And it's all my fault!" He began to weep bitterly.

"But he isn't dead!" said Jiminy, and read on.

"So now, dear son, we are living at the bottom of the ocean in the belly of the whale. But there is very little to eat here, and we cannot exist much longer, So I fear you will never again see

Your loving father,
GEPPETTO."

"Hurrah Hurrah!" shouted Pinocchio.

"Hurrah for what?" asked Jiminy somewhat crossly. It did not seem to him to be quite the time for cheers.

"Don't you see, Jiminy?" cried Pinocchio. "My father is still alive! There may be time to save him!"

"Save him?" said Jiminy stupidly. Then suddenly a light dawned. "You don't mean *you*—"

"Yes!" announced Pinocchio. "I'm going after him. It's my fault he's down there in the whale; I'm going to the bottom of the ocean and rescue him!"

"But Pinocchio, you might be killed!" warned the cricket.

"I don't mind," declared Pinocchio. "What

does life mean to me without my father? I've got to save him!"

Jiminy stared with open mouth. He hardly recognized this new Pinocchio—a brave, unselfish Pinocchio who stood there in place of the weak, foolish puppet he had always known.

"But think how far it is to the seashore—" he began.

Pinocchio looked thoughtful, but not for long. "I don't care. No place is too far for me to go after my father."

Just then, with a flutter of wings, a beautiful white dove settled gracefully down in the snow beside them.

"I will take you to the seashore," she said softly.

"You?" Pinocchio stared. But he did not see the tiny gold crown on the dove's head. It was she who had dropped the letter from the sky. She was his own dear Blue Fairy, disguised as a dove.

"Yes, I will help you," she assured him.

"How could a little dove carry me to the seashore?"

"Like this!"

And the dove began to grow and grow, until she was larger than an eagle. "Jump on my back," she commanded. Pinocchio obeyed.

"Good-by, Jiminy Cricket," he said. "I may never see you again." He waved his hand to his little friend. "Thank you for all you've done!"

"Good-by, nothing!" retorted Jiminy, and he too jumped on the back of the great white dove. "You're not leaving me! We'll see this through together!"

The dove raised her wide wings and rose from the ground. Higher and higher they flew, till the village disappeared and all they could see beneath them was whirling snow.

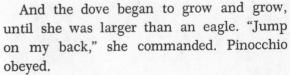

"Good-by, Pinocchio," the dove replied. "Good luck!"

And she grew small again and flew away. Neither Pinocchio nor Jiminy realized that she was the Blue Fairy, but they were very grateful.

As soon as the dove was out of sight, Pinocchio tied a big stone to his donkey tail, to anchor him to the floor of the ocean. Then he smiled bravely at Jiminy, who smiled back, and together they leaped off the cliff.

The weight of the stone caused Pinocchio to sink at once. By clinging desperately, little Jiminy managed to stay close by. They landed, picked themselves up and peered about. They were at the very bottom of the sea.

At first it seemed dark; they were many fathoms deep. Gradually Pinocchio's eyes became accustomed to the greenish light which filtered down into the submarine forest.

Giant clumps of seaweed waved overhead, like the branches of trees. Among them darted lovely bright objects, like birds or living flowers. They soon saw that these brilliant creatures were fish of all descriptions.

However, Pinocchio was in no frame of mind to make a study of the citizens of the sea. He walked along, peering into every cave and grotto in search of the great whale. But the stone attached to his tail made him move slowly, and he grew impatient.

"I wish we knew just where to look," he thought. "Jiminy, where do you suppose Monstro might be?"

"Don't know, I'm sure," replied Jiminy. "But we might ask some of these—er, people. I'll inquire here."

He knocked politely on an oyster. Its shell opened.

"Pardon me, Pearl," Jiminy began, "but could you tell me where we might find Monstro the Whale?"

To his surprise, the shell closed with a sharp click and the oyster scuttled off into a kelp bush as though frightened.

All night they flew through the storm. When morning came, the sun shone brightly. The dove's wings slowed down and she glided to earth at the edge of a cliff. Far below, the sea lay churning and lashing like a restless giant.

"I can take you no farther," said the dove. "Are you quite sure you want to go on this dangerous mission?"

"Yes," said Pinocchio. "Thank you for the ride. Good-by!"

"Hm! That's funny!" remarked Jiminy.

Just then a school of tropical fish approached, brightly beautiful and extremely curious.

"I wonder," Pinocchio began, "if you could tell me where to find Monstro—"

But the lovely little creatures darted away before he had finished speaking. It was as though Pinocchio had threatened to harm them in some way.

A bit farther along, they encountered a herd of tiny sea horses, grazing on the sandy bottom. Pinocchio tried once more.

"Could you tell me," he asked, "where I might find Monstro the Whale?"

But the sea horses fled, their little ears raised in alarm.

"You know what I think?" exclaimed Jiminy. "I think everybody down here is afraid of Monstro! Why, they run away at the very mention of his name! He must be awful. Do you think we should go on?"

"Certainly!" declared Pinocchio. "I'm not afraid!"

So they went on. It was a strange journey.

Sometimes the water grew very dark, and tiny phosphorescent fish glowed like fireflies in the depths. They learned to be careful not to step on the huge flowers which lay on the ocean's floor. For they were not flowers but sea anemones, which could reach up and capture whatever came within their grasp.

Striped fish glared at them from seaweed thickets like tigers in a jungle, and fish with horns and quills glowered at them. They saw wonders of the deep which no human eye has ever beheld—but nowhere could they find so much as one clue to the whereabouts of Monstro, the Terror of the Deep.

"The time is getting short!" said Pinocchio at last. "We must find him! My father will starve to death!"

"Father," he cried desperately. But there was no sound except the constant shifting and sighing of the watery depths.

"Let's go home, Pinocchio," Jiminy pleaded. "We'll never find Monstro in this big place. For all we know, we may be looking in the wrong ocean."

"No, Jiminy," said Pinocchio, "I'll never give up! Never!"

Not far away lay the Terror of the Deep, floating close to the surface, fast asleep. At times his broad back rose out of the water, to be mistaken for a desert island.

It was lucky for any ship close by that Monstro slept, for with but one flip of his tail he had been known to crush the sturdiest craft. As he snored the roars sounded like a tempest. It seemed impossible that anything could live within those crushing jaws.

Yet at the far end of the long, dark cavern formed by the whale's mouth lived a strange household. A kindly old man, whose skin was as pale as white paper, a small black kitten, whose ribs nearly pierced his fur, and a tiny, frightened goldfish, who swam weakly around in her bowl.

The old woodcarver had constructed a rude home, furnished with broken packing-cases

was now very low; the lantern sputtering above his table was almost out of oil. The end was near.

Every day he fished in the mouth of the whale; but when Monstro slept, nothing entered that dark cavern. Now there was only a shallow pool of water, and it was useless to fish.

"Not a bite for days, Figaro," Geppetto said. "If Monstro doesn't wake up soon, it will be too bad for us. I never thought it would end like this!" He sighed mournfully. "Here we are, starving in the belly of a whale. And Pinocchio—poor little Pinocchio!" Geppetto was obliged to raise his thin voice to a shout, to be heard above the whale's snoring.

The old woodcarver looked tired and worn.

from ships the whale had swallowed. He had salvaged a lantern, pots and pans and a few other necessities of life. But his stock of food

He had never been so hungry in his whole life. Figaro was hungry too. He stared greedily at little Cleo, swimming slowly about her bowl.

As Geppetto went wearily back to his fishing, the kitten began to sneak toward Cleo's bowl. But the old man saw him.

"Scat!" shouted Geppetto. "You beast! You *dog!* Shame on you, Figaro, chasing Cleo, after the way I've brought you up!"

The hungry kitten scuttled away to a corner to try to forget the pangs which gnawed him. Just then Geppetto felt a nibble at his line. He pulled it up in great excitement.

"It's a package, Figaro!" he cried. "Maybe it's food. Sausage, or cheese—"

But when the water-soaked package was unwrapped, it contained only a cook book! What a grim trick Fate had played!

"Oh, oh," groaned Geppetto. "I am so hungry! If we only had something to cook! Anything—"

He turned the pages, his mouth watering at the pictured recipes. "101 Ways to Cook Fish," he read. Suddenly his eyes were drawn, as if by a magnet, to Cleo. He could almost see the melted butter sizzling! As in a nightmare, he walked toward the goldfish bowl.

But as he started to scoop his little pet out and put her in the frying pan, the old man realized he could never do this thing.

"Dear Cleo," he begged, "forgive me! If we must die, let us die as we have lived—friends through thick and thin!"

It was a solemn moment. All felt that the end was near.

Then the whale moved!

"He's waking up!" cried Geppetto. "He's opening his mouth!"

Monstro gave an upward lunge, and through his jaws rushed a wall of black water. With it came fish—a whole school of fish! Hundreds of them.

"Food!" yelled Geppetto, seizing his pole. "Tuna fish! Oh, Figaro, Cleo—we are saved!"

And he began to pull fish after fish out of the water.

When Monstro woke, opened his eyes and saw the school of tuna approaching, he threshed the ocean into turmoil for miles around.

Pinocchio noticed every creature in the sea taking flight, but he did not understand the reason until he saw the whale coming toward him. Then he *knew.*

"Monstro!" he shrieked. "Jiminy, swim for your life!" For although he had long been in search of the Terror of the Deep, a mere look at those crushing jaws was enough to make him flee in terror.

But nothing in Monstro's path could escape. He swallowed hundreds of tuna at one gulp. Into that huge maw finally went Pinocchio!

At last, completely satisfied, the whale grunted and settled down in his watery bed for another nap.

"Blubber-mouth!" cried a shrill, small voice. "Let me in!"

It was Jiminy, clinging to an empty bottle, bobbing up and down outside Monstro's jaws, begging to be swallowed too.

But the whale paid no attention, except to settle farther into the water. The little cricket was left alone, except for a flock of seagulls, who began to swoop down and peck at him. He raised his umbrella and drove them away, got inside the bottle and prepared to wait for Pinocchio.

Inside the whale, although Geppetto's bin was already heaped, he was still at work pulling in tuna.

"There's enough food to last us for months," he told Figaro joyfully. "Wait, there's another big one!" He scarcely noticed a shrill little cry of "Father!"

"Pinocchio?" the old man asked himself in wonderment, and turned around. There, standing before him, was his boy! "Pinocchio!" he exclaimed joyfully. "Are my eyes telling me the truth? Are you really my own dear Pinocchio?"

Geppetto was not the only one who was glad. Figaro licked Pinocchio's face, and little Cleo turned somersaults.

"You see, we have all missed you," said Geppetto fondly. "But you're sneezing! You've caught cold, son! You should not have come down here! Sit down and rest! Give me your hat!"

But when Pinocchio's hat was removed, those hated donkey ears popped out into plain sight.

"Pinocchio!" cried Geppetto, shocked. *"Those ears!"*

Pinocchio hung his head in shame. "I've got a tail, too," he admitted sadly. *"Oh, Father!"* And he turned his head away to hide his tears.

"Never mind, son," Geppetto comforted

him. "The main thing is that we are all to-gether again."

Pinocchio brightened up. "The *main* thing is to figure out a way to get out of this whale!"

"I've tried everything," said Geppetto hopelessly. "I even built a raft—"

"That's it!" cried Pinocchio. "When he opens his mouth, we'll float out on the raft!"

"Oh, no," argued Geppetto. "When he opens his mouth everything comes in—nothing goes out. Come, we are all hungry—I will cook a fish dinner! Help me build a fire—"

"That's it, Father!" interrupted Pinocchio. "We'll build a great big fire!" And he began to throw into the fire everything he could get his hands on.

"Not the chairs!" warned Geppetto. "What will we sit on?"

"We won't need chairs," shouted Pinocchio. "We'll build a big fire and make Monstro sneeze! When he sneezes, out we go! Hurry—more wood!"

As the fire began to smoke they got the raft ready.

"It won't work, son," Geppetto insisted mournfully.

But before long the whale began to grunt and cough. Suddenly he drew in his breath and gave a monstrous SNEEZE! Out went the raft, past those crushing jaws, into the sea.

"We made it!" shouted Pinocchio. "Father, we're free!"

But they were not yet free. The angry whale saw them and plunged ferociously after their frail raft. He hit it squarely, splintering it into thousands of pieces. Pinocchio and Geppetto swam for their lives, with Monstro, the Terror of the Deep, in full pursuit.

The old man clung weakly to a board. He knew he could never reach land, but there was still hope for Pinocchio.

"Save yourself, my boy!" cried Geppetto. "Swim for shore, and don't worry about me!"

But the brave puppet swam to his father and managed to keep him afloat. Giant waves swept them toward the dark, forbidding rocks which lined the shore. Even if they escaped Monstro, they would surely be crushed to death.

But between two of the rocks there was a small, hidden crevice. By some miracle, Pinocchio and Geppetto were washed through this crevice into a small, sheltered lagoon. Again and again the furious whale threw his bulk against the rocks on the other side. His quarry had escaped!

But alas, when Geppetto sat up dizzily he saw poor Pinocchio lying motionless beside him, still and pale. The heartbroken old man knelt and wept bitterly, certain his wooden boy was dead.

The gentle waves carried a fishbowl up onto the beach. It was Cleo—and to the edge

of the bowl clung a bedraggled kitten, Figaro. But even they were no comfort to Geppetto now.

A bottle bobbed up out of the water. Inside it rode Jiminy Cricket. He saw what had happened and longed to comfort Geppetto, but his own heart was broken.

The sorrowful old man finally gathered poor Pinocchio in his arms, picked up his pets and started home. They too felt sad, for

they knew Geppetto was lonelier than he had ever been before.

When they reached home, it no longer seemed a home; it was dark and cheerless. Geppetto put Pinocchio on the workbench, buried his face in his hands and prayed.

Suddenly a ray of starlight pierced the gloom. It sought out the lifeless figure of the puppet. A voice which seemed to come from the sky said, as it had said once before:

"—and some day, when you have proven yourself brave, truthful and unselfish, you will be a real boy—"

The old man saw and heard nothing. But Pinocchio stirred, sat up and looked around. He saw the others grieving, and wondered why. Then he looked down at himself, felt of his arms and legs, and suddenly he realized what had happened.

"Father!" he cried. "Father, look at me!"

Pinocchio was alive—really alive. No longer a wooden puppet, but a real flesh-and-blood boy!

Geppetto stared unbelievingly. Once more he picked Pinocchio up in his arms and hugged him, and cried—this time for joy. Again a miracle had been performed; this was truly the answer to his wish—the son he had always wanted!

What did they do to celebrate? Geppetto made a fire and soon the house was as warm and cozy as ever. He started all the clocks and played the music box. Figaro turned somersaults, and Cleo raced madly about her bowl. Pinocchio flew to get his precious toys; even they seemed gayer than ever.

As for Jiminy Cricket, he was the happiest and proudest of all. For on his lapel he now wore a beautiful badge of shining gold!

INDEX